D1457483

The Warhol Incident

An Alexis Parker novel

G.K. Parks

Copyright © 2013 G.K. Parks

A Modus Operandi imprint

All rights reserved.

ISBN: 0989195813
ISBN-13: 978-0-9891958-1-2

For mom and dad

ONE

I stared out the restaurant window, completely mesmerized by the view.

"Like what you see?" James Martin asked from across the table. I turned to him and smiled. I couldn't help it. I was in full-on tourist mode tonight.

"It's breathtaking."

"Funny, I was going to say the same thing about you, Alexis." He was still trying to win me over with his playboy demeanor and smooth words, and I resisted the urge to roll my eyes. He sensed my displeasure at the comment and decided to select a more practical conversation topic. "Do you start work tomorrow?"

"Yes, I have a meeting scheduled with the insurance executives, and I'll take it from there." Currently, I was Alexis Parker, international traveler.

"Exactly what is it you're supposed to do?"

"Asset retrieval." I made a face. "The details are limited, to say the least. Honestly, I think Evans-Sterling, the insurance company, just wants to make sure the painting I was hired to escort gets back safely, so they aren't forced to issue a payout for any loss or damage."

"How did an insurance company in France even hear about you?" His forehead creased as he tried to work the details out in his mind.

"It's not a French insurance company. They're international with offices all over the world. The owner of the painting is American. My guess is one of your board members may have mentioned my name since people of your status tend to travel in small circles," I pointed out. "The real question," I gave him a suspicious look, "is why you suddenly needed to take a trip to Paris which coincided so perfectly with my travel itinerary."

"I have to make sure the Paris branch of Martin Technologies is operating efficiently. Plus, I've been hearing good things about my French counterpart. I might just have to offer him the VP spot since it is still available." Martin was the consummate workaholic, so the fact he was globetrotting with me still seemed a bit suspect in my mind.

It had been a few months since I worked as Martin's personal bodyguard and security advisor. Over the course of several weeks, I had uncovered a conspiracy within his company. After exchanging gunfire with some contract killers and watching Martin almost bleed to death, his company decided to keep me on retainer for their other security consulting needs. I opened my own small firm, thanks in large part to the money earned on that first private sector job, and now I was taking smaller, less dangerous jobs on the side.

"Well, you didn't have to let me fly over with you on the company jet. I was given a travel allowance."

Martin waved my protest away, which he often did.

"Yes, but you have to admit, a private jet is much nicer than commercial business class. And the nuts are actually warm." He smirked.

"I wouldn't know," I replied, "nor do I want to know."

Martin chuckled, amused by his own play on words. For a brilliant, capable CEO in his mid-thirties, he often reminded me of a teenage boy.

"Ready to get out of here?" he asked, glancing at his watch. I nodded, and he called for the waiter, spoke perfect French to him, and paid the bill. We exited into the cool night air and strolled toward our hotel.

"Where's Bruiser tonight?" I asked while looking out over the Seine.

"I gave him the night off. We are in Paris, after all." Martin expected some type of protest, but I remained silent. The city was too beautiful for an argument. "You do realize Bruiser really isn't his name, right?" Bruiser was the nickname I insisted on giving his current full-time bodyguard.

"He'll always be Bruiser to me."

We reached our hotel and headed up in the elevator. I caught a glimpse of our reflection in the mirrored doors. Martin was impeccably dressed as always, tonight in a black Prada suit, with his stylish dark brown hair, amazing good looks, and toned athletic build. Despite the jetlag, I was impressed how pulled together I appeared, wearing a black skirt, silk blouse, and the Jimmy Choo pumps Martin left in my possession from my previous stint working for him. My brown hair was pulled back and curled as it cascaded down my shoulders. If I didn't know any better, I would have thought we were a couple. Luckily, I knew better.

"Come up for a nightcap?"

"I have that meeting in the morning," I replied,

"and mixed in with the jetlag, I'd probably sleep through the alarm and miss the entire thing."

"You could stay with me tonight. I'll make sure you get up in the morning." His green eyes sparkled.

"Ha. Ha." Martin was the ever-optimistic lothario. "I won't date my boss, remember?"

"But I'm not your employer anymore. Martin Technologies is, and I didn't say anything about dating. I just asked you to stay the night, on the couch if you prefer. I remember how much you like to sleep on those." I narrowed my eyes at him. "Fine," his speech pattern became slightly more formal, "but there was something else I wanted to discuss with you. Business related, I promise."

"Okay," I cautiously agreed. "You didn't have to wait this long."

"Why ruin our weekly dinner, especially when we're in this exotic locale?" He smiled. The elevator doors opened on my floor, and we both looked out into the hallway. "Plus, I want you to see the view from my room." He pushed the close door button, and we continued the ascent to the penthouse suite. *Classic Martin*, I thought.

"Can't you just tell me now?"

"What fun would that be?"

The elevator doors opened again, and we exited onto the top floor. He pulled out his room key and unlocked the door, holding it open so I could step inside. Walking into the incredibly large and lavish suite, I was awed by the magnificent view of the Eiffel Tower lit up in the night sky.

"Maybe the ride up to your room wasn't a complete waste of my time," I gave in, turning around to find him already pouring drinks from the mini-bar. "I'm not drinking."

He ignored my protest and mixed a martini for me

and poured two fingers of scotch for himself. "In case you change your mind."

He brought the glasses over and handed them to me, so he could open the balcony door. We sat outside at the small table with our drinks. I slowly spun the glass on the tabletop, waiting for him to tell me what possible business agenda he needed my help with now. He leaned back and took off his tie, unbuttoning the first few buttons of his shirt a bit awkwardly, using only his left hand. Once he was situated, he picked up his scotch and took a sip.

"Anytime now." I stared at him, waiting for him to begin.

"I was thinking," he began slowly, prolonging this as much as possible, "if you have the time, maybe you could give the Paris branch of Martin Tech the quick once-over. Make sure the place is secure, no obvious security leaks, and check out Luc Guillot and make sure he isn't a murderous, conniving son of a bitch before I offer him the VP position."

"That can be arranged." Making a quick mental assessment, I tried to determine the most efficient way of doing things. "The painting isn't being moved until the end of the week, so I can swing by tomorrow after my meeting, or...," the time difference and jetlag were getting to me, "what's today?"

Martin chuckled. "Monday."

"Okay, so Tuesday afternoon or Wednesday at the latest. When are you flying home?"

"Thursday or Friday, depending on how things go with Guillot. The Board has already granted permission to offer him the position, and they have the paperwork all ready to be signed. I'm just a bit reluctant." Martin finished his drink and rubbed his right shoulder absently.

"Still going to physical therapy?"

"Uh-huh, it's getting there slowly, but in case you haven't noticed, I'm not the patient type. Then again, a follow-up surgery is always an option."

Picking up the martini and taking a larger gulp than I intended, I wanted to wash the images of Martin being shot and almost dying out of my mind. "I'll check into things and give you my assessment of Monsieur Guillot." I stood and headed toward the door, but I couldn't just leave, not when we skirted the edge of the dangerous precipice that was our past history of death and mayhem. "Martin." My voice was soft as I turned back to face him, but he was already up and behind me at the door. Our eyes locked.

"It's okay," he whispered into my ear, reaching around and pulling the door open. The closeness of his body to mine was almost intoxicating. I swallowed and turned, walking purposefully back into the hotel room.

"I'll call you tomorrow after my meeting and let you know when I can check out MT of Paris." I headed for the door.

"Okay." He was slightly distracted, pouring himself another drink.

Stopping at the door, I turned around. "Good night."

"Bonne nuit, Alex." He winked as I hastily retreated.

My room seemed much smaller now. Thanks a lot, Martin. I tossed my purse onto the table and kicked off my shoes. Turning on my laptop, I changed out of my clothes as the computer started up. I might as well run a background check on Guillot while it was fresh on my mind. I typed in the query and clicked the submit button. Scanning through the information, I found Guillot had a few minor traffic violations, but nothing screamed psychopath. Martin Tech was stringent in their hiring policies, but it never hurt to double-check these things. I sat, staring at the screen for a few minutes.

"The more you accomplish tonight, the less you have to do tomorrow," I said out loud to psych myself up because, at the moment, the only thing I wanted to do was crawl under the covers and sleep for a week. It was only eleven Paris time which meant it was five o'clock at home, but since I didn't sleep on the flight or very much the night before, I had a legitimate reason to be exhausted. Performing a quick internet search on Guillot before going to bed was all I was willing to do at the moment. I checked some news sources and other websites for any type of scandal, but Luc Guillot appeared to be an upstanding, scandal-free citizen. I shut my computer and was getting ready for bed when there was a knock at the door.

"You've got to be kidding me," I yelled. Opening the door, I expected to find Martin. Instead, it was the hotel concierge.

"Madame, sorry to bother you so late," the concierge apologized. At least in French being called ma'am sounded classier. "This package was left for you and marked urgent. I thought it best to deliver it tonight."

"Merci." I took the package and handed the man a few Euros which were scattered on top of the dresser.

Shutting the door, I stared suspiciously at the large manila envelope in my hands. My name was written on the front, but no other information was provided about the sender or the contents. I opened the flap carefully. Paranoia had become my constant companion, probably due to my previous career as a federal agent at the Office of International Operations. Luckily, nothing exploded.

As I dumped the contents unceremoniously onto the table, I flipped on the floor lamp. The package came from the Paris office of Evans-Sterling and contained information on the painting, the owner, the insurance protocols and claims procedures, and proper methods of transportation. It was now midnight, and I needed to be well-versed on all of this by the morning. Settling down in the chair, I began reading and taking notes. By the time I finished, it was a little after three a.m. I set the alarm for seven and crawled under the covers.

It was 5:18. *Damn time change*, I cursed inwardly. I hadn't slept at all, despite how tired I thought I was. I twisted and turned for another thirty minutes and finally gave up and dragged myself out of bed. Flipping the computer on, I did a more thorough search on Guillot. Still, nothing negative turned up. It was just barely after six when I got into the shower and dressed for the day. The plan was to get some caffeine pumping through my system as soon as possible. Heading for the small café across the street, I figured I'd have time to return to my room before leaving for my meeting at Evans-Sterling.

Finding a seat at one of the outdoor tables, I ordered an espresso. As I waited for the server to return, I noticed Martin, head buried in a newspaper, seated a few tables over. I got up and went over to him.

"Give Bruiser the morning off, too?" I asked a bit more combatively than necessary. Lack of sleep had the unfortunate side effect of making me bitchy.

"Alex?" Martin was surprised by my sudden appearance. "No, he's over there." He jerked his head toward a larger man sitting a few tables away, bemusedly watching our exchange. I smiled at him and sat down across from Martin. "Someone's up bright and early this morning." Martin scrutinized my appearance. "Did you even go to bed?"

"I had some unexpected work to do." I sighed. "Apparently, Evans-Sterling decided to courier over some information I needed."

"You should have stayed with me. They wouldn't have been able to track you down." He was joking, but I couldn't help but think his tone sounded a little too sincere.

It was my turn to examine his appearance. His eyes were bloodshot, and considering his breakfast choice of a plain croissant and black coffee, I had a feeling he was hung over. This was the kind of thing that made me such an astute investigator.

"I probably wouldn't have managed to get any sleep with the party you were having."

He shrugged and resumed reading the paper.

The server finally located me and brought my espresso over. I thanked her and inhaled deeply, taking a tentative sip. Definitely strong. Martin finished the paper and folded it neatly, watching me drink the espresso like it was water and I had been lost in the desert for a week.

"Slow down before your head explodes or you give yourself a heart attack," he warned, and I put the mostly empty cup on the table and leaned back, waiting for the caffeine buzz to kick in.

"Last night, I did some digging into Guillot. From what I can tell, he's clean. Seems stable, no real criminal record, and no scandals. It's like he's you, but French." Martin nodded but said nothing. "What time are you expected at the office?" I asked.

"Around one. I'm trying to be reasonable to the Board in case I need to teleconference." He was back in work mode. "Give me a call when you plan to head over. I should still be there."

"Okay." I put some money on the table for my coffee and Martin's breakfast. He looked at it, confused. "Breakfast is on me for once." I walked away before he could protest.

TWO

I took a taxi to the Evans-Sterling offices and was ushered upstairs and into a conference room where I was instructed to wait. I tried not to fidget, despite the jitteriness I was experiencing from drinking the espresso.

"Ms. Parker, I'm Salazar Sterling." He held his hand out, and we shook. "Please." He indicated the seat I just vacated, and I sat back down. "It's so good of you to come all this way just to escort a painting back to the United States for us."

"No problem." Given his accent, Sterling was an American or at least an ex-pat. "I was just surprised to be hired for such a simple job."

"Well, there have been issues lately." Sterling lowered his voice. "The gallery has misplaced the last three pieces of art scheduled to be transported elsewhere." The way he said misplaced led me to believe the more appropriate term would have been stolen. "Our investigators are looking into things, but since Mr. Wilkes is a high profile client, we thought it'd be best to avoid another mishap. You come highly recommended."

"What exactly am I here to do? I read the materials that were left at my hotel last night, but they didn't provide much to go on."

"My apologies. The item you will be escorting is a small painting. All you need to do is transport it to the States, and we'll have our people meet you at the airport and sign off on the delivery."

I'm just a glorified courier, I thought, but decided to be a bit more tactful than to say it aloud. I was working on being diplomatic. "Anything I need to do on this end to prepare the painting for transport?"

Sterling smiled, pleased by the question. "You used to work for the Office of International Operations. You're probably used to recovering art and dealing with transport issues." I nodded noncommittally. "I must admit, we ran a background and checked your credentials. Your past is rather impressive, and we thought it'd be best to have someone so well-versed to ensure the safe delivery of the art." This job wasn't as simple as it originally appeared. "We were hoping you wouldn't mind keeping an eye out over the course of the next few days just to make sure nothing happens to our precious cargo. When the exhibit closes, the painting will be taken down, authenticated once again, and our team will prepare it for transport."

"We aren't talking twenty-four hour surveillance, are we? I'm one person. I can't provide that type of around the clock coverage."

Sterling laughed. "No, of course not. I want to put you in contact with our lead investigator, Jean-Pierre Gustav. He's checking into the three other missing masterpieces, and he might be of some assistance to you. The gallery is under surveillance, but it's good to have a trained federal agent with experience in matters such as these on-site."

"Ex-federal agent." I left the OIO for a reason, and chasing down art thieves was a small part of it.

"Tomato, tomato," he pronounced the word two different ways. "I will pass your number on to Jean-Pierre, and he will be in contact with you shortly. He can show you the gallery, and the two of you can work the details out further, concerning how to ensure the painting's safe delivery."

"I have something pressing to do this afternoon." Some disclosure might be a good idea. "Will it cause a scheduling conflict?"

Sterling looked thoughtful for a moment. "Not at all. I'm sure Jean-Pierre won't contact you until tomorrow."

Good, I thought as I went outside to hail another cab. Pulling out my phone, I dialed Martin. When the call went to voicemail, I decided to get a jump-start at the MT building and do some snooping on my own. My MT ID card was in my wallet, and it ought to be sufficient to get me into the building, even if we were in a different country. I gave the cab driver my destination, and off we went. Allons-y.

The cab ride didn't take long. I just entered the Paris branch of Martin Technologies when my phone rang.

"Where are you?" Martin asked as soon as I hit answer.

"In the lobby."

With perfect timing, the elevator doors opened, and Martin emerged. I hit end call and put my cell phone in my purse. Luc Guillot stood next to Martin. The two were having a seemingly jovial conversation in very fast-paced French.

"Luc, allow me to introduce my security consultant, Alexis Parker," Martin said once he and Guillot reached me.

"Enchanté, Mademoiselle." Luc kissed both of my cheeks.

"Monsieur Guillot," I greeted, eyeing Martin suspiciously and wondering how he made such a perfectly timed entrance.

"I asked Ms. Parker if she would be so kind as to evaluate the security protocols in place since she was already in France on other business," Martin explained to Guillot. Guillot agreed and made sure my ID card was programmed with unlimited access to the building.

I glanced over at Martin and Guillot. They were wrapped up in their own little world. "I'm going to check out the equipment and procedures in place," I announced to the two oblivious men. "Do the security guards speak English?"

"Of course," Guillot replied, giving me a friendly smile. "If you need any assistance, they will be more than happy to help."

I thanked him and threw a sideways glance at Martin before heading toward the elevators. Clipping on my security badge, I planned to start at the top and work my way down. Martin caught me before I made it to the elevator.

"Thanks for doing this."

"This is exactly why you hired me. When I finish here, I'm going back to the hotel. I'll e-mail my findings to your corporate account by the morning."

"Dinner tonight?"

"I don't want you to get sick of me." I refused to explicitly answer his question.

"Never." He gave me a devilish grin before heading back to Luc and continuing on their way.

The next three hours were spent evaluating the safety procedures and security protocols in place at the Martin Technologies building. The French office was smaller than its American counterpart. The building was only a few levels and designed solely for import/export. There was a large docking bay on the ground floor for trucks to load and unload materials. The top floor contained offices and conference rooms, and the middle floors held smaller offices and cubicles with basic necessities like human resources and accounting. I gave the security officers the third degree about protocols for emergencies. With the exception of the docking bay, there wasn't much that needed improvement. The office itself seemed like a joke with limited resources, no corporate secrets, and not much worth stealing or protecting. I wondered if Martin asking for my input was just an excuse, but when it came to Martin and business, there was never any real way of knowing what he was thinking.

Finishing my tour of the building, I went back to the hotel, double-checked there were no other messages or packages left for me, went to my room, changed out of my clothes, and collapsed onto the bed. Screw the time difference and staying awake through the jetlag, I needed sleep.

I opened my eyes to the sound of knocking. It took a moment to remember where I was. Grabbing my robe from the chair, I tied it around my waist as I made my way to the door.

"Why aren't you dressed?" Martin asked, entering my room, uninvited. "It's eight o'clock."

"What?" I couldn't believe I slept through the entire day and night. "Shit." I was supposed to have written up the security evaluation for him, and I probably missed the call from Jean-Pierre. "How could I have slept so long?"

"Probably because you didn't sleep last night," Martin pointed out, taking a seat and watching me, amused. Nothing like making yourself at home.

"Wait. Last night?" I went to the window and pulled the curtain. It was dark. "It's still today." I was making no sense, and I blamed him. I slapped his good arm. "You're such an ass."

"Hey," he feigned injury, "I thought we had dinner plans."

"We did not have dinner plans." Grabbing some clothes, I stomped to the bathroom and shut the door.

"I told you I'd send you an e-mail."

"I'm pretty sure you agreed to go to dinner with me." There was a level of swagger in his voice. "I asked about dinner, and you didn't obviously refuse. Therefore, we have plans." Martin's unilateral decision-making and reasoning always irritated me. I stared at my reflection in the mirror, hoping he might be a figment of my imagination. Instead, he continued his diatribe. "Plus, you are obviously awake now and getting dressed, so there is no reason to cancel said plans."

I opened the door. "Do you ever actually listen to the things you say?" I tried not to chuckle at how utterly insane this entire exchange would seem to normal, rational people. Luckily, neither Martin nor I was normal, and one of us was definitely not rational.

"All the time. You must admit, I always make very valid points."

"Maybe to the clinically insane," I responded, sitting on the bed and grabbing my laptop off the table.

"What are you doing?" He genuinely seemed confused that I wasn't grabbing my purse and announcing I was ready to go to dinner. Ignoring his question, I typed out a quick e-mail and hit send. His phone immediately buzzed, notifying him of a new message. He opened the mail and read aloud. "Martin,

I am not going to dinner with you. <3 Alex." He looked at me and smiled. "I really like the heart."

"I thought you would. Now, please," I gestured toward the door, "I do have actual work to do." Martin understood and nodded, standing up. "Thanks for waking me. If you didn't, I probably would have slept all night."

He brushed my hair out of my face and tucked it behind my ear. "If you finish in a few hours and still want to grab a quick bite, let me know."

"Okay."

He left the room, shutting the door behind him. I resisted the urge to follow him into the hallway and announce that I changed my mind. Instead, I opened the word processing program and typed out a formal report on the strengths and weaknesses of the Paris office. Once my report with the suggested improvements was completed, I e-mailed it to Martin's corporate account as promised.

It was a little before eleven. Ordering room service, I ate my dinner while watching French-dubbed American television. After I finished eating, I attempted to look into the recent art thefts and see if I could discover anything useful. The only problem was the news stories were in French, and while I managed to go through French articles last night about Luc Guillot, I only accomplished this by gleaning information from the context. Here, I didn't understand the context. I should have paid more attention in French class. Picking up the phone, I dialed Martin. Unfortunately, he was the only person I knew who was fluent in French.

"Change your mind?"

"Actually, I have a favor to ask." Further ingratiating myself to him was not something I wanted to do, especially given our history of him taking a bullet intended for me. "I need a translator."

"Okay, I'm upstairs." He ended the call, and I grabbed my room key and laptop, slipped on a pair of sneakers, and headed for the elevator. Martin had changed into a t-shirt and jeans, instead of the suit he wore earlier.

"I'm sorry to bother you with this."

"It's no bother. I would have preferred getting to go to dinner than doing your homework, but whatever makes you happy." He grinned, indicating no hard feelings.

I provided a brief breakdown of my freelance job and the information I ascertained so far about the three other misplaced paintings. Initially, I was hesitant because of the potential for confidentiality issues, but it was Martin. He could be trusted, and I had little choice since I needed his help.

He nodded thoughtfully and read the articles. When he was finished, he supplied a summary of the information. Basically, the art had gone missing before being transported out of the gallery. There were no leads in terms of it being sold or stolen, and as far as surveillance showed, the paintings didn't leave the museum, leading to the theory they were simply misplaced.

"Hmm." A million theories formulated in my mind, but I reeled them back. The other paintings were not my problem. I had nothing to do with the investigation to find them. I just didn't want the one I was sent to retrieve to face a similar fate.

"You have that look." His eyes brightened as he stared at me. "The one that says I have a gut feeling about this. It's been a while since I've seen that look. It's a good look."

"It's not my problem. I'm just here to make sure the painting I'm bringing home stays where it's supposed to be."

"Sounds like a decent plan." He opened the mini-fridge. "Can I get you anything?"

I looked at the clock. "I don't want to keep you, if you have an early morning." I moved to get off the couch.

"Stay put. It's only six at home. Trust me, you aren't the only one having trouble sleeping."

I laughed, and he pulled out a bottle of French wine and two glasses. He handed me a glass as he took a seat next to me.

"Are you offering Guillot the job?"

"I already did. He has to find a permanent replacement, arrange for VISAs, and finalize the paperwork. I spoke with a couple of board members, and they are working on travel arrangements, finding him and his family a residence, and all that other fun stuff."

"He accepted the offer?" It was more a statement than a question.

"Yes. He realized it was the point of this trip and expected it. He's signing the official paperwork tomorrow, and I'm flying back Thursday morning to get the ball rolling on our end."

I studied Martin's reaction, but I couldn't figure out why he wasn't pleased by this decision. "And you're okay with this?" I had issues keeping my mouth shut and minding my own business.

"It's great." He glanced at me, and I looked at him skeptically. "Well, it's good. It will be less traveling I have to do. Far fewer business trips and service calls. I'm just having issues adjusting to...," he paused, trying to determine how to verbalize his misgivings.

"Trusting people," I supplied the words for him. "It'll come back with time." Reaching for the bottle of wine, I refilled our glasses.

"Thanks," Martin said, lost in his own world. Once again, I managed to bring the conversation to a crashing halt. Great talent you have there, Parker.

"Dinner, tomorrow night? It is your last night in Paris, after all. Plus, you did help me with my homework." I shot him a brief smile. "It's the least I can do."

"Sure, but don't stand me up this time."

THREE

"Ali Parker?" the undeniable voice on the other end of the line asked, sounding completely confused. There was only one person who ever called me Ali.

"Jean-Pierre?" I didn't connect the dots until now. "You aren't working for Interpol anymore?" I was astounded. Not to mention, Gustav wasn't Jean-Pierre's surname when I worked with him years ago. Of course, that might have been because he was undercover at the time.

"No, I went private sector, same as you. Things change, chére," Jean-Pierre said into the phone. The prospect of working this job significantly improved since I'd be working with an old acquaintance.

"My, my." I gave him the hotel name and my room number. We planned to meet in an hour, so he could fill me in on the investigation and take me to La Galerie d'Art et d'Antiquités.

My first international smuggling case had landed me in Paris, and the OIO had been partnered with Interpol to track down a ring of art forgers. Jean-Pierre had been working undercover, having made strong black market ties to illegal art sales. It was his expertise and contacts that helped bust the case open for us and led to the arrest of several key forgers and illegal art dealers. He had been an incredibly impressive UC operative. I couldn't imagine why he would have willingly left Interpol. Arguably, people said the same thing when I left the OIO. Things really did change.

Jean-Pierre knocked on my door, and I let him in. The last four years hadn't altered his look much. His blond hair was gelled into some slight spikes, and he still had the musculature of a military man. He wore a black leather jacket and jeans with wraparound sunglasses hooked behind his neck.

"Ali," he greeted, kissing me on both cheeks. Upon closer inspection, he had a few new scars on his face and neck. It appeared someone had gotten too close with a knife, but I didn't say anything.

"You're working permanently for Evans-Sterling now?"

"Things got too rough, and the pay wasn't cutting it anymore," he responded. "It was time for a change. I can't be running around, playing a badass every minute of the day." I laughed. "It is good to see you."

"It's been too long."

Jean-Pierre explained the layout and situation at the gallery concerning the missing pieces of art. Obviously, all of them were insured by Evans-Sterling, but the painting I was escorting was the most valuable.

After arriving at the gallery, I wandered the hallways and studios, pretending to be a patron in order to get a feel for the security measures in place. The gallery, while small and fairly unknown, did possess quite a few expensive pieces that dated as far back as the Renaissance. Security cameras covered all of the rooms, and tripwires were attached to the frames. I agreed with his assessment that the paintings were relatively secure, at least during business hours.

"Any leads on who misplaced the other three paintings?" I asked once we were outside and a couple of blocks away.

"I've been conducting surveillance at night, along with a few other Sterling employees. If I had to make a guess, it's either the curator or the art restorer. They are always the last two people to leave, never together, and given their positions at the gallery, they'd each have the access to pull it off." Jean-Pierre's gut instincts were good. He had been doing this for a long time, and I had no reason to question his assessment.

"How's the security? Do they have night guards on duty?"

"They have a couple of guys who work the desk and watch the security feed. Each of the individual studios inside has its own laser grid and metal gate. That's probably why nothing goes missing until after being moved into the back room for prep and transport." He seemed bored giving me the details since he'd already had this conversation with various other people, including the Police Nationale.

"Sorry, just trying to catch-up."

He nodded, unperturbed. "It's fine." We got into his car. "Why don't you come out with me tonight? The gallery is under surveillance, and you can witness firsthand how things are running."

"Okay." I thought briefly about my dinner plans with Martin, but this was more important. "What time?"

"Shift change is midnight. Meet me then?"

"You just want to take advantage of my internal clock's time difference and catch-up on some sleep while I keep an eye out," I teasingly accused.

"Don't you know it, chére." He grinned. "I'll give you a call if something happens between now and then. Sal probably wants you paying close attention Friday and Saturday morning, so tonight can be a dry run."

"Sal?"

"Salazar Sterling, the guy who signs our paychecks."

"Well, maybe yours. I'm only working this one job. I'm my own one-woman investigating and consulting firm."

"How'd you manage to get that gig?"

"Long story. Maybe I'll fill you in tonight," I teased, getting out of the car. At least I'd be able to make dinner with Martin and still work the stakeout with Jean-Pierre. Tonight was going to turn out well.

* * *

It was 7:30, and I was sitting across the table from Martin. He decided on a more native Parisian dinner, so we were in a brasserie close to the hotel. He wore jeans and a black dress shirt. I was dressed in a similarly casual manner in some tightly fitting denim, a sweater, and a killer pair of heels. We were on our second bottle of wine, and I realized I needed to stop now in order to sober up before meeting Jean-Pierre. Hopefully, I wouldn't fall asleep between now and then. Martin reached to refill my glass, but I put my hand over the top.

"I have to work tonight," I told him.

He looked at me like I was insane. "You're joking, right?"

"Actually, I'm not. I'm conducting some surveillance on the painting thing." I probably wasn't supposed to tell him any of this. But somehow, he had become my trusted confidant, and as it was, he had translated for me last night. He might as well be clued in. "What time is your flight tomorrow?" I inquired, changing the subject.

"It's my jet, so it leaves when I want to leave." I gave him my best *give me a break* look. "The flight plan is for 8:15 tomorrow morning."

We ate in silence for a while, enjoying the food and the company. I provided a vague run-through of my itinerary for the rest of the week and filled him in on my travel plans for Saturday morning. Unfortunately, those of us who didn't have private jets had connecting flights to Heathrow, then JFK, and from there, home.

"I can pick you up at the airport," Martin offered.

"No, I'm okay," I said firmly. "The Evans-Sterling guys are taking possession of the painting at the airport, so I don't need even more people in suits waiting for me. I might get confused with a celebrity or an heiress."

"I don't have to wear a suit." He indicated his casual dress. "I'm not wearing one now."

"No, you are not." My ability for clever banter was somewhat impaired at the moment as Martin stared at me with his classic lecherous look. "What?"

"Y'know, we're in a bar in Paris. I'm not wearing a suit. You aren't under my direct employ at the moment."

I could see where his argument was going. "I'm always employed by you. I'm on retainer." This was just another in our long list of arguments regarding my insistence to not become romantically involved with my boss.

"I could fire you," he looked wistful, "and rehire you in the morning."

"I have to work tonight." Although that wasn't the sound argument I should be making, my internal voice commented.

"And you say I'm a workaholic," he scoffed. "We don't have to be James Martin and Alexis Parker tonight." He tried a new tactic. "We could just be two lonely American tourists who met by chance in a foreign city." The two bottles of wine turned Martin into an incorrigible romantic and me into someone who might be stupid enough to fall for the bullshit.

"Martin," I sighed, "you're still you. I'm still me. We're the same people here or at home." I gave him a sad smile.

He reached over and brushed his thumb across my cheek, his signature move. "I guess you're right." I was drowning in the green pools of his eyes. "I might have to work tonight, too. I'm waiting for a call from the Board about Guillot." He glanced at his watch. "C'est la vie."

"Ha," I exclaimed. "And you gave me a hard time about working tonight."

He paid the bill, and we walked the few blocks back to the hotel. I stumbled, and he offered his arm for balance. It was the heels, not the wine; although, if I were being honest, it might have been a little bit of both. Acting more subdued than usual, we entered the hotel and rode the elevator to my floor. Martin exited when I did and walked me to my room.

"Have a safe trip home," I murmured.

His words from the restaurant played through my head on a loop. The prospect was becoming more appealing by the second. The warning bells blared in my mind, but I ignored them. Fumbling to pull my room key out of my pocket, I got distracted by how close he was standing. I looked into his eyes. Maybe he was right, and we didn't have to be us tonight.

My brain shut down, and on pure instinct, I grabbed the front of his shirt and pulled him to me. His hands tangled in my hair as we kissed. It was electric, like we were lightning, and the energy surged between us. One of his hands traveled slowly down my back. We continued kissing as if the world were about to end. His hand traveled lower, and he hiked my leg up. Wrapping both of my legs around his waist, I let him support my weight in his arms and lean my back against the wall. This was not appropriate hallway behavior, and it was about to turn even more graphic. But, at the moment, I didn't care. My phone buzzed in my pocket, breaking the spell temporarily.

"Don't answer it," he hissed in my ear as his lips traveled to my neck and began to do some absolutely fantastic things. I sighed in pleasure, giving up on retrieving the phone. Voicemail existed for a reason.

My hands were in Martin's hair now, and I was trying to remember where my room key was when his phone rang. This time, he stopped, cursing quietly. Rational thought reigned supreme in my brain, and I untangled my legs and stood, slightly shaky, back on the ground.

"I'm sorry. I have to take this." His apology was so sincere. I knew he would regret having ever answered the phone. The universe just sent a cosmic signal, preventing us from crossing that line and making a huge mistake. I found my room key and pulled out my cell phone. It had been Jean-Pierre, and I needed to call him back. Martin spoke a few words on his call and hung up. "I hate to say this, but I have to go. There is one more thing I need to get signed before I head home tomorrow. I'll be back as soon as I can." He smiled seductively. "Remember where we were, and we'll continue this as soon as I get back." He clasped my face in his hands and kissed me again before retreating toward the elevator. "Don't start without me," he called, getting into the elevator.

I watched the doors close and shut my eyes. "Stupid. Stupid. Stupid," I berated myself as I unlocked the door. Thankfully, we didn't have an audience in the hallway, and things stopped before they really started. Why did I have to be attracted to the one person I shouldn't be involved with? At least nothing serious transpired. I picked up my phone and dialed Jean-Pierre.

"What's going on?" I asked.

"I got a call from a fence I know. Tonight, there might be a scheduled buy for one of the missing pieces. Want to head over early?"

"I'll meet you there in an hour." Hopefully by then, I'd manage to sober up completely.

"À tout à l'heure." Jean-Pierre hung up.

I pulled a sports drink out of the mini-fridge and drank greedily, hoping replenishing my fluids and electrolytes would flush the remaining alcohol out of my system faster. It was only wine, but the sheer volume was the issue. Checking my reflection in the mirror, I noticed my pupils weren't dilated and responded to the light. Maybe I wasn't intoxicated but just stupid. Damn Paris. The fact it was the city of love was a mental manipulation by itself without Martin putting other idiotic and fanciful ideas into my head. I was angry for the mess I was making of things. I worked for Martin's company, and he was my friend. That was it.

Locating the hotel stationery, I decided it was best to leave a note: *Glad we were saved by the bell. Went to work. Have a safe flight.*

After leaving it at the main desk for him, I went outside and hailed a cab. My head was clearer now. My earlier intoxication might have had more to do with Martin than the wine.

The cab dropped me off a couple of blocks away from the gallery, and I walked the rest of the way to the proper street. I had my suspicions on which vehicles were being used for surveillance but decided it was best to call Jean-Pierre rather than to surprise someone who may be armed.

"Ali," he said from behind and opened the side door of a nondescript gray van. Climbing inside, I assessed the equipment and vantage point. "It ought to be an exciting night. The guys think the art restorer is moving one of the missing paintings."

"Why?" I stared out the window at the gallery.

"Watch and see." Jean-Pierre picked up a camera and snapped some photos as a man exited the building with a large portfolio.

FOUR

Jean-Pierre and I waited in the surveillance van outside Jacques Marset's residence. Marset was the art restorer employed by La Galerie d'Art et d'Antiquités. The other four Evans-Sterling investigators were in two other vehicles. One was still monitoring the gallery, and the other was parked farther down the street in a black sedan. Glancing at the clock on the dashboard, I realized we had been here for two hours, and so far, nothing happened. Maybe Mr. Marset went home and straight to bed.

"Why are stakeouts always so much more exciting in movies?" I mused aloud as I continued to stare out the window.

"Don't jinx us."

"Sorry." I adjusted the seat into a more comfortable position. "Give me the rundown on why you thought tonight would be so eventful."

"A fence I know heard the first painting, a Manet, was being moved out of the country and going up for auction in Luxembourg in three days."

"Reliable source?"

"I wouldn't consider him a source otherwise. Anyway," Jean-Pierre changed the subject in an attempt to make polite conversation and kill some time, "are you enjoying your trip so far?"

"It's okay. No sleep. Lots of work. The fun just doesn't stop," I responded sarcastically, and he smiled.

"You can sleep when you're dead."

Hopefully, that wouldn't be for a long, long time. My phone buzzed loudly. I pulled it from my pocket and looked at the display. It was Martin, and I pressed ignore.

Jean-Pierre watched me suspiciously. "Who was that?"

"No one," I replied just as my phone beeped, announcing a new voicemail message.

"No one seems persistent."

"You have no idea."

"Boyfriend?"

"No, just a lonely American tourist I met in a bar." Martin's story might as well come in handy for something.

"Slut," Jean-Pierre teased.

"He wishes. What about you? Wife and kids, or are you still keeping a girl in every port?"

Jean-Pierre smiled but shook his head. "I got out of the business for a reason. Settling down is the plan, but I haven't made it happen yet. I'm only on step one or two."

"Intrigue. Is there a lucky lady?"

"Clare." He smiled like a schoolboy with a crush. "She's actually working for Sal, too. She's in the other car with Van Buren."

"Sorry, I ruined your ideal stakeout fantasy." My phone buzzed again. Martin, you are killing me. I fished the phone out of my pocket. "I'm going to take this, so I can get this guy off my back." Hitting answer, I held the phone against my ear, decreasing the volume.

"I am so sorry." Martin's voice was full of remorse. "I never should have left."

"It's okay. The real world came knocking. Those two lonely tourists have lives they need to get back to. We would have regretted tonight."

"Alex, please." He understood the implications of my words. Tonight was an accident based on being in a foreign, romantic city and drinking too much wine. "Stay safe."

"Always."

"See you when you get home?"

"Have a safe flight. I have to go." Disconnecting, I blew out a slow breath.

"Think he got the message?" Jean-Pierre asked.

I nodded. He got it, loud and clear. "Whoa." I sat up straighter and grabbed the binoculars. "We have movement."

Jean-Pierre was on the radio to the other surveillance team. An SUV just pulled up, and two men got out of the vehicle, heading straight for Marset's house. We continued to watch as the men rang the doorbell, and Marset opened the door, allowing them to enter his home. It was almost four a.m. when the men left. The silver briefcase they had been carrying was no longer in hand; instead, they were carrying a large cardboard tube. Jean-Pierre told the other team to stick with the SUV since I was a liability, given my lack of weaponry and my tourist status in the country. The SUV pulled away, followed slowly by the sedan.

"Where do you think they're going?" I posed the question as he pulled out the radio and called the third team, who was still waiting at the gallery, to give them instructions on how to assist Clare and Van Buren.

"Could be anywhere. We'll try to keep a tail on them between the two cars." He was contemplating something when there was movement at Marset's. The art restorer exited through the back door with a large duffel bag in hand and went quickly down the alley. He stopped at the opening and looked around cautiously, eyeing our van suspiciously.

"We have a runner."

Marset made us and ran back down the alley and leapt the fence, making our ability to follow in the van nonexistent. I opened my door, prepared to give chase. Jean-Pierre was a few seconds ahead of me, and we ran down the alley after our suspect. Jean-Pierre leapt the fence in one fluid motion. Unfortunately, I had to jump and climb to get myself up and over. *If only I had longer legs*, I thought wistfully as I continued to run full-out down the avenue.

Marset was still in sight but had a decent lead. The avenue split, and Jean-Pierre signaled that I go right in the hopes of heading off the suspect. Turning the corner, we entered a parking garage from two different angles. I ran up the ramps while keeping a watchful eye on the stairs. Jean-Pierre was gaining on him. On the fourth level, Marset exited the stairwell and ran into a cluster of parked cars, disappearing into the darkness.

"Shit," I muttered.

Jean-Pierre emerged and looked at me. Unfortunately, neither of us knew where Marset was. The radio in Jean-Pierre's jacket squawked, and a woman said something in French about losing the vehicle, making us oh for two tonight.

While carefully walking through the rows of cars in search of Marset, I heard tires screech from the floor above. The SUV flew down the ramp, heading straight toward us. Throwing myself flat against one of the structural pillars, I reached instinctively for my gun.

"Dammit." I was in a foreign country with no firearm. Things could have been better. The SUV stopped, and Marset ran from his hiding spot toward the back door. Jean-Pierre lunged, knocking the duffel bag away. It skittered across the pavement, sliding to a stop next to another of the pillars. The two men struggled on the ground. Jean-Pierre couldn't get a good grip on Marset, who continuously squirmed out of the hold as he tried to reach the discarded duffel. I maintained a close eye on the SUV, quickly running through my options for detaining its occupants.

The two men sitting in the SUV seemed entirely untroubled by this unfortunate series of events. One barked orders to Marset in bored-sounding French, and the other exited the SUV, brandishing a pistol. He looked at me and fired. I dove to the next support pillar and ducked behind it. Why was I stupid enough to think chasing after some smugglers was a good idea? The struggle continued behind me, and I peered around the pillar, knowing I was going to be of little help. Jean-Pierre managed to kick the duffel bag farther away from the man and was now taking cover behind the parked cars as the gunman fired at him. If I could just reach the bag and distract them, Jean-Pierre could get clear. Playing decoy had to be my least favorite idea, but it was the only one I had. Staying low, I ran from my hiding spot to the bag and shoved it hard enough to slide across the asphalt and drop to the level below.

The solo gunman turned and fired at me. His aim left a lot to be desired, but it was France. Guns weren't nearly as prevalent here, thank goodness. Running in a zigzag pattern to make myself a more difficult target, I headed for the parking barrier, hoping to take the same path as the duffel. As I leapt over the barrier wall, my leg caught on the rusted wire, and I landed splayed on top of a parked car. Quickly rolling off the hood, I came to rest in a crumpled heap on the ground. The car next to me provided a place to stow the duffel bag, and I crouched between the two closely parked cars, hoping the SUV and its occupants wouldn't be able to locate me or the bag. My thoughts returned to Jean-Pierre on the floor above. Was he okay? The tires screeched again as the SUV drove past at breakneck speed and continued down the ramp and out of the garage.

"Ali, you okay?" Jean-Pierre called from above.

"Never better." I waited three counts before emerging from my cover position in case the SUV returned. Jean-Pierre was on the radio with the other two teams as he came down the ramp toward me. "What the hell did they want?"

"Je ne sais pas. Marset got inside the SUV, and they drove off. Nice move, playing decoy," he complimented.

Reaching under the car, I pulled on the strap of the bag until it popped free from the undercarriage. "You do the honors." My jeans were ripped at the thigh, and my leg was bleeding. Just my luck. Peering over his shoulder into the bag, I spotted the missing Manet, along with a few thousand dollars.

"Money and a Manet." He indicated the contents. "Why would Marset have both?"

"I don't know. Who were his friends in the SUV?" I asked, but he shook his head, perplexed. The other two Evans-Sterling teams were en route to meet us and help sort out this mess.

"I have to call the police," he seemed torn, "but you have a flight to catch on Saturday." If I were a witness or involved in a large-scale police investigation, I wouldn't be flying home with Mr. Wilkes' painting. "There's no reason why you have to be here, or why you were ever here." He glanced down at my leg and up at the wire that inflicted the damage. "We can clean this up. Just try not to bleed on anything."

"Are you sure?" I didn't feel right removing myself from the equation. This was not how I was trained, and this wasn't something I'd normally do.

"I'll call Sal and tell him what happened. We'll let him decide. It's his show." He dialed Sterling and filled him in.

While he was on the phone, the other two teams arrived in the parking garage to meet us. A man and woman exited the sedan, Clyde Van Buren and Clare Olivier. The other team in the van pulled up next to them, and Ryan Donough and Michel Langmire stepped out. Van Buren went to speak with the two men, leaving Clare to stare suspiciously at me. Although, I noticed Donough wasn't paying much attention to his pals and instead was eyeing me. We had never been formally introduced, but I skimmed through their Sterling dossiers. Donough stepped away from the group and was about to approach me when Jean-Pierre got off the phone.

"Clare," he said to her, "this is Ali. She needs a ride back to her hotel."

I looked at him, unsure how I felt about any of this. I guess I could take it up with Salazar Sterling myself.

"Come on," Clare said in English. Her French accent was much thicker than Jean-Pierre's.

I looked at the rest of the crew. They seemed to be in some type of exclusive club I wasn't supposed to be privy to even knowing about. Even Donough slipped back into his group, lost in discussion over the situation. I followed her to the sedan and got into the passenger seat. After I gave her the name of my hotel, she turned the car around and headed back into the heart of the city.

"What happened back there?" she asked, her eyes on the road. When I finished my story, she frowned, deep in thought. "I would suggest you get that leg cleaned up. You might need some stitches. See if the hotel doctor can do it for you. Tell him you fell or something."

I wondered why the Evans-Sterling employees seemed so covert and hostile. It's not like they were international spies.

"You used to work for Interpol like Jean-Pierre?" I tried to get a feel for Clare.

"I used to be with Interpol but not like Jean-Pierre." This meant she wasn't a UC, maybe an analyst.

"OIO," I volunteered, trying to put us on an even keel.

She nodded, glancing briefly at me. "I know. Sterling was pleased you were coming on board for this asset retrieval."

Finally, I understood the hostility. The full-time Evans-Sterling employees thought I was invading their territory and stepping on some toes. "This is a one-time only kind of thing. I'm just here to authenticate and retrieve Mr. Wilkes' painting, and then I'm going home."

Clare laughed cynically. "That's how it always starts. One job that leads to another and then another."

"No. I'm on retainer elsewhere. This was just a way to score a free trip to Paris."

She assessed my words, nodding to herself and

deciding I wasn't a threat to her job. "D'accord." We drove the rest of the way in silence. When we got to the hotel, Clare parked on the street, a block away. "It was nice to meet you, Ali..."

"Alexis Parker," I introduced myself. Better late than never, I suppose.

"Alexis," she repeated. "Clare Olivier." And people said I wasn't good at making friends. Obviously, they didn't know how incredibly personable I could be. "Stick with a simple story, and get that leg looked after. Sterling will call in the morning for an official debrief."

"Thanks, Clare."

It was just after five a.m., and the night shift clerk smiled as I stumbled into the lobby. I asked if there was a hotel doctor who could come to my room. The night clerk promised she would send him up as soon as she could. One of the luxuries of five-star hotels, the service was excellent.

Changing into a pair of shorts, I assessed the damage to the top of my thigh. It didn't seem too bad, but once it was no longer covered by my torn denim, I feared Clare was right. Stitches were going to be in my future. I cleaned my leg and poured one of the mini bottles of vodka over the wound to disinfect it.

"Damn," I hissed as the alcohol stung my skin. There was a knock at my door. Checking the peephole, I let the doctor in and told him my story as he assessed my injury.

"Let's get that stitched up," he informed me in a British accent. "I'd say twelve should do it. Are you up to date on your Tetanus vaccines?"

"Yes." I wasn't happy with the diagnosis. It was just a cut, but I let the man do his job.

"Keep it clean. If it gets swollen, red, or otherwise infected, you'll need to go to the hospital or your own doctor. Avoid physical activity or anything that might put undue stress on your thigh or rip your stitches." This was his way of avoiding a lawsuit.

By the time he left, it was almost seven a.m. Martin must be up and preparing to leave for the airport. I had too much on my plate right now to think about him and the mess I had gotten myself into with the asset retrieval and art smuggling investigation. I climbed into bed and sighed. Why was I acting so damn irrational when it came to everything?

FIVE

"Mr. Sterling, I can explain." I sat across the conference table from Sterling. He cocked his head to the side, waiting for some elaboration. "Olivier and Van Buren were called off to pursue the SUV, which we believed was in possession of the Manet. However, after they left, Marset exited his house with a suspicious duffel bag. Mr. Gustav and I were the only two people there to give chase."

Sterling nodded his head slowly, tapping his fingers subconsciously on the tabletop. "Do you think any of the men involved can identify you?"

"It all happened so fast. It was dark." Would I be able to recognize any of them? With the exception of Marset, I didn't think I could pick either of the SUV's occupants out of a lineup, so they probably didn't get a good look at me either. "I really doubt it."

"Okay. The parking garage has no surveillance cameras. We can't identify the SUV, and you can't identify anyone. So I see no reason why your presence needs to be divulged at this particular juncture,"

Sterling surmised.

I had a bad feeling about this, but I let it go. I wasn't a federal agent anymore, and with my limited knowledge, I wouldn't be able to help the Police Nationale with their investigation.

"What's going to happen to the recovered painting?"

Sterling considered if I needed to know this tidbit of information. "It will be re-authenticated and returned to its rightful owner. I would strongly recommend you keep an eye on Mr. Wilkes' painting and make sure it does not meet a similar fate."

I went back to my hotel and changed into one of the few designer suits I owned and curled my normally straight hair, trying my damnedest to look as different as possible. Heading to the gallery, I spent the entire day admiring the art and checking to see if I recognized anyone. The restorer, Marset, was not present, and I was certain he either fled or was in hiding. Clare Olivier and Clyde Van Buren were parked outside as I exited the gallery. Once I was a safe distance away, I called Jean-Pierre.

"I'm going to change and grab a quick bite. I'll be back to assist on the surveillance in an hour."

"Sterling's changed his mind. He wants you removed from surveillance," Jean-Pierre informed me. "We have this covered."

I spent the rest of the night in my room, determining the most logical reason why Marset had the Manet and what I assumed to be the buyer's money for the painting. Was the SUV Clare and Van Buren followed the same one from the parking garage? If it was, something must have gone awry with the trade-off.

The next morning, I was awakened by my phone ringing. "Is everything all right?" I asked Jean-Pierre.

"The recovered Manet is a fake. Our independent authenticator finished her analysis this morning."

"It explains why the money and the painting were both in Marset's possession." My mind was already turning around the facts. "I'm going out on a limb and guessing Marset was double-dipping." Given his ability to restore art, there was a good chance he could create a realistic facsimile. I wondered if the painting we suspected he sold was the genuine article.

"That's what I'd do," Jean-Pierre replied. "Sterling wants to move the timetable up on your retrieval. Make sure you are at the gallery at three p.m. today. Evans-Sterling security will meet you there. The painting will be authenticated on-site, and you will escort it back to your hotel. Just make sure it doesn't leave your sight until you deliver it Saturday to our people on the other end."

"Will you be at the pick-up today?"

"I'll try to swing it," he said before disconnecting.

At least it was Friday. I'd catch my flight tomorrow morning and deliver the painting to the Evans-Sterling investigators at the airport. I tried to think optimistically instead of imagining all of the things that could go wrong between now and then. Looking at the clock, I realized I could sleep for a couple more hours and rolled over, trying to quiet my mind and the incessant nagging feeling that things weren't as simple as they should be.

It was almost noon when my phone rang again. I reached over and picked it up, assuming it was Sterling or maybe Jean-Pierre. Unfortunately, I was wrong on both accounts. I needed to learn to check the caller ID before automatically hitting answer.

"Alex," Martin's voice broke through the last traces of sleep, "I thought I'd call and see how you are."

"You should be asleep. It's practically the middle of

the night," I scolded him, not wanting to have any type of conversation.

"You're flying back tomorrow, right?" Martin was using his professional tone.

"Yes, why?"

"There's a meeting set with our security equipment firm for Monday. Since I'm updating some office space for Guillot and our contract is almost up anyway, I thought you could come in and consult on the most cost-efficient ways to upgrade our security. I remember how much you complained about the low-resolution surveillance cameras."

The entire reason he had me assess the security of the Paris branch of Martin Technologies was to see how capable I was before asking if I would do the real job. It was amazing how frequently Martin liked to test his employees' qualifications. "Let me guess. The Paris office was a dry run."

"It needed to be done. Your report and recommendations were well-formulated and most helpful."

"Monday?"

"Yes, Monday at two o'clock, conference room three, next to my office."

"I'll see you then," I replied, ready to disconnect.

"Hang on." He stopped me, and his tone shifted. "The other night..."

"Nothing happened. Let's just leave it alone for now."

"See you Monday." Things were back to business as usual.

* * *

The pick-up of Mr. Wilkes' painting went off without a hitch. The painting was authenticated by the independent third party hired by Evans-Sterling. The armed Sterling employees secured the painting in its box and locked it in the cargo compartment of their vehicle, giving both me and the painting a ride back to my hotel. Jean-Pierre handed over the briefcase once we parked. I decided against using the hotel's safe to store the painting for fear I would have to go through the hassle of re-authentication. Instead, I placed it in my room and decided to babysit it until the morning when the same set of security guards would escort me to the airport. Luckily, it was a small painting that easily fit into my carry-on bag. It would never leave my sight.

Jean-Pierre watched as I packed. The painting was neatly rolled into a tube, and the tube was placed inside a reinforced briefcase. My clothes for the morning were left out, along with a few necessities, but everything else was packed and ready to go. It felt strange having to pack for a flight, keeping in mind certain things such as bag size and weight, when my trip over had been so easy and carefree. Working for Martin spoiled me. First, it was a private jet and a five-star hotel. Next, I'd probably need to hire a chauffeur or maid.

"It was good seeing you again," Jean-Pierre said. "We had some wild times on the first go-around. Do you ever miss it?"

"Sometimes," I admitted, thinking about working at the OIO for Mark Jablonsky, running ops, arresting people. "But when I think about all the red-tape, the long hours, and never knowing where I was going or when I was coming back, it wasn't worth it."

"You didn't feel like you were making a difference," Jean-Pierre filled in the blanks.

"Not really," I said. He chuckled at my response. "I realize playing fetch with a painting isn't making a difference either, but..."

"The hours are better, and the pay is pretty damn fantastic. And for the most part, you probably aren't going to get shot or killed."

I hedged on this fact. Since I started out in the private sector, I had taken three hits to the vest, and last night involved some bullets flying in my general direction. "Well, realistically, that's how it should be."

"Tell me about it," he retorted derisively. We spent the rest of the evening exchanging crazy stories from my days at the OIO and his days at Interpol. It had been a long time since I thought about my old life and the real reason for leaving it all behind.

"Have a safe flight, Ali. You just have to deliver the painting, and then you can wash your hands of this whole mess."

"True." I smiled. "You stay safe. Clare's a lucky woman, but don't put your life on hold for too long. There are no certainties in waiting."

He looked at me suspiciously. "Planning on following your own advice?"

"Those who can, do; those who can't, teach," I quoted.

He looked confused. "You Americans have such odd sayings."

*   *   *

That night, I twisted and turned. Sharing old war stories had brought back memories of my final days at the OIO. Mark Jablonsky had put me in charge to coordinate the infiltration of a warehouse thought to be used for the import and export of contraband. It was meant to be harmless, but as the first two-man team breached the perimeter, a booby-trap went off. Two agents were lost that day.

After finalizing the paperwork, being cleared of all culpability, and dealing with the mandated psychological evaluations, I stormed into the director's office and handed over my letter of resignation and my badge. It was one thing to be in the field and have your life threatened or even your partner's. It was something else entirely to give the command that sent men to an early grave. There had been countless hours of reassessing and searching for something that had been missed, but in the end, none of it mattered. They weren't coming back, so there was no reason why I should either.

Mark offered to have me reinstated, but the consequences far outweighed the benefits. Eventually, he gave up on his crusade to turn me back into a federal agent and instead helped secure the job with Martin, and I had been private sector ever since.

My flight the next morning from Paris to London went as planned. Evans-Sterling security escorted me and the painting to the airport. I checked in and kept sight of the briefcase the entire time. Once I got to Heathrow, there was a delay. I was sitting in the airport, the briefcase on my lap, reading a magazine when an announcement came over the intercom that due to bad weather, all outgoing flights were cancelled until further notice. *Crap*, I thought miserably. With the briefcase in hand, I decided to have some lunch and wait out the storm. Lunch soon turned into dinner, and dinner turned into wishing I left two days earlier when Martin flew home.

Settling into a chair far away from other travelers, I called the Evans-Sterling office back home and filled them in on the impending delay. They agreed to keep an eye out for my new arrival time in order to meet and take possession of the painting whenever I managed to fly home. Since I didn't feel like calling

Sterling with the news, I dialed Jean-Pierre and informed him of the delay. They had a few new leads on the missing paintings, and hopefully, the entire situation would be resolved soon. Once again, he insisted that I not worry about any of this but just get home and move on to whatever my next job was going to be. It felt odd playing only a small part in such a large-scale investigation, but I wasn't investigating. My job was asset retrieval and delivery only. Maybe I should be working for UPS or FedEx.

Finally, the storm passed and flights resumed, setting me back almost sixteen hours. Sunday morning, I arrived home completely exhausted, jetlagged, and ready to be free of the painting. The Evans-Sterling people were at the airport and took delivery. I was unburdened and relieved to be home. Retrieving my luggage from baggage claim, I went outside to hail a cab. Parked in the pick-up zone was a very familiar town car with an even more familiar driver.

"Miss Parker," Marcal, Martin's personal driver, greeted, "need a ride home?"

"Marcal, why are you here?" I asked, exasperated. I peered into the car suspiciously, hoping Martin wasn't waiting inside.

"Mr. Martin sent me to pick you up. He had other business to attend to, but he thought you might like a ride."

I was too tired to argue, so I lugged my bags into the car. "How did you know when I was arriving?" After all, I was delayed sixteen hours.

"Mr. Martin gave me your flight number."

"For future reference, if Mr. Martin asks you to do something like this again, please disregard and take the day off." Martin could overstep his boundaries. Although, I knew him, and this was the tactic he chose to use in order to get me to speak to him. Too bad I wasn't falling for such childish games. I settled into the back seat and shut my eyes. At least I didn't have to worry about giving a cabbie directions to my apartment building.

"Miss Parker," Marcal woke me from my nap, "we're here. Do you need any help with your things?"

"No, but thank you." Perhaps I should tip him or something. Instead, I lamely picked up my luggage and exited the car, heading straight for my building.

I climbed the six flights of stairs and pulled the key from my purse to unlock the door. My apartment was dark since the lights were off and the curtains were drawn. Putting my bags down next to the door, I pulled it shut as I reached for the light switch. Before I could flip the switch, a strong pair of hands grabbed me, securing my arms roughly behind my back.

SIX

I bucked wildly, trying to free myself from my captor's grasp. Kicking off the floor, I knocked the man backward into the wall. I jerked my head back hard, making contact with the man's nose. His grip remained tight, and the unmistakable sound of the slide of a gun clicking into place resonated from within my apartment.

"That will be quite enough, Ms. Parker," an unfamiliar voice commanded from the direction of my kitchen table. I stopped fighting and was roughly shoved forward, my arms still pinned tightly behind my back. In the dark, I could barely make out the shape of someone sitting at my dining room table. The silver from his handgun reflected the light from my stove clock ever so slightly. "Why don't you try to act more civilized to your guests?" His voice sounded like a sneer, and I detected a very obvious French accent.

"Maybe I would if my guests weren't of the uninvited variety. Who the hell are you?" I snarled, staring into the darkness and hoping my eyes would adjust further.

"That's not your main concern."

Running through my options, I knew whoever had me was much larger and stronger than I was, and the man in front of me had a gun. It didn't leave much possibility for escape or retaliation. Were there any other men present in the shadows? There was no way to tell, so I couldn't be sure.

"What should I be concerned with?" I asked.

The man behind me tightened his grip, fearing I would lunge forward or try a different tactic. Most likely, I could get free but not with a gun trained on me at this distance. The man at the table stood up, flipped on my table lamp, and walked slowly toward me. He was in a cheap business suit, wearing a ski mask. He was average height and a little overweight.

He stood directly in front of me, exhaling his foul breath into my face. "It's come to my attention you've recently delivered a painting. No matter what you hear or see, it would be in your best interest to step away from this particular endeavor." My breathing was harsh as I stared at this guy. His eyes seemed off, and I suspected he was wearing colored contacts to further disguise his physical appearance. "This is your one and only warning to walk away."

"Kinda hard to go anywhere with this monkey on my back." I didn't take kindly to threats, especially by some asshole in a ski mask who ambushed me in my own apartment.

Ski Mask stepped back and nodded almost imperceptibly to my captor. He grabbed both of my wrists in one hand and used his other meaty paw to slam my head against the wall. Pain erupted through the side of my face, and I crumpled to the ground once he released my wrists. Fighting away the waves of blackness, I was taken by surprise when the man slammed his boot down on my stitched-up thigh. White hot pain shot through me, and I screamed as every single stitch ripped through my flesh. Instinctively, I curled myself into a ball as he delivered another few kicks to my injured leg. "That's enough. We need to go before the neighbors report her screams," Ski Mask commanded, and the onslaught stopped. Ski Mask leaned down, grabbing a fistful of my hair and jerking my head off the ground. "Remember what I said." He slammed my face against the floor for emphasis. As soon as he stepped away, I opened and closed my mouth carefully, checking to see if my jaw was broken. Two sets of footsteps walked to my door, and then the door opened and closed.

I forced myself into a seated position and looked around the room cautiously. When no other attackers presented themselves, I dragged myself to my desk drawer and pulled out my nine millimeter. Loading a clip into it, I leaned against the desk and waited for them to return. After a few minutes passed and no one came back to finish the job, I got off the floor. Using the desk for support, I slumped into my chair. My leg was bleeding profusely, and my vision was impaired by my quickly swelling left eye.

"Holy shit," I gasped, reining in my thoughts. The painting was delivered. My job was finished, so why did some goon and his henchman threaten me? "I'll just sit here for a minute and regroup," I said aloud to myself.

Between the bloody, sticky mess that was my leg and my damaged, swollen face, I couldn't bring myself to move. Finally, I got up, limping, and made my way to the front door. No one was in the hallway. Locking the door, I put the small security chain into the latch and picked up the phone to call Detective Nick O'Connell. He had helped me before, and I knew I could trust him.

"O'Connell," he answered as I slowly made my way through my apartment, making sure Ski Mask and his friend didn't leave any other unpleasant surprises.

"It's Alex Parker. How good are you at changing locks?"

"What's wrong?" He knew I would never call unless the shit hit the fan.

"I need your help. I don't know if I want this to be official." I was uncertain how well-connected Ski Mask was and if he'd know I ratted out his conversation to the police.

"Okay, I'll meet you. Where are you?"

"At home."

Sterilizing a pair of manicuring scissors and tweezers, I was in the process of removing the remnants of my stitches. Having pieces of thread attached to only one side of my injured flesh wasn't doing me any good. "Holy fucking hell," I cursed, pulling the last piece of thread out of my leg. As I poured rubbing alcohol over the gaping hole in my thigh, I tried not to scream. Finally, I wrapped it in gauze and taped it in place, anything to avoid a trip to the ER after being awake for the last twenty-four hours.

After slipping on a pair of loose fitting shorts, I assessed my face. My left eye was swollen shut, and the area from my eyebrow to my cheekbone was red and swollen. I was about to go in search of an ice pack when there was a knock at my door. Immediately tensing up, I grabbed my handgun off the bathroom vanity.

"It's Nick," O'Connell called from the hallway. Cautiously, I unlatched and unlocked my door, stepping aside and allowing him to enter. "What's the other guy look like?"

"I wouldn't know. This was a present from my welcome home party," I retorted, relocking the door. From the freezer, I pulled out a bag of peas. Taking a seat on the couch, I gave Nick a summary of what happened.

"You should file a report." He carefully assessed my face, gingerly touching the damage in order to determine if anything was broken.

"I don't know who this guy is or how connected he might be." I winced at his touch. "I don't want to start stirring the pot until I know what's cooking."

O'Connell thought it was a bad idea not to implement any official channels. "I'll write up a report but keep your name off of it. In the event anything happens, at least we'll have that much." He would simply follow the same procedures in place for dealing with confidential informants.

"Fine," I acquiesced and gave him a more thorough description of the man and the events surrounding my assault. O'Connell walked around my apartment, checking for any evidence. "Ski Mask was wearing gloves. They both were wearing gloves, actually." I thought about the man's hands against my arms.

"Professionals?" O'Connell asked, and I nodded. He went into the hallway and checked the lock. There were no signs of a break-in. "Were you wearing the same clothes?" My bloody jeans were on the bathroom floor, but my shirt was the same. "Get changed. If you were that close to the guy, maybe you got some kind of transfer on you."

Limping to my bedroom, I changed my shirt, and he bagged it. "You always come prepared?"

"You always in such a good mood after getting the shit knocked out of you?" he asked.

"No, it must be your bubbly personality." Sarcasm was my attempt to hide the exhaustion and fear. "Do you know any good locksmiths willing to work Sunday nights who can install a deadbolt or four?"

O'Connell made a call to a retired cop he knew who was nice enough to come over and install two deadbolts and a security bar on my door. The man looked at me suspiciously. He probably thought I was the victim of domestic abuse. *That really served as a great commentary for how often crimes and abuse happen against women*, I thought cynically. I wrote the man a check, and he left without another word.

"Will you be okay by yourself?" O'Connell asked.

"Of course."

"I'll have a few cars keep an eye on things tonight in the neighborhood, just in case."

When he left, I locked each of my new locks and turned on all the lights in my apartment. It was the only way I would feel safe enough to sleep. I left my nine millimeter on the nightstand for easy access. I changed the gauze on my leg since I already bled through it, grabbed the bag of peas, and put them on top of my face before closing my eyes and going to sleep.

I awoke late Monday afternoon after sleeping for almost eighteen hours straight. The gauze on my leg was soaked through with blood, but the bleeding seemed to have stopped. And my thigh didn't look as bad as it did the day before. Despite the fact my pillow was soppy from the melted peas, my eye was no longer swollen shut. However, I still looked like I went twelve rounds in the ring with a heavyweight champion who mistook my face for a punching bag. I showered and dressed, re-bandaging my leg.

When I checked my phone, there were four missed calls. *Glad I'm so popular*, I thought as I listened to my voicemail messages. The first was from Martin, asking where I was.

"Shit." I forgot about the meeting. The second was from Evans-Sterling, asking for a call back. The third was from Jean-Pierre, but the words were garbled from a bad connection. The fourth message was Martin again. He sounded worried and wanted me to call him back immediately when I got the message.

Deciding to prioritize, I dialed the home office of Evans-Sterling. The receptionist transferred my call to Mr. Evans, the namesake partner in charge of the American branch.

"Ms. Parker," he sounded frustrated. Join the club. "The painting you delivered yesterday was a fake. Can you please account for your whereabouts surrounding the sixteen hour delivery delay?"

"What? What do you mean it's a fake? It was authenticated Friday afternoon. The paperwork is included in the briefcase. It never left my sight. Evans-Sterling security transported the painting to the airport. It was a carry-on, and I had it with me the entire time I was waiting for the flight to be rescheduled. Your guys signed off on delivery at the airport." I recounted all of the events. Suddenly, the threat from yesterday made a lot more sense. *Dammit*, I thought angrily.

"I see. Can anyone verify the authentication?"

"Jean-Pierre Gustav was there when the painting was authenticated and transported to my hotel room."

"I have some other things to check, but we'll be in touch." Evans hung-up.

I rubbed the intact portion of my face. How the hell could they think I stole a painting? My mind raced around my threatening houseguests. I was never one to frighten easily, but at the same time, I wasn't sure how far down the rabbit hole I was willing to go for a painting, especially when my employer was accusing me of the theft. It was a good thing I called O'Connell yesterday and he insisted on making a report, even if it wasn't filed through the normal channels. At least I had a paper trail and some corroboration.

Glancing at the clock, I hadn't eaten since the London airport, and I needed to get some pressure bandages and other first-aid supplies. Clipping on my shoulder holster and handgun, I put on my jacket and made sure to take my wallet out of my still packed bags. I placed my P.I. license and carry permit inside. Trying to obscure as much of the left side of my face as I could, I parted my hair on the side and put on a pair of oversized sunglasses. With my two new keys, I exited my apartment and made sure to lock the deadbolts. There would be no more surprise visitors for me.

Each step down the six flights of stairs was excruciating. I didn't want more stitches after having the last set ripped out. Truthfully, I was a baby when it came to doctors. After stopping at the deli on the corner for a quick sandwich, I bought some antiseptic, bandages, and a few ice packs since peas weren't practical when they had a habit of melting into goo. I returned to my apartment building and hobbled back up the steps. *Why couldn't I live on the first floor or even the second?* I thought as my leg repeatedly threatened to give out on me. Emerging onto the sixth floor, I was confronted by a man in an expensive suit, standing outside my door.

"Go home, Martin," I ordered. If Ski Mask and his friend were keeping an eye on me, then Martin could inevitably get caught in the crosshairs.

"Alex?" My odd appearance confused him. "Where have you been? You missed the meeting. You're always so punctual. If Marcal hadn't picked you up yesterday, I might have thought you were still in Paris."

"Something came up. Now, if you wouldn't mind leaving." My angry tone outmatched his, and I ducked my face down, hoping he wouldn't notice. Maybe he would get the hint and go away.

"What the hell is wrong with you?"

I pushed past him toward my door and attempted to remember which key unlocked which lock. Why did they all have to be the same color?

"I've had other things to deal with. If you don't like it, fire me. I don't care. Just leave." I was doing my best to piss him off so he'd storm out and away from any potential danger that could theoretically be waiting on the other side of my door.

"Are you on some kind of bender?" he asked, sounding shocked and incredulous. One of the keys got stuck in the lock. I was trying to coax it out when his words took me completely by surprise.

"Yes, of course, I'm on a fucking bender. How did you ever guess?" I replied sarcastically and impulsively turned to look at him, realizing my mistake too late. "Shit." His features shifted from angry to concerned. "Dammit." I couldn't get the key out. Nothing was cooperating today, not Evans-Sterling, not Martin, and not the damn lock. I kicked the door with my good leg in frustration.

"Here." His voice was gentler now as he reached out and maneuvered the key out of the lock and proceeded to unlock my door.

"Please, just go away," I begged, feeling absolutely defeated as I entered my apartment. My hand rested on my gun, and I performed a quick walkthrough of my apartment, making sure there were no other intruders present. Martin stood in my doorway, watching curiously.

"I'm not going anywhere until you explain what the hell is going on."

"Then get inside and close the door before the rest of the neighborhood sees you."

SEVEN

Martin entered my apartment, looking around casually. He had never been inside before, and I felt like a panda at the zoo with the way he surveyed everything. I bolted my door, and put my newly purchased ice packs in the freezer.

"Might as well make yourself at home."

"Thanks for being so hospitable," he replied sardonically, taking a seat at my kitchen table and waiting for me to say or do something.

I ran through scenarios, trying to determine the best way to deal with the situation. Pulling out the chair across from him, I sat down and slowly took off my sunglasses.

"Don't say anything," I instructed because the last thing I wanted at this moment was sympathy, concern, pity, or whatever it was Martin was going to utter. His green eyes spoke volumes on their own. "I was asleep and missed the meeting. I'm sorry. I should have called or remembered. Yesterday was crazy. My flight was delayed sixteen hours, but you already know that since you sent Marcal to fetch me." My words were biting, and I couldn't be bothered to keep the contempt from my voice.

"I thought you could use a ride."

"No, you thought if you supplied a ride, I would call you. But just so you know, I'm perfectly capable of taking care of myself." I put my hand up to keep him from speaking. "I don't need you, Marcal, or anyone else stopping by here or at the airport or wherever. I have enough to worry about without having to worry about anyone else getting caught in the crossfire." As I spoke, I realized I was too stubborn to back off from tracking down the real painting and hopefully nailing Ski Mask to the wall in the process. "You being here is really not a good idea right now."

"Why?" Martin could be so clueless. Some shock value might drive my point home. He was a showman at heart, after all, so I got up from the chair and moved to my front door.

"Because when I got home yesterday, I was grabbed here," I put my hands behind my back, "and shoved here." I pantomimed the movements. "Where a man sitting in the exact same spot you're in right now pointed a gun at me and threatened to kill me if I didn't back the fuck off. Then I got my face slammed into the wall right here." I slapped the surface with my palm. "So perhaps today isn't a great day for you to show up, uninvited and unannounced." It was overly dramatic, but he needed to understand this was the world in which I lived.

"Alex," he stood up, "I didn't know."

"That's right. You didn't know. You shouldn't know, and you shouldn't be here because I don't know who the hell they are or what they want. If they know who I am and where I live, just imagine how tempting it must be for them to find a few more targets to focus on." I stared fiercely into his eyes.

"That's even more reason why you shouldn't be by yourself." He reached the completely wrong conclusion to my story. "Did you call Jabber or O'Connell?"

"No, I didn't call Mark." Asking Mark Jablonsky, my former boss and colleague at the OIO, to keep an eye out wouldn't be helpful.

"But you called O'Connell, and he just left you here. Alone."

"He took care of things. I'm fine. I don't need a babysitter." I gave Martin my most lethal glare. "So you can go."

Despite my insistence, he remained unperturbed and took a seat on the couch in my living room. "Sorry, can't do that." He loosened his tie.

"Do you want me to call the police and have you arrested for trespassing?"

He shrugged, contemplating the threat. "Not really, but do what you have to." He nodded resolutely. "Given the excellent job Detective O'Connell's done so far, I doubt he'd arrest me." Martin's tone was disdainful. Sitting on the other end of the couch and glaring at him, I tried to remove him with the power of my mind. Unfortunately, the blow to the head last night obviously impaired my telekinetic powers because he remained seated. Eventually, the glaring and quiet got a little too boring for him. "I rescheduled the security equipment meeting until next week. Think you'll remember to show up this time?"

I snorted and shook my head. He was unbelievable. "You really need to get out of the office more," I muttered, pausing briefly. "Fine," I sighed. Maybe now, he would leave. Instead, my phone rang.

"Parker," I answered. The number had a French country code. The call was staticky, and I moved around the room, trying to get better reception.

"Jean-Pierre..." I recognized Clare's voice on the other end of the line. "I needed to call...was a fire..."

"Clare, you're breaking up."

Her voice sounded on the verge of hysterics, but it was hard to tell with all the static. "Jean-Pierre's dead." There were sobs and French spoken quickly by someone else.

"What?" This couldn't be right. He left a voicemail message earlier today. "How?" I paced the room.

"Body...car fire...erre's wallet." The reception wasn't getting any better, and Clare's words were getting more garbled. "Wanted you to know...call later." She disconnected.

"Alex, what's wrong?" Martin asked, but I couldn't process his words.

I shook my head and continued pacing the length of my apartment. Jean-Pierre was dead. He died in a car fire. That was all I got out of Clare, but it made no sense.

"Oh god." Whoever tried to scare me off did even more than that to Jean-Pierre. Could this be about the authentication of Mr. Wilkes' painting? Poor Clare. I dialed the OIO offices and waited for Mark to answer.

"Hey there, stranger," he greeted.

"Mark, I need you to get everything you can on a car fire in Paris that occurred sometime today. The decedent is Jean-Pierre Gustav. Maybe you remember him. He helped us out on that art smuggling case four years ago." My voice broke slightly, so I shut my eyes and took a breath to steady myself.

"Alex?" Mark asked, concerned. "Is everything okay?"

"No. Just see what you can get." I hung up, still

pacing back and forth, trying to piece together everything I knew.

According to Mr. Evans, the painting was a fake. It had been authenticated in France; Jean-Pierre witnessed it just like I did. It was delivered to the Evans-Sterling employees at the airport. But when I came home, Ski Mask and his lackey were in my apartment, warning me to back off, and now Jean-Pierre was dead. What the hell was going on? I absently bit my lip and continued to think as I strode the length of my apartment.

"Alex, stop." Martin stood in front of me, but his tone was gentle. He pulled out a chair and placed it in my path. "Sit down. You're bleeding all over the place."

I looked down. A small stream of blood ran from my thigh to my ankle. "Hmm." I couldn't feel it, probably because I was too preoccupied to notice. "It's fine, just some ripped stitches. Don't worry, I'm not going to bleed to death." Great choice of words. My morbid sense of self-preservation was being callous again.

Martin went into my bathroom and came back with the bag of supplies from earlier. He tenderly guided me into the chair and bandaged my leg, despite my protests, when I realized something and shot up.

"Did I hurt you?" He instantly pulled his hands away.

"They were in the parking garage. No. Wait. That doesn't make sense. They wouldn't have known anyway." Speaking out loud to myself was freaking him out. This would have amused me more if I wasn't working the details out in my mind. Who knew I had a screwed up leg? Jean-Pierre, Clare, the hotel desk clerk, the doctor, and maybe the rest of the Evans-Sterling team, if they had been paying attention. Being kicked in the exact place of my previous injury wasn't a coincidence.

Martin grabbed my hand and pulled me back toward the chair. I sat down obediently and let him finish playing doctor. "There," he patted my knee, "little trick I learned when bandaging my shoulder. It should keep it from re-opening." He was kneeling on the floor in front of me.

"Stay there," I instructed. Pulling another chair over, I placed them both on either side of him.

He looked at me as if I lost my mind. I walked around the chairs slowly, scrutinizing from different angles as I tried to recreate the parking garage. It had been much darker, and Marset, the gunman, and their buddy drove past quickly. None of them could have seen my injury.

"What?" Martin asked as I tapped my pointer finger against my lips.

"It's an inside job. That's how they got my address, knew what time I was getting in, everything." That must have been how the painting was authenticated as real but turned out to be a fake. Perhaps the Evans-Sterling security team switched it, or the third party authenticator was on the take. I dragged one of the chairs back to my table and sat down. They killed one of their own for what, a doodle on some canvas? My attacker was French. Could he have flown over ahead of time to lay in wait just to threaten me and then head back on another flight and kill Jean-Pierre? How many people were involved? Evans-Sterling had offices around the world. My head spun. Was there anyone I could trust from the insurance firm?

I went to my still packed luggage which hadn't left the spot where I dropped it yesterday afternoon. Retrieving my laptop, I dug around for my power cord. Finally, I found it and plugged my computer in, logging in to the Evans-Sterling site. Martin came around and peered over my shoulder. Automatically, I closed my laptop lid and glared at him.

"I need to work, and you need to leave."

"What are you doing?" He sounded frustrated and hurt. "You went and picked up a painting and brought it back. You're done. Why are you doing this?"

"Because a good man died," I stared into his eyes, "and I can't let that go. Not again. Plus," my tone became slightly more threatening, "I don't take kindly to threats." I turned toward the computer and opened the lid.

Martin wrapped his arms around my shoulders. I sighed and put my hand on his forearm. "I'm sorry about your friend."

"Me, too."

He leaned down and kissed my good temple. "Get to work. I'll make dinner, and then I'll get out of your hair. I promise." He was being sweet which made me feel like an ass for being so harsh with him. I still didn't like him being here, but the damage was already done.

The employee database for Evans-Sterling listed the few people I had been in contact with: Jean-Pierre Gustav, Clare Olivier, Clyde Van Buren, Salazar Sterling, Ronald Evans, Ryan Donough, and Michel Langmire. All the information was perfunctory and not very helpful. The two namesakes had large photo spreads and business experience listed, but the investigators were little more than names and photos.

Jean-Pierre mentioned a source who ousted Marset's plan to sell the Manet. Perhaps Clare would know something about that. Clare genuinely seemed upset by Jean-Pierre's death, but a transcontinental phone call full of static wasn't the greatest way to judge a person's sincerity. I wasn't ready to rule her out just yet.

I needed details on the scene and a much more thorough list of everyone who could be involved or even remotely involved. I had no idea who comprised the Evans-Sterling security team who escorted me to the airport on Saturday morning or who the men were who signed off on the delivery of the painting Sunday afternoon. Maybe there was a way I could get access to French nationals who flew into the country between Friday and Sunday. But the list would be too long and extensive to even think about going over. It might not even help. Ski Mask could be a local, hired to make a threat, and the killer may never have left Paris. I was spinning in circles and needed to stop and get a grip.

Changing gears, I carried my luggage into my room. I needed to do something more productive than run myself into the ground. I pulled out my dirty clothes and tossed them into the hamper and placed my toiletries back in the bathroom. Then I put my empty suitcase in the closet.

"I don't see how you don't starve living here," Martin called from the kitchen. Apparently, my unpacking signified it was safe to attempt conversation. "It's no wonder you're so thin."

"Why? Pizza guy delivers. Chinese food delivers. Indian food delivers. There's even a sub place around the block that will deliver." Going into the kitchen, I sat at the table. Every single cabinet was open, as well as over half the drawers. Martin had no idea where I kept anything. "And let's not forget, I do own a microwave. Frozen dinners can stay in their cardboard boxes for years without expiring." I smirked, glad to get out of my own head for a few minutes. It was nice having him here, even though it was a risk he shouldn't take.

He was making some kind of sauce and found a few

cans of crushed tomatoes in my cabinets, along with a box of penne. "This will take a while to cook." He indicated the sauce. "I hope you aren't hungry, or I guess you could call one of those delivery joints." I narrowed my eyes, knowing his tricks all too well. He decided to buy as much time as possible to avoid leaving me alone.

"And if I were, what would you do?" If only he would admit to his manipulative tactics.

"Hand you the phone and let you order whatever you wanted, my treat."

"I take it you're staying for dinner." It wasn't a question since I already knew the answer.

"That would be lovely. Thanks for the invitation."

"Just so you know, I am on to you and your pathetic attempts at psychological manipulation. The only reason they work is because I let you get away with them. Apparently, I've somehow learned to tolerate you."

"Duly noted."

I left Martin in the kitchen to continue to cook or pretend to cook while I went into my bedroom and called O'Connell. I updated him on current events and gave the go-ahead to stick my name and pertinent detailed information on the report and file it. The best way to see how wide-reaching this thing was was to throw some matches at the powder keg until something exploded. O'Connell assured me patrol cars would drive past my place every now and again to see if things stayed quiet. I thanked him and hung up, heading back into the kitchen.

"Martin, please tell me you didn't leave Marcal sitting outside in your town car this entire time." I hadn't actually thought about how Martin arrived at my apartment so much as I had focused on getting him to leave.

"Of course not. I told him if I didn't come out in fifteen minutes to go home," he said matter-of-factly. Looking out the window of my fire escape toward the parking lot, I didn't spot any suspicious cars or anything of the sort outside. "Don't worry, I wasn't thinking anything sordid. I just figured I'd call when I was ready to leave."

The fact he felt the need to mention he didn't have any ulterior motives made me think perhaps he originally did, but I let it go. "When you got here, did you see anyone suspicious or any suspicious vehicles?" If I had anything concrete to report to O'Connell, I'd rather do it sooner instead of later.

He thought for a moment. "No. I noticed your car was parked outside and figured you must be home. I didn't consider you might have walked to the store." Which was exactly what I did.

"Okay, just wondered." My anxiety lessened since O'Connell's guys were keeping an eye on things, and neither Martin nor I had seen anyone suspicious outside. But I couldn't be too careful, especially when it involved him potentially painting a target on his back.

Pulling a couple of plates and some silverware out of the open cabinets and drawers, I set the table. "So how's everything coming along with Guillot's transfer?" It was a safer, more civil conversation topic.

Martin spoke about the paperwork he'd been working on and estimated Guillot would be able to transfer in within a couple of months, depending on how quickly his temporary work VISA could be obtained.

Finally, dinner was ready. Although, it probably could have been ready an hour or so earlier. We were almost finished eating when there was a knock at the door. I tensed immediately and went to the coffee table to retrieve my gun.

"Who is it?" I called warily.

"Mark. I brought you some files, special delivery." I put my gun down on the table and went to the door, unlocking the two deadbolts, sliding the security bar out of the way, and unlocking the doorknob. "What is this, Fort Knox?" Mark asked before I managed to open the door. As the door opened, surprise and concern dawned on his face.

"Hey, come in. You're just in time for dinner." I stepped out of the way, so he could enter. He had a stack of folders in his hands.

"Are you okay?"

"I'm fine. If you were hoping to jump onto the overprotective bandwagon, you're a little late to the party," I said pointedly for Martin's benefit.

"Jabber," Martin greeted Mark. They had been friends from way back, and the only reason I even knew Martin was because Mark had gotten me hired as his security consultant.

"Marty." Mark nodded, putting the files down on my coffee table. "I hope I'm not interrupting."

"Not at all," I said quickly, after relocking the door. I grabbed a plate and fork from the kitchen and put them on the table for Mark.

"No French wine?" Mark teased.

"Definitely not," I replied a little too quickly, and Martin got a devilish glint in his eyes.

"I have a few bottles at my place. I figured I'd save them for a special occasion. I'll send one home with you the next time you stop by," Martin promised. Going to the fridge, I pulled a beer out for Mark while glaring at Martin, who pretended not to notice.

"Alex, what's going on?" Mark asked, concerned.

I gave him the same rundown Martin heard. The details surrounding Paris and the chase through the streets which led to the pathetic shootout in the parking garage were excluded due to Martin's presence. Mark nodded as he listened thoughtfully.

"Wait," Martin interjected, "you told me you had ripped stitches. When did you get stitches?" Why did he always pay attention?

"In Paris. Don't worry about it. I cut my leg on a piece of rusted wire in a garage. It's not important." Martin seemed satisfied with the answer, but Mark was aware of a few missing pieces.

After dinner, Martin offered to clean up, despite my insistence he should go home instead. The sink ran full blast while Mark and I went into the living room, and I filled him in on the misplaced paintings, the fake Manet we recovered from Marset, and the SUV in the garage.

"Sounds like you had a hell of a time in Paris."

"The only thing worse was coming home. Why can't anything ever be simple?"

"I got the files you wanted. You can thank our Interpol friends."

I picked up the folder, not wanting to open it yet. Once I did, Jean-Pierre would officially be dead. The ball would be rolling, and there would be no stopping it. I put the file back on the table, pulling my hand away like it might bite.

"Thanks." Changing the subject, I glanced back at Martin, who was still washing dishes. He was doing this deliberately slow as well. "He won't leave," I whined, and Mark chuckled. "I missed the damn meeting at Martin Tech today, and he just shows up at my door and sees this," I indicated my face, "and won't leave."

"He's worried about you and with good reason. Plus, he's trying to make up for the weeks you spent taking care of him."

"I was paid to take care of him. It was a job," I insisted. Mark gave me a *yeah, right* look but kept his mouth shut. "I'll be honest with you. I'm scared. If Ski Mask and his little friend come back, I don't want them to target anyone else to get to me."

"I get it. I'll have a talk with Jones, you know him as Bruiser, and I'll make sure he keeps an extra close eye on Martin. Once Marty realizes you're okay, he'll back off. Trust me."

I picked the folder up and opened it, reading the information presented inside. A body, so badly burned it was unrecognizable, was discovered in a burnt-out car identified as belonging to Jean-Pierre Gustav. It was discovered this morning. The identification was made based upon the driver's license found inside the wallet that had somehow been protected from the fire, likely because it was leather and inside the inner pocket of Jean-Pierre's leather jacket.

"Car bomb?" I asked. Given the graphic photos enclosed, it must have been a quick blast that blew out the entire interior of the car and charred the body, leaving only the leather intact.

"That would be my guess. It's still a new and open investigation, but this is the preliminary report," Mark said. I shut the folder and put it on the table. "Parker, you can let this one go. Interpol's investigating. He used to be one of theirs. They will get whoever is responsible."

"I know it's someone from Evans-Sterling. Or at the very least, someone from Evans-Sterling is involved." I found the list of people I dealt with and handed it to Mark. "Give this to whoever gave you the report, and let them check out backgrounds and alibis."

EIGHT

"Are you sure you're okay?" Mark asked again. I nodded. I wasn't some fragile flower that was going to crumble. "All right." Mark walked to the door. "Marty, I can drop you at home."

Martin turned and looked at me, unsure if he should stay or go. "I'll meet you downstairs in ten. I have some private business to discuss with Alex."

Oh joy, I thought cynically. "What now?" I was emotionally drained from the news about Jean-Pierre and anxious to get started on tracking down the party responsible.

"I'm sorry," Martin said simply, his eyes full of remorse. "I should never have left you in Paris."

"Look. We are both adults."

He smirked. "I meant I shouldn't have left you in Paris, the city. I should have insisted you fly back with me. Maybe this wouldn't have happened."

I felt like an idiot. "This has nothing to do with you. This," I indicated my face, "is why you need to stay away from me. Enough people try to kill you just because you're you. You don't need them to be after you because of me, too. This is the life I've chosen. It comes with the territory." Jean-Pierre left Interpol for the chance at a life too, but he didn't get one. It wasn't fair.

"Alexis," Martin's voice was gentle, "I wish I could ask you not to do this, but it's what makes you, you. I'll stay away, but if you need anything, I expect a call." He walked to the door, and I got up to lock it behind him. He stopped and turned to me. "Don't forget the security equipment meeting next week."

"E-mail me the details." After locking up, I headed to the coffee table and picked up the file Mark brought. It was going to be a long night.

I pulled dossiers on every Evans-Sterling employee who worked with Jean-Pierre on the investigation. Everyone had a squeaky clean background that I found infuriating. On the gallery's website were names of all the employees. Maybe if there was a connection between one of my squeaky clean suspects and a gallery employee, the dots would connect. The hotel desk clerk and doctor probably weren't part of the conspiracy to threaten me and murder Jean-Pierre, which did very little to rule out the list of suspects who could be involved.

I brewed a pot of decaf coffee since I needed to do something besides stare at the computer screen. I listened to the garbled voicemail Jean-Pierre left on my phone. Why didn't I hear the phone and answer? Maybe I could have done something. The message remained fairly indecipherable, so I'd have to bring it to Mark tomorrow and see if it might be of some help to the Interpol investigators. The last conversation I had with Jean-Pierre was during my layover at Heathrow. He said they were making progress on recovering the paintings. Was this what led to his death?

Backtracking, I tried to recall the precise threat I

received. No matter what happens from here on out, I was to step away from the investigation. What kind of horseshit was that? Recalling Ski Mask's physical characteristics, I determined he was somewhere between 5'9 and 6'0 and weighed maybe 200 pounds. I looked through the small photos on everyone's dossier. The description didn't match any of them. Everyone at Evans-Sterling was in decent physical shape, except for the men in charge.

I was attacking the problem from too many different angles and ending up lost in the middle. Looking at the clock, I realized it was almost two a.m. I closed my computer, double-checked the locks, and decided to get some sleep with half of the lights still on in my apartment. *This was progress*, I reasoned. I was just about to drift off when the phone rang, causing me to jump up, startled.

"Parker," I answered.

"I'm sorry if I woke you," Clare said from the other end.

"I wasn't asleep." I went into the kitchen where I had left my notes. "How are you doing?"

She made a nondescript sound, followed by a lighter clicking and a lengthy exhale. "I can't believe he's gone."

"I am so sorry for your loss." The words came out automatically. "Do you want to tell me what happened?"

"They called me to the scene to identify what was left. It was his jacket and his wallet." It sounded as if she were trying very hard not to cry. "It wasn't his face. He was scorched." Clare was tortured by the indelible images she had seen, which broke my heart.

"Are they sure it's him?"

She let out a horrible sounding laugh. "Not yet, but I'm sure." She exhaled another breath. "They think it was a car bomb." I waited patiently for her to continue. "The blast shattered his teeth, making dental recognition impossible, and the amount of burns to the flesh." She choked the sobs back down. "I understand. I'm sorry." I picked up my pen and crossed her name off my list. No one tortured this much could be responsible. She was weeping. "Listen," I needed her to focus on something else, "when I got home...," I stopped. I was so close to telling her about Ski Mask, but something didn't feel right. "Jean-Pierre left a voicemail message, but I don't know what it was in regards to. Do you think he was on to something involving the Evans-Sterling investigation?"

"Je ne sais pas," Clare reverted back to French, but if she kept things basic, it'd be okay.

"Has anyone been threatened?" Hopefully, she wouldn't ask my motivation for this particular question.

"No. I don't think his murder," she paused, fighting to regain her composure, "has anything to do with the investigation." I sat down on the couch, waiting for her to continue but willing to give her as much time as she needed. "Jean-Pierre got himself in too deep with gambling debts."

"I had no idea." I was dumbfounded, not expecting the conversation to go in this direction.

"He always says he can handle it," she was crying again, "but this time, it got away from him."

"Clare, if there is anything I can do," I felt useless, "please don't hesitate."

"I barely even know you, Alexis, but I saw how happy it made Jean-Pierre to work with you again. I thought I should call and let you know what happened." She was ready to disconnect. "Interpol is looking into things. I will let you know how it ends."

"I am deeply sorry."

"Moi aussi." Clare hung up.

I leaned back against the couch cushion and closed my eyes. *Pull it together, Parker*, my mind instructed my emotions to obey.

I was back to the most basic question imaginable. Was Jean-Pierre's murder related to Ski Mask threatening me? There was a thought already formulating in my brain, but I didn't like where it was going. If Jean-Pierre needed to pay off his debts, what was he willing to do? Did he help misplace the lost paintings? It was hard to fathom him being crooked, but then again, I couldn't imagine my threat and his death weren't related. It didn't make any sense. If he was dirty, why would they kill him? Rule number one of loan sharking, if you kill your client, you'll never get paid. No, his death had to be related to the art theft. Maybe it was simply made to look like a loan shark getting revenge for unpaid debts.

I went back to bed and stared at the ceiling. There was nothing I could do at the moment, so I decided to get some sleep. Tomorrow, I would come up with a plan of attack.

*   *   *

The next morning, I showered, dressed, and headed to the Evans-Sterling building. It was time I had it out with Mr. Evans. I entered the lobby and spoke to the receptionist, insisting Mr. Evans meet with me. She took my name and relevant information and informed me he was in a meeting right now, and I should make an appointment.

"I'll wait," I replied, sitting down in a chair and picking up a magazine. She eyed me carefully and finally got on the phone and spoke in a hushed tone.

"Ms. Parker, Mr. Evans can see you now." It was amazing how quickly meetings could come to an end, particularly when they were of the made-up variety.

"Thanks." I headed toward his office.

"Ms. Parker." Evans was in his doorway, waiting for me. "Please, have a seat." He stepped back and allowed me inside. I took off my sunglasses and sat down. He came around the desk, surprised by my appearance.

"Mr. Evans," I forced my voice to remain neutral, "are you aware one of your investigators was found murdered yesterday morning in Paris?"

"Yes, but," he began, but I cut him off.

"And did you realize, sir," I practically spat the word, "that not only did you accuse me of stealing the painting I was hired to retrieve, but also upon arrival, I was greeted by two very friendly gentlemen who suggested I have nothing further to do with the painting or the subsequent investigation." I watched Evans for any micro-expressions or suspicious behavior. Despite his faults, he seemed genuinely frightened and properly concerned.

"I was not aware."

"Well, now you are." He gaped at my bruised cheek, a bit unnerved. He probably prided himself on being more of a lover than a fighter. Although, given his physical characteristics, he'd be lucky to call himself either. "I would strongly recommend you check into your employees' backgrounds because I wouldn't be surprised if one of them was involved." I stood up. I said my piece, and it was time to leave.

"Ms. Parker," Evans finally spoke, "you will still be compensated for the job, even though the results were not what we expected."

Resisting the urge to tell Mr. Evans what he could do with his money, I stomped out of his office and out of the building. This wasn't about the money or the job. This was about getting answers.

In my car, I sat smoldering for a few minutes. Things could have been handled a little more professionally. On the plus side, I didn't threaten anyone or cause any property damage, so I suppose I could still write the entire event off as an overall win. While I was determining my next course of action, a few employees exited the building. Maybe it wouldn't hurt if I waited a bit longer, just to make sure no one matching my recollection of Ski Mask entered or left the Evans-Sterling building.

After almost an hour of waiting, nothing surfaced. Staring out the window, I ran through scenarios in my head until my phone rang. I glanced at the caller ID before answering.

"Mark," I greeted.

"If you're still dead set on looking into this case, I have some more information to add to the Gustav file. Do you want to come by and pick it up?"

"Yeah. Okay." Turning the key, I pulled away from the parking spot. "I have a voicemail that might be of some interest. Maybe you could have someone clean it up for me before you pass it along."

"You're going to make sure I end up racking up a ton of favors with Interpol, aren't you?"

"Of course. You know me, completely into fair trades."

He snorted and hung up.

NINE

After leaving Mark's office, I knew it was about time I checked in at my own. I was leasing a small office space at a strip mall. It was designed for meeting clients and appearing to be a competent and established investigator. So far, I met with exactly one client in my office, and that was Martin when he brought the retainer contract for me to sign. Other than that, it was basically just a drain on my limited income.

Picking up the mail, I unlocked the door. The stack of letters was mostly addressed to *current resident*, until I came across a delivery notice. The slip advised a package was not delivered this morning, and another delivery attempt would be made later today. I'd just have to stick around until the courier graced me with his presence.

Taking off my shoulder holster and placing my gun in the now open top drawer of my desk, I opened the bottom drawer and propped my injured leg up. Leaning back in the chair, I stared out the door, waiting. People went about their business, to and from the other shops. At least my lack of clients wasn't because of a zombie apocalypse.

After a few minutes of waiting, I figured I might as well get some work done. Turning on the computer, I perused the new information Mark provided. I checked into Jean-Pierre's background and ran checks on any and every one he had been in contact with. Interpol provided the OIO with a list of Jean-Pierre's CI's, the ones they knew about anyway, as well as his other black market contacts.

Every single person had a rap sheet, which didn't surprise me. I just didn't know if he had been in contact with any of them or if they would have turned against him for the right price. Rubbing my eyes, I searched the police databases for anyone involved in illegal gambling. I wanted a clear picture of what the gambling and racketeering world looked like in Paris and if it was strictly tied to organized crime. Gambling existed on so many different levels that whoever Jean-Pierre owed could have been a small-time bookie, looking to make a big impression, or someone running a large-scale crime syndicate.

Looking for bomb specifications in the updated file was futile since none were provided. The cause of the explosion was still under investigation, as were the DNA results for the victim. The only positive identification was the VIN of Jean-Pierre's car.

I turned off the computer and pulled out a pad of paper. It was time to try this the old-fashioned way. Here were the few facts I had. Jean-Pierre was murdered. Ski Mask and his goon threatened me and knew of my previous injury. The painting was a fake. Marset had a fake Manet and quite a bit of money in his possession, and the SUV and its two occupants were assisting Marset. I added Jean-Pierre's gambling debts to my list with a question mark. Was Marset ever located, and did the painting go up for auction in Luxembourg as Jean-Pierre suspected?

I stared out the door, unseeing, as I slowly ran through the few contacts I had in the underground art world. Unfortunately, every name I came up with had been arrested or worse. Maybe Clare or another Sterling employee knew who Jean-Pierre's contact was. Although, who could be trusted? At least one person on the team had to be involved in this. No one else would have known enough about me to send Ski Mask to deliver a message.

The bell above my door dinged, and I jumped despite the fact I was staring at the door. It was the courier. Plastering a pleasant smile on my face, I signed the sheet and accepted delivery of my parcel. After he left, I carefully examined the exterior of the box. It had French stamps and international, overnight airmail stickers. There was no return address. *I really needed to invest in a bomb sniffing dog*, the paranoid part of my brain thought as I pulled out a letter opener and sliced through the tape. Slowly peeling back the brown paper to reveal a white cardboard mailing box, I tried not to think what my remains would look like after being flash-burned by a letter bomb.

Inside the box was a VHS tape. It was unlabeled, and there was nothing else inside. It was a good thing I was one of the few people left with outdated equipment. I rummaged through the small storage closet, looking for the TV and VCR combo. This was probably why most people considered me a packrat. I pulled the TV out and set it on top of my desk, finding an extension cord and inserting the tape into the player. Hitting play, I waited.

The image was grainy, and the tape was low

quality. The tracking lines scrolled up and down the screen. The scene looked vaguely familiar, and I watched Jean-Pierre's spiked blond hair emerge from the bottom right-hand corner of the screen. He walked over to a dark colored car and unlocked the door. The screen went bright white, followed by a few moments of nothing but static and fuzz, and then I saw the remnants of the still burning vehicle. I gasped. Why would anyone send me this? The tape played for a few moments, but there was nothing else on it. Hitting stop, I sat down in my desk chair. My hands trembled as I fumbled with the remote, shutting off the blue glow from the television

I pulled out a pair of gloves and ejected the tape, placed it back in the box, and grabbed my belongings. I headed straight to Mark's office. He looked up as I entered.

"What's wrong?" He reached for the box, but I pulled it out of his reach before he could touch it.

"Might be evidence. I already touched the whole damn thing but figured I might as well be retroactive with the gloves." I was in a bitch of a mood. Watching a friend get murdered tended to have that effect. "In case you were wondering, someone was kind enough to let me watch Jean-Pierre's last few seconds. Do you think they were being helpful or just sending another message?" I placed the box on Mark's desk and pulled out the failed delivery notice from my purse and handed it to him.

"Are you okay?" He motioned to some agents in the hallway to come and properly claim the box.

"I'm fucking wonderful."

The agents came in and removed the box and packaging from Mark's desk. He nodded to them as they walked out. "Are you sure you don't want to let this one go?"

I stared him down like he was a speeding train, and we were in the midst of a game of chicken. "Funny, the more forcefully that point is made, the less likely I am to listen." There was another trip to Paris in my future.

*   *   *

I went to the shooting range to blow off steam. I had just gone through two magazines, firing in the classic two-handed stance most law enforcement agencies insisted on. I pressed the button, and my paper target moved toward me. The center of the paper was decimated, just the way I liked it. I replaced the target with another and was reloading my gun when my phone buzzed.

"If it isn't my favorite detective," I answered, putting the safety on.

"What an honor," O'Connell teased. "How many other detectives do you even know?"

"Don't belittle my compliment. I'm assuming your call actually has a point." Gunfire sounded in the background as a few other people shot at their targets.

"Is this a bad time?"

"I'm at the range."

"It must have been a slow week for the tech guys because they got a match on some blood from the back of your shirt." My attempt to break my captor's nose had been successful. "His name's Aaron Ramirez, local guy, bit of a thug, used to do odd jobs for the Sanchez gang until they got disbanded. He has quite a few assaults and drug offenses, nice assortment of felonies and misdemeanors. We have a BOLO on him."

"Uh-huh." Why would a French national hire a local guy to assist? Maybe Ski Mask wasn't really

French but pulled off a convincing accent.

"Are you doing okay?" O'Connell interrupted my thoughts.

"Peachy." I informed him of the delivery this morning and Jean-Pierre's murder.

"Shit, Parker. You don't half-ass anything, do you?"

"Apparently not. Let me know when you collar the guy."

Disconnecting, I flipped the safety off and fired one-handed in a sniper stance until the magazine clicked empty. All head shots. At least my aim was improving. I repeated the process with my left hand, aiming this time for center mass, making about seventy percent of the shots in the ten ring. It would do in a pinch. Cleaning up my spent bullet casings, I went back to my car and drove home.

Once again, I carefully entered my apartment and made sure everything was as I left it. I thought about the VHS tape. An attempt had been made to deliver it to my office early this morning, but I wasn't there. It didn't matter. I already knew Jean-Pierre was dead, and watching him die had little impact on that conclusion. But something was gnawing at my subconscious. I just couldn't put my finger on it.

The databases provided detailed arrest information on Ramirez, but there was little to be gained that O'Connell didn't already tell me. I cross-referenced Ramirez with the employee list from Evans-Sterling. There was no overlap or connection to be found. Not to mention, Ramirez didn't even possess a passport. He must have been hired for his sparkling personality and ability to grab women who were half a foot shorter and a hundred pounds lighter than he was.

A thought crossed my mind, and I looked into the Sanchez gang to see if they had any connections to black market art smuggling. There must be some kind of connection between Ramirez and Paris. *Talk about a French connection,* my mind filled in the pathetic joke. After a couple of hours of searching, the pieces connected. A few members of the Sanchez gang had been arrested for running an illegal gambling ring. The items recovered in the raid included an Andy Warhol print with an estimated value of $60,000. Gambling and art, my two favorite things at the moment.

Tracking the history of the Warhol backward, I was scrolling through ownership and bills of sale when my phone rang, destroying the mental trail I was so carefully following.

"What?" I asked, annoyed.

"I just wanted to make sure you were okay," Martin said.

"I am." I blinked a few times. The hours of staring at the computer screen made it difficult to focus on things at a distance. Maybe I could use a break. It was almost seven. "I need to get back to work."

"Okay."

"Just remember to stay clear of me for a while." I wasn't going to tell him about the videotape.

"Sure. Good night, Alex."

I went back to clicking away at the keyboard, but my concentration was shattered. Looking for something to eat, I rummaged around in the kitchen. I ate dinner and stared out the window of my apartment, wondering why everything had to be so complicated. I thought about Jean-Pierre and Clare. I was firmly planted in the anger stage of grief. To top it off, I was even more pissed someone had the audacity to send such a heinous tape. The anger was just the motivation I needed to get back on track.

I went to the computer and traced the Warhol's ownership back two years when it was in the possession of a Mr. Wilkes, who insured the painting with Evans-Sterling.

"Hot damn." I leaned back in my chair and tried to digest the full implications of my discovery.

TEN

I failed to consider the significance of the painting's owner. Mr. Stanley Wilkes was simply a name attached to a file provided by the helpful bastards at Evans-Sterling. It was mixed in with their welcome package of 'do's and 'don't's on procuring and transporting valuable art, making it even more difficult to ascertain any useful information on the man. The law enforcement databases found nothing on Wilkes. He didn't exist, or he didn't have a criminal record. A general people search came up with quite a few Stanley Wilkes, but none matched the address or contact information Evans-Sterling provided. After an internet search, I still had nothing. Did Evans-Sterling screen their clients at all?

It was almost ten p.m., so calling the office building now would be a fruitless endeavor. I shut down my computer and decided to get some sleep. The jetlag, my welcome home party, and Clare's late night call fucked up my Circadian rhythms even more so than usual.

Leaving a couple of lights on in my apartment, I

changed the bandage on my leg. Amazingly, it was healing, thanks to Martin's little trick. I assessed my face in the mirror. It was severely bruised but no longer swollen. As long as I didn't touch it, things were good.

I slept until six a.m. *Maybe I was turning into a morning person,* I thought ironically as I dressed in workout gear and did a few hundred crunches, some push-ups, and finished with a couple basic combinations of punches and blocks, avoiding anything that might put undue stress on my thigh since it didn't need to start bleeding again. I had a lot of pent-up energy from all the hostility I was harboring toward Jean-Pierre's murderer. After showering and dressing, I took a seat at the computer and double-checked that I didn't miss finding the proper Stanley Wilkes.

By nine o'clock, I was out the door and heading for the Evans-Sterling building. Mr. Evans would be absolutely delighted to see me again. This time, the secretary went straight to the intercom and informed him I was in the lobby. Once I entered his office, my tirade began.

"Who's Mr. Wilkes?" I asked before taking a seat.

"Ms. Parker, our client confidentiality is very important."

"Cut the bullshit. Wilkes doesn't exist. So whose painting did I bring back?"

Evans tried to intimidate me with his stare, which didn't work since his face reminded me of a pug. Sure, he could probably snort loudly and maybe let out a bark every now and again, but his bite wasn't dangerous. I waited him out.

"This is a very well-endowed, high profile client. Wilkes is the name we have selected in order to ensure the utmost level of privacy."

"Despite your penis-envy for the guy, he often has issues in the procurement of his paintings, doesn't he?" I narrowed my eyes at Evans. If I gave him my death glare, he would keel over.

"I don't know what you mean." He fidgeted with the pen on his desk. He must make a lousy poker player. "Now if you wouldn't mind leaving, or I can have you escorted from the building."

I stood up and walked slowly toward the door. "It's a real shame about that Warhol getting caught in the police raid a couple years back. It would be a disgrace if the press got wind of how Evans-Sterling was failing to protect client assets from being used in some illegal form or fashion." I would burn the whole place to the ground in order to get what I wanted.

"You wouldn't dare," Evans barked. "You signed a confidentiality agreement. We'd own your ass."

"Actually, I'm pretty sure my contract only pertains to the painting I was hired to return, and quite frankly, I don't remember a strict confidentiality clause anywhere. If you want to call the legal department and have them explain it to you, I can wait."

He turned blood red but realized he wasn't going to win this. "Sit down," he commanded. Victorious, I went back to the chair and took a seat. "If I tell you what you want to know, it can't leave this room." I shrugged. "Stanley Wilkes is the codename we use for suspect pieces a high-end brokerage firm has hired us to procure."

"Suspect?"

"The company has its own investments and eccentric clientele. Every once in a while, one of their buyers locates a piece they must have, but sometimes, the art they acquire may not be, shall we say, legitimate. All of the verified pieces are later sold or surrendered to institutions and private dealers. However, since these pieces aren't always reliable, we're paid to handle the procurement, authentication, and delivery in order to maintain the brokerage firm's reputation."

"You're involved in the sale of illegally obtained works and fraudulent art?"

"Of course not." Evans was genuinely offended. "Nothing black market, but sometimes, we play in the gray." If I were still an OIO agent, I'd have him in cuffs. "We hire former federal agents, like yourself, in order to ensure laws are not broken." In other words, so they could cover their asses.

"Why did the brokerage firm want to acquire this particular painting?"

"I don't know," he sounded sincere. I couldn't be positive he wasn't lying, but my gut said he was on the level about this.

"How did the Warhol end up in a raid?" It didn't matter, but my interest was piqued.

"It belonged to a gang. One of the lackeys transferred ownership for a decent price. We were handling the delivery." Evans was covering by making the sale sound legitimate. "Unfortunately, not all of his cohorts agreed on the price. Things got a little messy. It wasn't our brightest moment."

Nodding, I left the office. I had a lot to think about.

*   *   *

I went to Mark's office, positive he must be sick and tired of seeing me by now. When I knocked on his door, he looked up wearily.

"Please don't give me anything else," he begged. "I have enough casework of my own without doing you or Interpol any favors."

"Maybe I just came to see you. It's been almost twenty-four hours. I don't think I can make it a full day without getting to see your smiling face," I said.

"What do you want, Parker?"

"Is there an ongoing investigation into Evans-Sterling?"

He adopted a shifty-eyed look. "What did you hear?"

"Not a thing. I just thought if there wasn't one in the works, there should be."

He sighed, exasperated, and rubbed his forehead. "What did I just say about giving me more work to do?"

"You were looking for an excuse to score some overtime," I suggested, smiling pleasantly. After telling Mark everything I uncovered from Evans, he didn't seem surprised. Evidently, things like this were common occurrences. It was nothing earth-shattering or worth starting a new file or investigation on, at least not at the present.

"While I have you here, you might as well know, our guys checked the box, the tape, and the content. We haven't identified the sender. However, the VHS tape appears to have been cut. Unfortunately, there's no way to determine what was removed, but I thought you'd like to know." I was about to speak, but Mark cut me off. "Oh, and yes, I did pass it on to our friends at Interpol."

*　　*　　*

O'Connell called during my drive home. Ramirez was brought in late last night. They were still holding him. Making an illegal u-turn, I headed for the precinct.

"That was quick," O'Connell commented as I took a seat in the vacant chair across from his desk.

"Traffic was light." I neglected to mention the one or two minor traffic violations I committed on my way here. "You do realize there is no way I can legitimately identify him."

O'Connell's nod was barely perceptible. "That doesn't mean we can't suggest he cooperate on his own volition." He winked. "Are you willing to get back in the ring, slugger?"

If I went along with this ruse, there was a good chance I'd have a few more unexpected visitors knocking on my door or worse. Although, if I didn't, my opportunity to identify Ski Mask would be nonexistent. "Okay."

I followed O'Connell into the interrogation room and remained near the door as he went around the table and sat in front of Aaron Ramirez. Ramirez stared at the table. As far as I could tell, he didn't notice me.

"Mr. Ramirez," O'Connell spoke slowly, "are you sure you want to stick with your story that you have no idea why you're here?"

"That's right." Ramirez rocked ever so slightly back and forth in his chair. He was cuffed to the bar in the table. "This is jus' some kind of racial profilin' shit. You see me out and think he mus' be guilty of somethin'."

"Hmm." O'Connell glanced at me. I leaned against the wall, making sure it was sturdy, with my arms crossed over my chest. "So you don't want to tell me who hired you for the assault on Sunday afternoon?"

"I don't know nothin' 'bout that." Ramirez stared at his nails.

"Funny," I spoke up, "I know you're lying."

Ramirez turned his head in my direction, watching me carefully. There was maybe a flicker of recognition, but this thug was a pro. He wasn't even dazed by my presence.

"Do you realize, Mr. Ramirez, assaulting a federal agent is a felony?" O'Connell might have left out the word former, but I wasn't about to correct him. An assault was an assault.

"Who's a federal agent?" Ramirez seemed curious but not flustered or nervous. I wasn't sure we'd get him to roll. "She a federal agent?"

I gave him a big, fake smile.

"So you see," O'Connell got his attention, "it'd be a shame if something horrible were to happen to you in lock-up before you get transferred out of here. You know how things work when you attack a cop." O'Connell leaned back in the chair; we had all the time in the world.

"What do you want?" Ramirez asked after a few minutes of complete silence.

O'Connell glanced at me again. This was all for show.

I cocked an eyebrow up and shrugged. "A name would be nice." I stood up straight, away from the wall, and sauntered toward the table, staring Ramirez down. My expression conveyed one simple truth; I'm not intimidated by a son of a bitch like you. "Give us the suit with the accent, and I'll make sure you get out of here this afternoon."

Ramirez pulled back on his cuffs, making them clang menacingly while he eyed me. Finally, he shifted his gaze to O'Connell.

"This on the level?" he asked.

"I'll make the paperwork disappear myself," O'Connell promised.

"He don't got a name," Ramirez responded.

"Fine. Throw the son of a bitch in lock-up." I turned and headed for the door. "I'm done."

"Sorry, pal," O'Connell said. The chair squeaked

against the floor as he got up. I was one step into the hallway when Ramirez spoke again.

"Wait, what if I roll on who paid me?"

I turned around slowly and glanced at O'Connell. It was his call what he wanted to do.

"I guess that would suffice." O'Connell retook his seat, and I shut the door and resumed my leaning.

"Guy named Clyde Van Buren wired the money."

I nodded once to O'Connell and left the interrogation room. If I stayed a moment longer, I would want to even the score. Back in the bullpen, I sat down in O'Connell's chair, waiting for him to finish with Ramirez. He was giving him the stay away or else speech. Finally, O'Connell met me at his desk.

"Was that helpful?" he asked, staring at his chair forlornly. Surrendering his chair, I took a seat next to his desk.

"Just confirmation it's an inside job." Tilting my head up, I stared at the ceiling, asking, "Do you think he'll tattle to his buddies?"

"No. He's getting out of town and taking a nice long vacation. At least he will if he knows what's good for him." O'Connell could be intimidating when he wanted to be.

"Looks like I might be taking a trip, too. Thanks, I owe you one."

"We'll call it even for everything you gave me last time," he countered. "Fair enough?"

"Sure." I left the precinct and headed home. All the lights were staying on tonight.

ELEVEN

Clyde Van Buren, former American Customs agent, was hired by Evans-Sterling two years ago. The first large-scale asset retrieval he worked was the Warhol, which would explain how he had Ramirez's name. Van Buren had no criminal record, a decent enough credit score, and had recently applied for permanent alien resident status in France. But that didn't explain why he would be willing to kill Jean-Pierre and threaten me. There didn't seem to be any reason besides the fact the guy must be a greedy, sinister asshole.

Clare had been partnered with him during the stakeout at the gallery. Could there be a potential love triangle in my midst? I clicked the mouse a few times to close the opened windows. It didn't matter what Van Buren's motivation was. All that mattered was stopping him. I informed Mark of the situation, and he put me in direct contact with the Interpol liaison, Patrick Farrell.

Farrell was a cooperative man and promised to keep me in the loop. Interpol was now working with the Police Nationale on tracking Van Buren's movements and attempting to build a solid case against him for the murder of Jean-Pierre. Theoretically, my work should have been finished at this point.

Unfortunately, I had a horrible habit of failing to let things go. I spent the rest of the week spying on the Evans-Sterling offices. If Clyde Van Buren was dirty, how did I know there wasn't an equally corrupt American investigator working with him? I ran license plate numbers, backgrounds, and followed a few of the more suspicious types. Everyone at the American branch of Evans-Sterling appeared to be on the level. I even followed Mr. Evans once or twice when he left the office. Nothing conclusive turned up. On the plus side, no one noticed the tail since I wasn't pulled over or arrested for stalking. On an even more positive note, no one came to my apartment to deliver any more messages.

When I wasn't stalking Evans-Sterling employees or running background checks, I was digging up information on the French team Jean-Pierre led. Once again, no one appeared dirty, except Van Buren, who had the blip on his radar with the Warhol incident. With more digging, I discovered Jean-Pierre was partnered with him on that retrieval. Maybe this was when things went awry between the two. Clare was removed from the entire situation since she was one of the latest newcomers to Evans-Sterling, causing my theory on a love triangle to fall to the wayside.

If I wanted more concrete answers, I needed to go back to Paris and do some legwork. During my search for cheap flights, a new e-mail message popped up. Martin had forwarded the pertinent information regarding the security firm meeting which was scheduled for Tuesday afternoon. I could go to the meeting and leave Tuesday evening or Wednesday. I wasn't being paid to investigate Jean-Pierre's murder, but I was being paid to consult at Martin Technologies. My priorities were skewed toward tracking a killer instead of worrying about updating security cameras but whatever pays the bills.

I sent Martin a response guaranteeing I would be there this time and booked a flight for ten o'clock Tuesday night. Assuming an eight hour flight and the obvious time difference, if I slept on the plane, I could hit the ground running Wednesday afternoon. It seemed like a solid plan, minus the fact I had no idea what I intended to do in Paris. I wasn't a cop. I wasn't a federal agent, and I wasn't even an Evans-Sterling employee anymore. Was this entire trip completely ludicrous? *Yes*, my internal voice answered. However, the constant gnawing feeling made it painfully apparent I had to be there, even if it was just to watch the real cops put the screws to Van Buren. I felt I owed it to Jean-Pierre, which was an equally ridiculous notion. We worked a case together four years ago and spent a few days together recently. I didn't owe him anything. In all honesty, I barely knew him.

I tried to rationalize why I shouldn't go to Paris to avenge Jean-Pierre. The problem was, for whatever the reason, he had been a kindred spirit. We both left our government jobs to start over in the private sector in the hopes of making a name for ourselves and living the life we wanted. If Jean-Pierre couldn't do it, how good were my chances of succeeding before someone blew up my car or waited in my apartment to put a bullet through my skull? Maybe I just wanted to know if it was me, someone would be fighting to find answers. God, I was turning into an insecure mess.

The next day, I called the hotel and requested a

room reservation. The desk clerk was more than happy to assist. Boxing up some items, I would overnight them to my hotel room since I didn't want to piss off the TSA agents. My handcuffs, pepper spray, taser, and Spyderco knife were brought to FedEx for delivery. I might not need any of it, but considering I had yet to determine what my actual plan was, it didn't seem like a bad idea to be prepared. The hotel would hold my parcel until I arrived. Pulling out my duffel bag, I packed only the necessities and a few items to help me blend in with the seedy underground gambling scene. And they say women can't pack light.

The next day, I dressed as a business professional in a skirt, dress shirt, and jacket, put on a pair of pumps, and covered my slightly discolored face with concealer. The bruises were in the final stage of healing, and my thigh, while still not completely closed, was well on the way to becoming a pink scar. Marching into Martin Technologies, I was greeted by the security guard, Jeffrey Myers.

"Ms. Parker, long time, no see." Jeffrey smiled. "Go on up. Mr. Martin is expecting you."

The place was a ghost town. The only office still on this level was Martin's and maybe mine, if it hadn't been turned into a janitor's closet. I knocked on his door and waited to be buzzed in.

"Alex." Martin looked up from his desk, acknowledging my presence. Picking a spot in front of the wall of windows, I stared outside while he finished whatever he was doing. He clicked away at the keyboard, and the printer fired up. "Are you ready to listen to the spiel about the latest developments in security cameras and fiber optics?" He sounded cynical in his mocking.

"That is why I'm here. Are you joining me for the

festivities?"

"I can spare a few minutes," Martin said, "but Charlie Roman's sitting in on the meeting, in case you need assistance." I briefly met Mr. Roman, a board member, at a charity function with Martin. "Can you provide your official recommendations before close of business today?"

"Of course." Looking in the direction of my old office, I asked, "Do you mind if I borrow the old office space?"

"It's your office." Martin seemed confused by my request. "You are still a Martin Tech employee. You are entitled to have your own space in the building."

"Good to know."

He was clearly busy, so I went across the hallway and unlocked the door. Besides being vacuumed and dusted, the office didn't look like it had been used in months. I put my belongings down and sat in my chair. It felt strange being back in this building for work. I shook the feeling away and rifled through the drawers for a legal pad and pen. Once prepared, I went to the conference room to wait until Martin freed himself from his desk chair and the security equipment representative showed up.

I was trying very hard not to spin in circles in the office chair when Martin entered the conference room. He no longer seemed interested in work, and it was reflected in his posture. I shot him a questioning look.

"Charlie's waiting in the lobby. Our sales rep is running late today." He pulled out the chair next to mine and carefully examined my face. "How are you?" he asked softly. Work-mode Martin was taking a break.

"I'm okay." I stared at the lines running across the legal pad. He reached to touch my makeup covered cheek, and I automatically jerked away. He pulled his hand back as if he'd been burned. "Sorry, it's almost healed, just a reflex."

"I wanted to check on you."

"No reason." I shook my head, dismissing his sentiment. "I'm actually," I was about to tell him of my impending trip when Mr. Roman and an exquisitely dressed woman entered the room.

"James Martin, Alexis Parker, this is the equipment representative, Dani Heller," Roman introduced us. There were rounds of handshakes and nods. I didn't quite like the way Dani looked at Martin, but I needed to let that go. She was a saleswoman. I just wasn't sure what she thought she was selling.

Dani came prepared with a slideshow and presentation on the newest and latest equipment from lasers to fiber optics to remote-operated cameras and motion sensors. She was fifteen minutes into her presentation when Martin picked up my pen and scribbled a note on my legal pad. I looked down, assuming he was wondering what my opinion of the biometric locks was, only to be surprised by 'dinner tonight?' I tried not to smile. It felt like we were in high school passing notes. I gave Martin an almost imperceptible headshake.

"Excuse me, Ms. Heller," Martin interrupted, standing up. "I hate to run, but I'm leaving these decisions in the very capable hands of Mr. Roman and our security consultant, Ms. Parker. Please, carry on." He gave her a charming smile and headed for the door. "Ms. Parker, if you'd be so kind as to hand deliver those recommendations personally at four this afternoon, that would be lovely."

"Yes, sir," I replied as he made his way out of the conference room and back toward the elevators.

Dani continued her sales pitch, completely unfazed

by Martin's disappearance. That kind of professionalism was admirable. At the end of the presentation, Roman thanked her for rescheduling. He didn't have any questions or anything else to add. I, on the other hand, was hired to consult on matters such as these.

"Ms. Heller, if you'd be so kind," I stood up, nodding to Roman that I could take it from here, "I would like to take you through the building and hear what types of improvements you think would be most beneficial." Most of what she was selling was too advanced for the MT building. It wasn't like Martin was protecting weapons-grade uranium, but maybe she would have some interesting ideas I failed to consider.

We began in the lobby and worked our way up. I flipped my notepad to a clean sheet of paper and noted her suggestions. Surprisingly, she wasn't insisting on solely top-of-the-line replacements. At the end, I escorted her back to the lobby and thanked her for her time. I reiterated that Martin would send her the list of upgrades he wanted very soon. She had been pleased by my questions and probably assumed she would make a nice commission.

In my office, I typed a thorough list of the most beneficial equipment upgrades. Basically, new cameras with a larger hard drive to store the digital files and some biometric locks wouldn't be a bad idea when used strategically. Overall, the security at Martin Tech was decent enough as it was. I recommended adding a few more cameras in the elevator and in the blind spots of the hallways but nothing earth-shattering or costly. Martin should be pleased. I printed out the report and e-mailed him a copy, just in case.

It was 3:45 when I opened my office door to wait

for him to return. At 4:12, he came down the hall, scanned his ID card, and entered his office.

"Here's the report you wanted." I placed it on his desk and sat down in his client chair, waiting for him to finish filing whatever it was he needed to leave the equipment meeting to do. When he was done, he glanced at the two-page report and focused on me.

"Still avoiding me like the plague?" he asked playfully.

"Actually, what I wanted to tell you earlier was I'm leaving tonight."

He got up from behind his desk and poured himself a drink. "Want one?"

"No, thank you." I moved to the couch. Business was obviously over for the day, and now I was afraid I'd have to justify my leaving.

"Going back to Paris?" He carried his drink to the couch and sat down next to me. He didn't sound surprised.

"Yes. My flight leaves tonight at ten. I don't know when I'm coming back. I just thought you should know in case you needed me to do anything here." I gestured obliquely around the office.

"We'll manage." He didn't sound pleased by my revelation.

"Okay, well, if there's nothing else, I should get going."

"Alex," his questioning tone almost sounded wounded, "what are you doing?"

"What?"

"Why are you going to Paris? What do you think you can do that isn't already being done?" He studied my face, hoping to gain some type of understanding.

"I don't know, but it doesn't mean I shouldn't try." I paused, determined to make him understand. "I have to do this."

He still didn't get it, probably because it was completely illogical. He got up from the couch, put his glass down, and knelt in front of me.

"This is purely platonic, so don't get mad," he whispered, wrapping his arms around me in a hug. I held him tightly for a few minutes, not wanting to let go. "Stay safe and please come back in one piece."

Finally, I let go and picked up my purse. Boundaries, Parker. We needed firm, clearly defined boundaries. "I'll see you later."

*   *   *

Dressed in comfortable travel clothes, I grabbed a quick bite and called a cab to take me to the airport. I checked in the recommended two hours early and sat in the terminal, trying to decide if this was actually a good idea. Just because something wasn't a good idea didn't necessarily mean I shouldn't do it.

I called Patrick Farrell and informed him of my impending trip. Farrell tried to be helpful by smoothing the waters with the Paris Interpol office. They knew I would be snooping around in their investigation and were willing to grant a slight professional courtesy as long as I agreed to stay out of their way. This helped to comfort my questioning mind. I dialed Clare to give her my flight number and arrival time. She sounded pleased to have someone to assist in the investigation she was conducting on her own.

An hour later, I boarded the plane and tried to get comfortable in the cramped, little seat as I closed my eyes. If I could just fall asleep and stay asleep for the next six hours, things would work out well. It was sheer willpower alone that let me sleep as we crossed the Atlantic Ocean. I woke up at ten a.m., Paris time.

We still had another couple of hours left in the air, but I could entertain myself for that long. Finally, the plane made its final approach and landed. I stood around baggage claim for what felt like an eternity before my single duffel bag emerged onto the carousel. Grabbing it, I hailed a taxi to my hotel.

TWELVE

The box I sent ahead was waiting in my room. Opening it, I regarded the contents before unlocking the room safe and placing everything, except the pepper spray, inside. My first stop would be the Paris branch of Interpol, and I didn't want to risk setting off the metal detector. Quickly unpacking my bag, I hung up my clothes and took a shower. Some breakfast and coffee would have been nice, but I didn't want to waste the time. Hailing a cab, I headed to the Interpol offices. During the ride, I sent Clare a text message to let her know I was in Paris and offered to meet later. She responded with a location and time to get together for drinks.

Entering the Interpol building, I was given a visitor's pass to wear. I informed the man working the main desk I was here in regards to the Gustav murder, and Agent Farrell should have contacted them about my impending arrival. In a small office, I was introduced to Agent Delacroix, who thanked me for all the information I supplied: the videotape, my suspect list, and the connection between Clyde Van Buren and

Jean-Pierre. I updated Delacroix on the connections concerning Ramirez, the Sanchez gang, and the Warhol that had been confiscated in the police raid. There were quite a few strangely shaped pieces to this particular jigsaw puzzle. Once I was finished dithering on about my conclusions, Delacroix asked what I planned to do now.

"Look around and see if anything pops up," I replied.

He wasn't happy with my answer. "Ms. Parker, I understand you used to be an American agent, and you still work in security. But this is Paris. We have an investigation in the works, and quite frankly, we don't need you bumbling about and getting in our way."

"I understand, but the thing is, I believe whoever killed Gustav is connected to the creeps who broke into my apartment and threatened me. I can't walk away, thinking they're still out there." Maybe I was being dramatic, but Delacroix considered my point.

"You can look around, but if you blow any part of this investigation for us," his gaze was unyielding, "I will personally make sure you are on the first flight out of here."

"Understood."

"If you find anything, you will report it directly to me. Think of me as your commanding officer."

I didn't like having no say in the matter, but there wasn't much I could do. I nodded my head in acquiescence.

"Good." He gave me a brief smile. "Enjoy your stay in Paris."

On the way back to the hotel, I felt like I sold my soul to the devil, and all I got out of the deal were the cheap seats. Oh well, I would make do with what I had. Right now, everything was pointing toward Van Buren being the mastermind behind my threats and

Jean-Pierre's murder. If I worked the case carefully, I could work around the Interpol investigation without getting in the way. There were always loopholes. I just needed to make sure I found the right one.

Back in my room, I resisted the urge to lie down. If I fell asleep now, I'd be doomed. Instead, I called the concierge and arranged for a rental car. Having my own means of transportation would make surveillance a lot easier. The car would be delivered, charged to my credit card on file with the hotel, and be waiting in the parking lot whenever I was ready to go out. I pulled up some maps, locating the gallery and a few other key locations, figuring Clare could point out where Jean-Pierre's car was found, where he went to gamble, and other similarly important locales.

Studying the city maps, I was familiarizing myself with the cross streets and traffic patterns when my phone rang. It was Clare. She was on her way and wondered if I needed to be picked up. It would make things easier and allow me to pay attention to the roads while she drove, so I gave her my room number and waited.

*   *   *

"Alexis," Clare intoned in her thick French accent, "I can't believe you came all this way."

"That's the general consensus." We sat at a small table in the corner of the bar. "How are you holding up?"

She shrugged. Her eyes held a question, and she hesitated to ask as she stabbed at the ice cubes. Eventually, she met my eyes and spoke softly. "Were you and Jean-Pierre lovers?"

"Oh god, no," I said, completely surprised. "I spent a couple of months working with him years ago. That was it." I swirled the straw around my glass. "I regret that I didn't know him very well." Signaling to the waitress for another round, I studied Clare's appearance. Her eyes were puffy and dark. The news of his death weighed heavily on her, but I detected the smallest sign of relief. Jean-Pierre might have been a lot of things, but at least he wasn't a philanderer.

"Then I don't understand. Why come here to avenge him?"

My original knee-jerk reaction to Jean-Pierre's murder was to hunt down the person responsible. That was also the same knee-jerk reaction I had when reading particularly gruesome news stories. This was often what separated our first responders and military from ordinary civilians. Some of us had the unquenchable need to do something. It was probably because we were all just closeted control freaks. The difference here was one too many people told me to back off.

"I want justice for him," I looked at Clare, knowing I needed to admit to my own selfish motivation, "but I've also received a few violent suggestions to walk away. Needless to say, I'm not the most obedient. It's more like, *oh really, then watch this, asshole.*"

A brief, knowing smile crossed her face. "Je comprend."

Glancing around the bar, I made sure no one was interested in us or our conversation. "What have you found?"

Clare gave a run-through of everything. The Police Nationale strongly suggested Evans-Sterling conclude its business at the gallery. The surveillance teams were pulled, and everyone who worked any aspect of the missing painting investigation was questioned in conjunction with the thefts. Passports and VISAs were confiscated, and no one was permitted to leave the country. Marset had not been located, but as far as Clare was aware, the Manet never went up for auction in Luxembourg.

In regards to the car bombing, the Police Nationale were working with Interpol to determine the cause of the explosion. The working theory was Jean-Pierre's accrued gambling debts were the motivation for the bombing. I was aware of most of these facts, but I didn't want to share my Interpol connection just yet. I didn't know why I was having trouble trusting Clare, but it was usually best to err on the side of caution.

"Do you know who Jean-Pierre owed money to?" I curled the corners of my napkin.

"We did not normally discuss such things. I followed him once to a private club in the second arrondissement." Clare laughed bitterly. "I thought he was cheating on me. Too bad I wasn't so lucky."

"Either way, Jean-Pierre still had a mistress on the side."

"C'est vrai."

"Find anything out about the club? Was it strictly illegal gambling? Are we talking sports betting? Cards? Casino games?" Gambling could cover any of a million different things.

"I don't know." She found a pen in her purse and wrote a name and address on a napkin and slid it across the table. "This is where Jean-Pierre went to bet. From the outside, it doesn't look like much. Nothing glitzy or sinister. It's just a dilapidated warehouse, like much of the area. It's all I know." It didn't seem like she wanted to find out any more than this. She wanted to remember him in the most positive light possible.

"Okay, I'll look into it and see what I can find." I tucked the napkin inside my purse.

"I've been following the bombing." She picked up

her glass and finished the rest of her drink. "So far, it looks like whoever is responsible knew Jean-Pierre well enough to know his habits, where he parked, what he drove, when he'd return." I could tell where her suspicions were headed. "It must have been someone he trusted."

I took a deep breath. "I think it was someone working on his team at Evans-Sterling." It was too soon to give up Van Buren.

"What?" The shock resonated in her voice and read all over her face.

"I got home Sunday night, after delivering the painting, and two men were in my apartment. They roughed me up, and they knew about my leg." I tapped my thigh.

"Shit." My revelation frightened her. "I can't imagine."

"Anyone at Evans-Sterling ever take issue with Jean-Pierre? Some bad blood or a past history?" I wanted to find out more about Van Buren and the tainted acquisition of the Warhol, but Clare just sat there, flummoxed. Perhaps this was too much for her to absorb all at once. First, her lover was murdered, and she's told it's because of his gambling. Next, she's brought in for questioning on some missing paintings, and now I was telling her one of her teammates was responsible. It was a lot for anyone to handle, and Clare being a desk jockey, not an operative, probably made this all the more difficult to stomach.

"I don't know." She looked to me for help.

"It's okay. It's a lot to process. Take some time. Sleep on it. If you think of something, we'll look into it."

She sat silently, lost in her thoughts. We left the bar, and she dropped me off at my hotel on her way back to her apartment without uttering a single word.

I went to my room, changed out of my clothes, and sat in bed with my laptop, checking into the address and name she provided. There were no raids or reports made. Whoever or whatever was operating out of this club managed to remain undetected or unreported to the police. I'd have to do things the hard way. At least it was a starting point which hopefully wouldn't interfere with Interpol's investigation.

*   *   *

The next morning, or afternoon since it was a little after one o'clock before I awoke, the valet brought my rental car around, and I drove to the address Clare had given me. The club appeared to be an old, abandoned warehouse, at least during the day. Maybe there was a weekly organized game, or it shut down and moved to another clandestine location to avoid detection. I would have to keep checking at various times to see if I could spot any obvious action going on.

Despite Delacroix's insistence that I stay out of the way, I found myself parked outside Van Buren's residence. I pulled public records and found his address and the model of his vehicle, complete with tag numbers. I was observing him from a distance. He had been a U.S. Customs agent, so I didn't expect him to be cognizant of being watched.

Van Buren appeared to live a boring and normal existence. He went to the market, the bookstore, and back to his house. Based on the flickering of the lights, he was watching television. For a murderer and potential smuggler, he wasn't particularly active. It was midnight when the lights went off inside his apartment. I waited another hour to make sure nothing else occurred before leaving. Driving back to the club, I didn't see any signs of life. Finally, I returned to my hotel room, raided the snack section of the mini-bar, and went to bed.

I continued to observe Van Buren for the rest of the week. He always stuck with a similar routine. Out to run errands in the afternoon, home the rest of the night to watch television, and then bed at a decent hour. I was becoming convinced he was the most brilliant mastermind ever. Who could pull off a murder, send trans-Atlantic threats, and still fit so perfectly into a humdrum, innocent existence? The man must be an evil genius.

Clare refused to join in the reconnaissance and insisted she was following her own leads on the car bomber. She had some friends at Interpol, but no one gave her any useful information. There was no way to be sure if it was because the investigation was still in the preliminary stages or if for some reason they didn't want it divulged. Being alone in Paris was making me paranoid. Everyone was turning into a suspect, including Clare. Deciding it best to rely only on people I could trust, I would go it alone as much as possible.

At night, after leaving Van Buren's, I was working my way into the underground gambling world by constantly barhopping in the hopes of locating some shady sports bars. This led to ordering and spilling enough drinks to make my presence seem realistic. I would then ask, often loudly, where to go for some action on the game. It didn't matter what game or sport. I was just looking for connections. So far, I had been directed to a few low-level bookies.

It was Friday night, a little after two a.m., when I located a pool hall. This was the fourth one I stumbled upon, but it felt different. This was the right atmosphere, judging by the patrons. I entered, smelling of the cheap tequila I intentionally spilled on my top two bars ago. Instinctively, I knew I was on to something. The pool hall had the right seedy feel to it and enough hired muscle for protection and enforcement.

A man playing pool said something, likely sexist, in French. His smile could make Martin's lechery look like it belonged to a choirboy. I returned his smile and made a pretense at drunkenly sauntering over. This was easily achieved by stumbling into the pool table and a barstool.

"Hey there," I said, making it painfully obvious I was American.

"Hey yourself, babe." The man spoke English. Maybe he deserved a prize, so I let him continue to stare down my top. "Looking to play? Or are you lost?"

I sized up the guy from the moment I stepped inside. He was one of the hired guns, large, burly, and covered in street tats. He would know how to deal with unpleasant outsiders. I noted the scar tissue around his knuckles and eyes. He had been some type of fighter, or he just really liked to hit people. Unfortunately, some of those people had hit back, maybe because he stared down their tops too.

"I need a drink first to warm up before I hit the tables," I slurred. "Are they open to anyone? Or just to people you like?" I attempted to be seductive, and he smiled.

"Francois, a drink for the lady," he yelled to the bartender.

I glanced over, watching the bartender mix the drink. I was suspicious by nature, but I couldn't risk being roofied. Francois mixed the drink and slid it down the bar.

"Mercy." I downplayed any and all French speaking

ability I possessed. When in doubt, best to play dumb. Taking a gulp from the glass, I put it on the edge of the table.

"Warmer?" Burly tat guy asked.

"You betcha. Do you wager here? I can never remember these things. I just came from Monte Carlo, and they wager on everything. I still have some of my winnings left." I pulled a hefty stack of Euros from my pocket and saw the man's eyes light up. Clearly, he thought he found an idiotic, drunken American girl, willing to hand over her money and who knew what else by the end of the night. That would make whoever was in charge happy and maybe give Burly guy enough of a raise to go get another tattoo.

"We only play for money here."

"Well, that is the only reason to play, now isn't it?" I cooed, cocking an eyebrow up at him.

THIRTEEN

"What's your name, baby?" the man asked as he racked the billiards.

"Alex." I took off my leather jacket and placed it on a nearby chair. My knife was folded into the top of my ankle boot, but the pepper spray was in my jacket pocket. Figuring it was an everyday necessity for women, I didn't think it would be touched or thought of as suspicious. "And you are?" I asked, trying to sound playful and slutty.

"Claude," he replied. "My pleasure to meet you."

"Not yet," I gave him my best sexy eyes, "but we'll see how things go." I picked up a cue. "What's the going rate on games?"

"Two hundred, starting." He watched my reaction, and I wondered if I was exuding cop instead of drunken slut.

Maybe I needed to step up the act. Pulling out a handful of Euros, I slapped them down on the table. "How about we play for whatever that is, and we can take it from there?"

He picked up the money, counting it quickly in his head and adding an equal amount to it before putting it into one of the side pockets for safe keeping. I was permitted to break, and I played well but not too well. I wanted to hook this guy by showing competence in the game play and betting without being an easy mark, but I made sure he won.

"Double or nothing?" I made a pouty face. "Come on, you have to give me a chance to win some of it back." Ordering another drink from the bar, I expertly spilled most of it between the bar and the table without anyone noticing.

"Okay." He was delighted by this prospect. Maybe he wasn't used to getting five hundred a game.

I leaned over the table, making sure he got a nice eyeful before standing up and walking around to the other side to line up my shot. Leaning against the table in front of him, I wiggled my ass before I finally took my shot. I wanted him to be distracted, so when I won, he wouldn't think it was because I was hustling him.

The game was close, but I scraped by at the last minute. It was a good thing I spent most of my four years at college playing pool late at night, and people said college didn't prepare anyone for the real world. Ha. Claude cursed in French. I smiled and picked up my glass, swallowing the remainder in one gulp before turning the glass upside down on the table.

People around us were watching now, and I could differentiate the regulars from those being hustled. One man, dressed slightly more sophisticated than the others, sat in the corner of the room, watching everything. He was the guy in charge. Taking a mental picture, I noted his close-cropped dark hair, eyes that had seen too much, and his flair for the decadent. His entire presence radiated power. This wasn't a small racket. I accidentally stumbled into some serious shit. Parker, you're playing with the big boys now.

"Another game," Claude demanded, and I agreed.

I needed to demonstrate my willingness to throw a significant amount of money around if I wanted to be taken seriously. I also knew I needed to scrape by until the end and then lose. The house always wins was the only rule that mattered when it came to gambling.

"Sure, but only if you buy me another round." I walked my fingers up his chest. My skills at flirtation sucked, but hopefully, it wouldn't matter.

"Francois," Claude called to the bartender, "one more."

I sipped this one slowly, knowing now that I had the attention of the man in charge, I couldn't get away with spilling half of it on the floor. "Let's make it an even grand this time," I suggested, placing the entirety of my winnings on the table.

He was ecstatic. The next game continued, and I scratched at the last possible minute, giving him the opportunity to win.

"Again?" Claude asked.

Boss man got up from the booth and went into the back room. Was he coming back, or did he see enough? Hopefully, my drunken tourist act had done the job. I made a pretense of reaching into my pocket.

"Sorry, I'm flush tonight." I absentmindedly ran my hand up and down Claude's bicep. He had some muscle, but it was mostly blubber from drinking too much. "Maybe another night. You have to give me a chance to win my money back." I made a pouty face.

"Come back anytime. I'm always here."

"Maybe pool just isn't my game." Was now a good time to broach the subject? "Any other games you think we could play?" I picked up the glass and finished it off. "I remember doing pretty good playing blackjack."

Claude turned away from me and glanced toward the room Boss man disappeared into. The door was open, and the man was seated at a desk inside. He nodded almost imperceptibly.

"Come back tomorrow, and we'll find something more to your liking."

I left the bar and headed to my hotel, keeping a careful eye on the rearview mirror to make sure I wasn't followed. There was no way of knowing if the bar I happened upon tonight would eventually lead to the men Jean-Pierre owed. Underground gambling might not run in just one circle, but I was certain I stumbled upon a powerful presence. There was no other explanation for the hired muscle and the back room head nod.

As I continued driving, my mind wandered to Van Buren and his humdrum life. From what I observed, he was a homebody who stuck to a stable routine. No friends, no visitors, nothing. I slammed on my brakes and turned down the next street, reversing direction and heading toward Van Buren's apartment. Maybe something new would surface at this late hour. It was almost four a.m. By my reasoning, Van Buren should have been asleep for the last four hours, but maybe I was wrong. Maybe he was like Marset, waking in the middle of the night to have clandestine meetings with strange men. I found a spot and parked.

All the lights were off, and there didn't appear to be any movement in the apartment. I'd wait an hour and then go to my hotel. I was sitting in the car, trying to stay focused on the apartment but not managing very well. Stakeouts were incredibly boring, especially by yourself. It was dark, and I was tired. I fiddled with the radio for a while, but that got boring fast.

Checking my phone, I debated if I should call Clare to keep me company, but it was the middle of the night. I thought about calling Mark or Martin. But Mark would want an update, and Martin would be confused by my call. I leaned back in my seat and stared out the windshield.

"Holy crap." I jumped when someone knocked on the passenger's side window. I glanced over while reaching for my knife. *Dammit*, I thought, hitting the unlock button.

Agent Delacroix opened the door and got into my car. "Parker, are you lost?" he asked in a demeaning tone.

"Not exactly." With my luck, I'd be going to the airport in the morning.

Delacroix sniffed the air cautiously. "Are you drunk?"

"Not exactly. My shirt might be."

He nodded at my comment as if it made perfect sense. "Just thought you'd like to know we've cleared Van Buren as a suspect. You can stop tailing him."

"What?"

"He isn't responsible. Airtight alibi." Delacroix was all business. "I know you've been surveilling him all week. I've had a couple of guys watching you watching him."

Dammit, I was so consumed by watching Van Buren I didn't worry about who was watching me. That was a rookie mistake, and if it had been the bomber, it could have cost me dearly. "Wait a minute, if he isn't the guy, why the hell are you out here at five in the morning, giving me this update?" Especially since this was my first late night stakeout. I was getting an uneasy feeling about Delacroix and carefully reached toward the door handle, preparing to flee if necessary.

He genuinely smiled, a look I had never seen on his face. "Maybe you need to do some more homework." He opened the door and got out of the car. "Go back to your hotel and get cleaned up. Come see me tomorrow afternoon. We have a couple of things to discuss." He walked down the street and got into a black sedan. I waited for a few minutes to see if he was leaving. He remained parked a few cars away. Finally, I gave up and slowly pulled out of the space, executing a three-point turn and driving past the sedan. Someone else was in the car besides Delacroix, but in the dark, there was no way of knowing who it might be.

Back in my room, I was more confused now than when I left. I pulled up the addresses on the other Evans-Sterling suspects, but no one lived near Van Buren. So why were Interpol agents in the neighborhood if Van Buren wasn't involved? But he had to be. He wired the money to Ramirez.

Wait a minute. I thought about the wire transfer. To wire money all someone needed was photo identification. Could someone have forged an ID using Van Buren's information in order to throw investigators off the scent? Great, Van Buren was likely a dead end, and I was back to square one. Whoever was behind this was an Evans-Sterling employee who worked the gallery case. I skimmed through Jean-Pierre's information, figuring if I was back at square one, I might as well start at the very first building block.

"Huh," I said to the computer screen. Jean-Pierre lived across the street from Van Buren. Could Delacroix have been staking out Jean-Pierre's apartment to see if the killer might be coming back for something? A missing painting perhaps?

I shut off my laptop and went to bed. There would be no way of knowing what was actually going on until

Delacroix read me in on his investigation, unless of course his entire plan was to lure me to his office in the afternoon just so he could personally escort me to the airport. I pushed the second thought aside, figuring he wouldn't have wasted his time if that was the case.

*   *   *

That afternoon, I arrived, looking professional. For what, I didn't yet know. I sat in Delacroix's office, waiting for him to return from a meeting and resisting the urge to rifle through the files on his desk, looking for information. Instead, I watched the second hand on the clock slowly tick by. When Delacroix returned, he glanced at the stack of files suspiciously as he sat behind his desk.

"Did you do your homework, Parker?" he asked in an attempt to disgrace my intellect.

"You're watching Gustav's place." I glared at him. "Are you waiting for someone to return to the scene of the crime, so to speak?"

He nodded to himself as a smug, omniscient grin crinkled the corners of his eyes. "I was on the phone a few minutes ago with Patrick Farrell. Seems you called in quite a few tips on this case." He wasn't answering my question, so I figured I might as well return the favor. We stared each other down for a few minutes.

"Are you sending me home?"

He seemed to consider something before he replied, "I heard you could be a hard ass. Stubborn, opinionated, difficulty playing well with others, probably means you don't let people push you around."

I remained unresponsive to his commentary. I

could be a team player, just ask Mark Jablonsky. Maybe I was a bit headstrong, but I always followed orders. Well, almost always.

"Is there a point?" I finally asked.

"Just thought it might be fun to see what you shake loose on your own. You know Van Buren is clear, so from now on, stay clear of Gustav's place. If we spotted you, someone else could too." I continued staring at him, wondering what the hell he was thinking. "You're free to go. Remember, report back anything you find. This is still my case."

"You know, I normally get paid for my services."

"Funny, you don't seem like a street-walker."

I headed for the door, more pissed off than when I arrived. Out of the two of us, I was not the one who couldn't play well with others.

"Parker," he called as I reached the hallway, "there might be some kind of reward for information that leads to the arrest of the bomber."

I snorted and continued walking.

FOURTEEN

That night, I went back to the pool hall where I met Claude. This time, I dressed in a black miniskirt, high-heeled leather boots, a matching jacket, and a light blue tank top. Hopefully, he wouldn't confuse me with a street-walker either.

Entering the bar, I noticed the same guy who appeared to be in charge sitting in the same booth. Claude was nowhere to be seen. Surveying the room, I took a seat at the bar and waited. When in doubt, patience was a useful tool. My back was to the wall, so I would have the tactical advantage of spotting anyone who might be coming. The barstools were half-full with other patrons, probably regulars. From what I gathered, I was the only tourist.

I ordered a drink and nursed it, waiting for something to happen. Ordering a second drink, I continued to wait. The man in charge finally approached me. He took a seat next to mine and said something in French. I gave him a slight smile and responded in English.

"I'm sorry. My French isn't too good."

He nodded and began again in English. "You were here last night playing billiards?" he asked, even though he already knew the answer.

"Yes. Claude said to come tonight if I wanted to win some of my money back. Do you know Claude?"

"Oui, Mademoiselle," he replied. "This is my bar. Allow me to introduce myself. I'm Louis Abelard."

"Alex," I replied, smiling. I offered my hand to once again inundate my Americanness. "Abelard, like the philosopher?"

"Ah, intelligent and beautiful." He took my hand and kissed it. "How did a girl like you happen upon my bar?"

"Just looking to have some fun. My girlfriends and I spent the last couple of weeks in Monte Carlo, and I didn't get the gambling out of my system yet. This was the first pool hall I found. I was hoping Claude could help me locate some table games."

Abelard considered my request. "Maybe I can help you." He got off the barstool. "Come with me." I followed him around the bar and toward the back room. He opened the door and ushered me inside.

"Where are we going?"

Following a man into a small, dark, enclosed space didn't seem like a good idea. The room was dimly lit with a folding card table in the middle and a couple of chairs. Two guys sat at the table, smoking cigarettes. I tried to stay near the door in case I needed to make a quick escape. The only problem with this plan was that everyone in the bar worked for Abelard. If this man wanted to make me disappear, it could happen. Why didn't I tell Clare, Delacroix, or even Mark where I was going? *Too late now*, the voice in my head responded. Remaining outwardly clueless, I tried to play along.

"Forgive me," Abelard said, "but what you are asking is illegal. Precautions must be taken."

One of the men not so gently frisked me, locating the pepper spray in my pocket but failing to locate the knife strapped to my ankle. I was then checked for a wire, which I obviously wasn't wearing since I wasn't good enough to be one of Delacroix's team players.

"Satisfied?" I asked, annoyed. The man nodded to Abelard, and he wrote an address on a sheet of paper.

"My apologies." He handed me the piece of paper. "If you are still interested in some high stakes action, go to this address Tuesday night, and when you knock on the door, tell the man I sent you."

"You mean I went through all this and I still can't get any action until Tuesday?" I regretted my wording and thought briefly of Martin, who needed to stay out of my head.

"You may play pool," he encouraged, "but if you want a casino experience, you have to wait." I was shown to the door. Abelard followed me out of the back room and went to his corner booth. Our interaction for this evening was over.

Trying to blend in, I ordered another drink as if I were interested in the prospect of picking up a game or two of pool. After twenty minutes, I left. Once outside, I dropped my keys in the parking lot as an excuse to turn around and make sure I wasn't being followed or watched. When I was certain it was clear, I got into the car and drove away. I needed to recruit some reinforcements before Tuesday night.

*　　*　　*

I ran extensive background checks on Abelard and the address he gave me. The location was another abandoned warehouse in the second arrondissement.

Whoever Jean-Pierre owed money to had to be at least peripherally connected to Abelard. However, I didn't know if Jean-Pierre was killed because of his gambling debt, as everyone insisted, or if it was because of the paintings. The most reasonable explanation was Jean-Pierre mixed his personal life with his professional one and tried to pay off his debt with the missing paintings, but I had no real evidence of this.

Calling Mark the next day, I filled him in on everything that had transpired. He didn't like my involvement with Abelard or the prospect of further embedding myself in the underground gambling world.

"You are not an agent," he pointed out, in case I forgot. "You're going to get yourself arrested."

"What else can I do? Delacroix doesn't want me here. I don't have Interpol watching my back."

"Alexis," Mark sounded compassionate but firm, "as your friend, I'm telling you to let this one go. O'Connell tracked down one of the guys responsible for the break-in at your apartment. No one else is going to pay you another visit. You did enough." He was being the voice of reason, but I was already in too deep.

"I promised Clare," I said, and Mark exhaled in the background.

"Do you trust her?" I didn't respond immediately, and he took this as a bad sign. "You cannot do this unless you have someone you trust watching your back."

"I know. The only thing I'm certain of is Clare didn't kill Jean-Pierre."

"Is that enough?"

"It has to be." I sighed. "I'll talk to you before Tuesday night. If you find anything else out which

---

may be helpful, I'd appreciate it." We ended the call.

Before phoning Clare, I wanted to have another chat with Agent Delacroix. I found the number for his office and dialed, hoping he wouldn't instruct me to stay away from the warehouse too.

"Delacroix," he answered.

"It's Parker. I was wondering if you made any headway concerning the motivation for Gustav's murder."

"Why? Did you find anything out?" This was not the way this conversation was supposed to go, but what choice did I have.

"Look," I paced my hotel room, "I know whoever is involved has to be on the Evans-Sterling team with Gustav." I paused, waiting for some type of acknowledgment. Unfortunately, Delacroix was better at playing this game. "I also know Jean-Pierre owed someone a lot of money." Still no response. "I'm going out on a limb and assuming maybe he planned on paying off his debt with a few misplaced paintings."

"Interesting idea," Delacroix finally said. "So what you're saying is someone working for Evans-Sterling was also working for the debt collectors?"

"Maybe. I thought that person was Clyde Van Buren. He and Gustav were involved in a raid a couple of years ago with the Sanchez gang and a misappropriated Warhol. Maybe this was his in with that kind of crowd."

Delacroix went back to being silent, and since I had nowhere else to go with this, I waited. "Did you ever consider it could be Gustav's connection to that kind of crowd?" he asked, breaking the silence.

I hadn't considered this because, in my mind, Jean-Pierre was still the good guy. "Was it?"

"Maybe Gustav brought someone else into the gambling world. If they racked up their own debt,

maybe they found a more creative way to pay it off."
Delacroix was simply giving me more possibilities to
ponder but never letting on if any of these theories
could be correct. It was infuriating.

"Who?" I didn't want to play twenty questions. I
just wanted a name.

"I don't know. There were only four other people on
the team, aside from you."

"Are you sure I didn't do it?"

"You weren't in the country when it happened. If
you had been, I would have considered you a suspect."

"That leaves Ryan Donough, Michel Langmire, and
Clare Olivier." I named off the three remaining team
members as I scribbled the names on a list. "If I start
staking out their places, will you to tell me to back off
again?"

"Try it and see." Delacroix disconnected, and I let
out a frustrated growl and sat down at the table.

I didn't want to call Clare for assistance when there
was a one in three chance she was involved. She
couldn't have killed him, but what if she inadvertently
let it slip where he would be and his debt collector did
the job? There couldn't be any doubts.

"Dammit," I cursed, putting my head in my hands,
cognizant of the clock ticking away my remaining two
and a half days.

Pulling up profiles on Donough and Langmire, I
began perusing the data. Donough had been Police
Nationale for a few years before being injured on duty.
The details were not included in the report, but he was
honorably discharged and sought employment
elsewhere, landing a job at Evans-Sterling. This
occurred within the last year and a half. Initially, I
assumed Clare was the newest member of the Evans-
Sterling team, but I must have missed this.

Pulling up the news articles regarding Donough's

injury, I found they were all in French, and the translation software was useless. It was a joke, trying to read through the gibberish it spat out. Unless I wanted to translate a children's book, the software couldn't put the sentences back into the proper structure.

I switched gears and searched Langmire. He had an eerily similar background to Gustav, former military turned Interpol agent turned Evans-Sterling employee. Did he and Jean-Pierre have an overlapping past in either the military or at Interpol? The connection couldn't be made since they had been stationed in different locations at different times. Although, if I were a betting woman, and at the moment I was pretending to be, then I would have guessed he was the next most likely suspect. Staring at the wood grain on the table, I tried to figure out what the best course of action would be. When brilliance failed to strike, I went with my secondary plan. Here goes nothing.

"Are you okay?" Martin asked immediately, answering on the first ring.

"Hi to you, too," I responded glibly, ignoring his worry. "Are you near a computer?"

"Hang on." He was moving around. "Okay."

"I'm sorry. This should only take a few minutes." I forwarded the link to the news story on Donough's injury and asked that he read and translate it.

Apparently, Donough had been chasing a suspect when he was hit by a vehicle and suffered a spinal fracture. His recovery had taken several months, and during that time period, he decided to leave the police force to pursue other opportunities. There was something strange about Donough, but I was having trouble deciphering what I was thinking.

"Alex? You still there?"

"Sorry." I shook my head and thanked him for his help. "You can get back to enjoying your Sunday."

"I wasn't doing anything special. How's Paris? When are you coming home?"

"I don't know yet." I pulled up addresses for Donough and Langmire, figuring I'd check them both out within my limited timeframe. A background check had already been conducted on Clare, so it wasn't necessary to do it again. Maybe she could be persuaded to take me to the crime scene where Jean-Pierre's car exploded. It might lead to something helpful.

"Make any progress?"

"Some, maybe. I don't know." I stopped typing and leaned back in the chair and closed my eyes. "Do you think it's crazy I'm here?"

"No, it's not." His voice was soft. "You live by your own moral compass. You do what you think needs to be done regardless of how insane it might seem." There was a smile in his voice.

"So you think I'm insane?"

"Just a little bit," he teased. "Be careful."

"Always."

We said our goodbyes, and I stared at the map some more, scribbling down directions.

FIFTEEN

Clare agreed to go to the garage where Jean-Pierre's charred remains had been found. The vehicle had been moved. Only a few torn remnants of crime scene tape remained, but overall, if I didn't know what happened here, I wouldn't be able to guess there was an explosion or a fatality. I walked around the parking structure, looking for surveillance cameras and checking for any obvious vantage points or easy escape routes. I located the place where the camera that provided the videotape should have been, but the camera itself was missing. Only the telltale mounting equipment remained stuck to the wall. It was odd there were no other cameras anywhere in the garage, not on any of the other three levels of the parking structure.

"Do you know if the investigators got a copy of the surveillance tape?" I asked Clare, who stood timidly at the entrance to avoid coming inside. Revisiting a crime scene could be traumatic, and I didn't want to push her too hard.

"There was no surveillance. No cameras in the garage."

"Except for the one that had been set up right here." I pointed to the camera mounting equipment still on the wall.

Clare took a step inside and glanced up. "That looks like an antique. I'm sure it's not connected to the explosion."

I judged her speech and expression. Obviously, she didn't want to be here. However, her insistence could be interpreted as covering up her collaboration in Jean-Pierre's murder. I filed that thought away and continued to examine the scene.

There wasn't much more to do. On a whim, I used my cell phone to photograph the mount where the camera had been and held my phone in front of it and photographed the area the camera would have covered, just to make sure my assumptions were correct. Forwarding the pictures to Agent Farrell's e-mail, I asked if the tech support at his office could verify the location. Looking around the garage once more, I gave up. In the event I was struck by a brilliant idea, I could revisit on my own.

Clare was standoffish for the rest of the ride. I assumed she would want to talk about the progress she was making in regards to tracking down her lover's killer, but she remained silent. She didn't even ask if I discovered anything. Regardless, I shared the small tidbit of information I had.

"Van Buren isn't behind this," I said quietly once she stopped at a traffic light.

"I'm aware," she responded coldly. "It doesn't bring us any closer to tracking his killer."

I kept my mouth shut even though knocking one of four suspects off the list was a huge accomplishment. "Clare," I began slowly, trying to be comforting or supportive or whatever it was she needed at the moment, but she interjected.

"I don't care. It doesn't matter. No matter what happens, it won't bring him back. Nothing can bring him back." Her eyes burned holes through me. I finally understood. The realization that Jean-Pierre was dead dawned on her, and she felt helpless.

"I am so incredibly sorry."

She made a harrumph noise, and we made the rest of the trip back to my hotel in silence.

"If there is anything I can do, call me, please."

"There is nothing anyone can do," she said dejectedly and drove away.

I sighed. She was right; there wasn't anything anyone could do to bring him back. The only thing left was to figure out what happened.

I picked up the directions to Donough's and Langmire's residences and got into my rental. My first stop was Langmire's apartment. He seemed the more likely of the two, but no one was home. The curtains were opened, but there was no light or movement coming from within his apartment or any suspicious sedans or SUV's to indicate Langmire was under surveillance. Maybe I was barking up the wrong tree. I waited almost an hour before giving up.

Next, I headed to Donough's apartment. The drive took about forty minutes, and I debated what to do if he wasn't home. I guess I'd just have to wait him out. Today was quickly turning into a bust. Finding the correct avenue, I parked a block away from Donough's apartment building. Before I could look for any surveillance vehicles, I spotted him, walking down the street. I slouched down in the driver's seat, hoping not to be noticed. He continued toward his building but stopped suddenly in front of a garbage bin. Carefully, I lifted my camera off the passenger's seat and zoomed in, watching as he glanced around before surreptitiously reaching into the dumpster and removing a plastic bag.

"What the hell are you up to?" I asked. He pulled something from inside his jacket pocket and placed it in the dumpster. This was a dead drop. I never imagined I'd get lucky this fast. Donough headed away from the dumpster and down the street, straight toward me. Shoving my camera onto the seat and slumping down further to avoid detection, I hoped he wouldn't notice me as he continued in my general direction.

Donough was half a block from my car when he sat down at the bus stop. He opened the bag and removed the contents, placing them inside his jacket pocket. I had no idea what he retrieved or what he left at the dumpster. I was still watching him intensely when he turned and looked right at me. Standing up, he walked at a fast clip toward his building.

"Shit." I was torn. He was involved in something shady, and he knew he'd been made. The problem was I didn't know what I was going to do with him if I caught him, but if I did nothing, he could destroy evidence or flee. My only lead might escape. Getting out of my car, I pursued him down the street, feeling the reassuring weight of the taser in my right jacket pocket. My handcuffs were hooked on my belt, hidden from sight. Hopefully, I could subdue the subject and then figure out the rest.

Donough turned and disappeared down the alleyway between his apartment building and a local cafe, past the dead drop dumpster. Even though I lost sight of him, I continued pursuit and cautiously entered the alley. He was nowhere to be seen, but the alley opened onto a parallel street. He could be anywhere by now.

Edging closer, I made sure he wasn't behind the dumpster. A door connected the apartment building to the alley. I pulled on the handle, but it didn't budge. I took a few steps past and heard the door open as I simultaneously felt the muzzle of a gun pressed against my side.

"Stop," the Irish brogue of a man's voice growled in my ear. I stopped and raised my hands. *Dumb move, Parker*, the voice in my head scolded. He grabbed my right arm and twisted it behind my back as he maneuvered me into the building, the gun still at my side. "Don't make a sound." I ran through my options. In this tight, enclosed space, I had no chance of putting up a fight. Relenting, I let him escort me through the narrow hallways of the apartment building. Donough got to his apartment and put the key in my hand. "Open the door, slowly."

I unlocked the door and turned the knob. He pushed me inside and kicked the door closed behind him. We were now in a large enough space that I had a decent chance to fend him off. He was acutely aware of this because he cautiously circled around, stepping out of my striking zone. The gun remained pointed at me.

"It's you," he sounded shocked as recognition dawned on him. His aim faltered, and I lunged. He held the gun in his right, so I used my right to shove it away as I spun around and tried to elbow him with my left. He blocked my elbow and twisted my arm behind me. "Stop," he repeated forcefully.

My foot slammed down on his instep, causing his grip on my arm to loosen. Pulling free, I let go of his gun hand as I spun my body around and delivered a right cross to his jaw. He stumbled backward, and the gun clattered to the floor. I dove for it, but he recovered and launched himself at me. We were both on the ground. I tried to roll him off, but he held on. Reaching into my jacket pocket for the taser, I had just gotten a grip on it when he grabbed my wrist and pried it from my fingers. I dropped the taser, and it slid out of my reach. I tried to knee him. But he straddled my thighs, and I couldn't get free from under his weight.

I was trying to maneuver out of his hold when I noticed a coffee mug on the floor next to his couch. Reaching for it, I grabbed the handle and slammed it into the side of his head. He crumpled sideways, dazed, and I scrambled for the gun. He cursed in French and launched himself at me, knocking me sideways to the floor. All I accomplished was pissing him off, which was not a good thing. He had my legs pinned and my wrists held tightly against the ground above my head.

"Bloody hell. Stop fighting," he angrily commanded. "I'm a cop." I wasn't about to fall for this line of bull. He used to be a cop.

"I don't know any cops who make suspicious dead drops outside their apartments," I practically spat, "especially when they were discharged from the police department." *Great job pissing off the guy who's going to kill you.* My internal voice could be a sarcastic bitch sometimes.

"Apparently in America you don't do undercover work," he sneered. He held both of my wrists firmly in one hand as he pulled a pair of cuffs from his jacket pocket and bound my wrists together around the table leg. "Now would you please just stay there." He got up cautiously, making sure I didn't kick him. Then he retrieved the gun from the floor, putting the safety on and sliding it into the holster on his belt. I got into a semi-seated position and watched him.

"What are you going to do with me?"

"I'm going to show you my badge, and if you can behave like a lady, I'll consider taking the handcuffs off." He went to the bookcase and pulled a thick volume from the shelf. Opening the book, he produced a shield and identification. Apparently, the book had been hollowed out. He tossed them in my general direction. It wasn't easy manipulating my bound hands around the table leg to examine his identification, but it looked legitimate.

"I'm supposed to believe these are current?" I asked. "I know you were a cop. Ryan Donough, honorably discharged after sustaining a spinal fracture. I can read the newspapers just like anyone else." Well, at least Martin could, but that didn't seem important at the moment.

"I never sustained a spinal fracture." Donough spun and lifted his shirt. From what I could tell, there were no scars or signs of surgery, but maybe he was just a lucky son of a bitch who healed well. He took a seat on the couch, rubbing his head absently. "Alexis Parker, former OIO agent, currently private security consultant."

"Maybe you should have tried this type of introduction in the first place." I was working on the handcuffs, trying to get the hinge to unlock, but I needed to buy some time.

"You should have just knocked on my door instead of watching me from your car. I can't afford that right now. It could blow my cover."

"What's your cover? Evans-Sterling douchebag who killed Jean-Pierre?" Leaning against the table, I hoped to lift it enough to slide the cuffs from under the leg before he noticed.

"Evans-Sterling employee investigating the missing paintings. It's an inside job, after all. I know you're aware of this. You wouldn't be here otherwise." He tried to crack a friendly smile, but it looked more like a challenge. "Paintings have been going missing for the last three years. A lot more than the three you heard about. They've always been insured by Evans-Sterling, and since the insurance company was responsible for the retrievals, my cover was established. Each of the paintings would inevitably encounter a delivery problem. Either they would arrive or depart as forgeries. It's happened at numerous galleries and museums all over France. The accident was staged along with my discharge. I was hired on to Evans-Sterling, and I've been in deep cover for the last eighteen months. It's just about over, and here you are, trying to fuck it up."

"What did you get from the dead drop?" His story was plausible, but without proof, he could be playing me. He opened his jacket pocket and pulled the items out. There were a list of addresses and a burner phone. "Doesn't prove anything."

"Listen, you can't tell anyone what I've told you," Donough said. If he was in deep cover, telling me was a total violation. So either he was close to wrapping it up, or he needed something. This was assuming he wasn't lying.

"You find a way for me to verify your story, and I'll keep my mouth shut. Maybe you could work on taking these cuffs off too." I tried a more civil approach, hoping he wasn't about to disprove the entire story and shoot me where I sat. He rubbed the side of his head where I hit him with the coffee mug, brushing pieces of ceramic from his hair.

"That can be arranged." He got up from the couch and approached cautiously. Since I was docile, he unlocked the handcuffs. "Does this earn some trust?"

"We'll see." I rubbed my wrists absently as I tried to make sense of the last twenty minutes.

SIXTEEN

Donough offered the name of his commanding officer and the code word for the operation. Taking his suggestion under advisement, I called Police Nationale Headquarters and spoke with Capt. Reneaux, who corroborated Ryan's cover story. Ryan Donough was one of the boys in blue. Deciding not to throw caution to the wind, I made a quick call to Mark to see if he could verify this through more official channels. Better safe than sorry, especially since I was sick and tired of having guns pointed at me.

"Here." Donough placed a bowl of ice water on his dining room table in front of me. He wrapped a few pieces of ice in a towel and sat down, pressing it against the side of his head. "Shall we try this again?"

"Alex." I stuck out my hand. "I'm checking into Gustav's murder. Congratulations, you're officially off my suspect list."

He shook my hand and chuckled at the absurdity of our second introduction. "Ryan." He leaned back in the chair. "You have one hell of a right cross."

I put my hand into the bowl of ice water. My knuckles were already swollen. "Sorry about the coffee mug. At the time, I thought you were a murderer." My apology lacked in sincerity, but I was in a playful mood since I finally identified an ally in this uphill battle.

"I'm sorry I approached you in that particular manner. I had no idea you were the one watching me all this time," he sounded relieved.

"I hate to burst your bubble, but I was outside your place for maybe ten minutes before you made me."

"Well, that's just bloody fantastic." He went to the window and pulled back the curtain just a sliver so he could look outside. "They're still out there."

Joining him at the window, I recognized the dark sedan and the Interpol agents in the vehicle. "Looks like I'm not the only one who thought you were responsible for Gustav's murder. Those are Interpol agents." I glanced at Ryan, still uncertain about our new level of trust.

"Are you working for them?"

"Not quite. From home I supplied them with information on the case, but once I got here, Delacroix told me to back off unless I had something useful to give him. Shouldn't you be working with them?" I was confused why the Police Nationale and Interpol weren't cooperating on this case since they were supposedly cooperating on the car bombing and Gustav's murder investigation.

"Interagency politics." Ryan shrugged. It was the same reason the FBI and NYPD never knew what operations the other was running at any given time.

"How close are you to closing this case? I know how things work, and you wouldn't have broken cover unless you needed something."

He assessed me for a few moments. "After you

appeared at the Evans-Sterling office, I ran a full security check on you. You'll be happy to know you were cleared from any and all suspicion quickly. I was hoping, if you were sticking around, that we could be allies. Recently, I raised a few suspicions during the course of my investigation and needed someone else to provide a distraction, but you left." Ryan provided the narrative from his point of view. I sat patiently, waiting for him to get to the point. "When the painting you were hired to retrieve turned out to be a fake, I had the hard evidence needed to prove Gustav was involved in the thefts. I called it in Sunday night, and we were set to move on Jean-Pierre."

"But he was killed before you got the chance." The pieces were falling into place. Jean-Pierre wasn't killed because of debts or betting. He was killed because he could have rolled on the people in charge.

"Exactly." Ryan stared intensely at me. "One of the other members of the Evans-Sterling team must have made me and informed their boss. The ringleader must have decided to cut ties."

"Clare?" She made the most sense. She always did, even though I was stubborn enough to believe she couldn't have done it.

"That's what I assumed. When I first grabbed you in the alley, I thought you were her, coming to finish the job." His comment about it being me now made more sense.

After I filled him in on everything from my meeting with Ski Mask and Ramirez to the frantic phone conversations with Clare to the video footage I had been sent, he had the complete picture in front of him. "I came back to Paris to find justice for Jean-Pierre, not to get mixed up in a smuggling conspiracy turned murder." I needed to learn to mind my own business. "To be perfectly honest, I'm shocked he was this corrupt."

"I do believe the gambling and the thievery are related. He had a problem and was looking for an easy way out. You know how one thing can turn into another."

"Which brings me back to my original question." I stared at Ryan. "You told me this for a reason. What is it? What do you need me to do?"

"I can't very well go anywhere without alerting my tail," he sounded annoyed. "We're so close. I've been under for a year and a bloody half." The time in seclusion was getting to him, and all he wanted was to be free to resume his normal life. "My commander is only in the beginning stages of establishing a cover for my relief replacement, but you have a legitimate cover. You've been investigating the murder all along. Will you help us?"

I took a deep breath. "Okay."

Ryan and I spent the rest of the day going over every piece of evidence he had and everything I uncovered. Given the intel from the last eighteen months, it was apparent Louis Abelard was in charge of both the underground gambling and the art thefts. The connection had been particularly daunting, and if it wasn't for Jean-Pierre, it might never have been made.

Jean-Pierre was a gambler at heart and somehow happened upon Abelard. I assumed in a similar fashion to the way I happened upon Abelard, completely by accident. Abelard's venture was costly, and the police suspected he had turned his small business into a large enterprise through forgery and black market art sales. He had made a name for himself as he sought to establish his own underground gambling empire. Millions of dollars in stolen art, over the course of the last few years, had bankrolled his entrepreneurial endeavors, but the police failed to get any hard evidence against him. Any time a lead, such as Jean-Pierre, seemed promising, something horrific occurred.

"At least I was on the right track." I smirked once we were done with the show and tell portion of the evening.

"Incroyable," Ryan reverted to French for a moment. "I don't see how you put so much together on your own. Eighteen months and only now are we compiling hard evidence."

"It's easier when you don't need evidence, and you get handed some very fundamental facts on a silver platter."

"You have a meeting scheduled with Abelard for Tuesday evening?"

"I wouldn't call it a meeting so much as an open invitation to spend a few grand on table games."

"It'd be enough. If Abelard's there and you can verify it, then we can move in, confiscate everything, and at least have enough to get him on some bloody illegal gambling charges. Who knows, maybe our compatriots at Interpol can make murder stick to him, too." The relief showed on his face.

"What about Clare? You're going to let her get away with everything?"

"Do you think she intentionally killed Jean-Pierre?" he asked. I shook my head. "Neither do I, so I'd be willing to let her bloody well suffer in silence for the rest of her life if we can't find anything to tie the two of them together. Who knows? We won't know what we have until that warehouse gets raided. Maybe it's just a wet dream, but I hope we find some of the missing art in that warehouse."

"You want me to be wired, don't you?" I flashed back to my lovely frisking at the bar. Where could I hide a wire?

Ryan thought about it for a few moments. "Maybe we can come up with a less obvious alternative."

This was absolutely crazy. I came to Paris for one reason, and now I was here for a completely different reason and working for the Police Nationale no less. Jeez, how in the world did I get myself into these things? When I get home, I'd have to shred my passport and ask Mark to place me on the no-fly list.

We each made a couple of calls and formulated a decent plan of action. The commander and a technician were meeting me at my hotel for a proper briefing and equipment check before Tuesday night. I also had to sign the paperwork, indemnifying them from any injury sustained. Legality and fear of litigation were always such a pleasure to deal with. Mark would have to forward my personnel file and any other pertinent information the French police needed before I could become their informant.

"Care for some dinner?" Ryan asked as I concluded my overseas calls and got the ball rolling. It was past ten, and I was considering going back to my hotel. It had been a long day. "It's the least I can do after taking you hostage."

"Fine," I relented. He ordered delivery from the deli down the street. While we waited, I glanced out the window. The surveillance vehicle was still outside. "Any idea how I'm going to get out of here undetected?"

He joined me at the window before going into the back bedroom. "There's another van out back."

"Great, if only I had an invisibility cloak," I muttered. Ryan looked at me like I was an idiot. "C'mon, you and that accent, you must be familiar with Harry Potter."

"I'm Irish, not English," he insisted, even though I

was very much aware of this fact, given his name and his accent.

"Such a cliché," I teased. Ryan and I were slowly forging a friendship of sorts.

Dinner arrived, and while we ate, he explained how his family had moved from Belfast to Paris when he was four years old. It made sense why English was his first language. After our meal, I looked out the window. The surveillance van wasn't going anywhere. What the hell, if Delacroix had a problem, he could kiss my ass. I investigate my way; he investigates his.

"I'm going out the front. I'll deal with the fallout if and when I have to," I announced.

"Hang on." Ryan wrote down the number for his new burner phone. "If you need anything, I'll be there."

"Okay. And Ryan, the next time you put cuffs on me, they damn well better be the pink fuzzy kind."

"I'll make a note of it." He smiled slyly.

"You do that."

I shut the door and headed out the front of the building. As I passed the Interpol surveillance van, I gave them a big smile and a friendly wave. *You guys are complete idiots*, I thought as I passed. They were annoyed by my overt actions, ruining their pathetic attempt to be stealthy. I was just pulling away when my phone rang.

"Parker, what the hell did I tell you?" Delacroix sounded angry.

"You know what? I don't work for you. I don't actually work for anyone at the moment, so unless you want to argue that I'm doing something illegal, stay out of my way." I hung up before he had a chance to respond. I was tired of his attitude and his inability to run a productive operation. Everything he had done so far seemed counterintuitive, and I no longer needed him or his help.

I got to my hotel a little before midnight. Ryan's CO, Captain Reneaux, would be stopping by first thing in the morning. I needed to be well rested for tomorrow, but I was too keyed up. Turning on my computer, I attempted to learn the finer points of basic table games from blackjack to roulette to craps. With the exception of watching some celebrity poker shows, I knew absolutely nothing about casino games. By two a.m., I had the proper terminology down, and by four a.m., I familiarized myself with the odds of each game. Hopefully, this would be sufficient enough to make me a believable enough player while I waited for the cavalry to ride in and save the day.

SEVENTEEN

At seven, my alarm woke me from what I considered a nap. Three hours of sleep didn't count for much, but it was the best I could do. I was dressed and anxious to get everything worked out. A few minutes past eight, the hotel phone rang, and I was informed a couple of gentlemen were waiting in the lobby. Giving the front desk permission to send them up, I was nervous. Although, I had no idea why.

"Madame Parker?" a male voice bellowed. Opening the door, I found two men standing in the hallway. "Captain Reneaux," one of the men introduced himself, pulling his credentials from his jacket pocket. "We spoke on the telephone yesterday. This is our technical specialist, Monsieur DuVall." The other man presented his identification.

"Please." I gestured for them to enter.

"Merci," Reneaux replied. "I would like to thank you for your willingness to assist us, but are you positive you want to undertake such an endeavor?"

This was my last chance to back out, but that wasn't

going to happen. "I'm in."

Reneaux reiterated everything Ryan said yesterday but provided a more elaborate explanation of the role the support team would play. Basically, all I needed to do was get inside the warehouse, verify the presence of Abelard and the illegal gambling, and stay out of the way until the police breached the perimeter. It sounded easy enough with one exception.

"When I first stumbled upon Abelard at the pool hall, I was thoroughly searched." I emphasized the word thoroughly. "I can't be wired."

"We've thought of that," DuVall piped up. He reached into his briefcase and retrieved a small square. "This is a tracking device, so we will be aware of your location at all times. It's petite. You can place it almost anywhere." I looked at it skeptically, not impressed. "Also," he pulled out a burner phone similar to Ryan's, "it's the twenty-first century. Everyone has a cell phone. As a precaution, we can track your whereabouts through the phone's GPS. Plus, you can use it to call in or send a text." *This is the great technical specialist for the French police*, I thought sarcastically. "If they confiscate phones at the door," he continued, holding up a small earwig, "we can communicate this way. It has a microphone and speaker, allowing for two-way communication."

"The only thing is," Reneaux cut in, "it transmits on a higher radio frequency. If you're wanded, it will be detected. Keep it off until after they check you."

Great, I get a low jack, a cell phone, and half a set of headphones. What could possibly go wrong?

It was almost noon by the time we finished going over the location, schematics, where the tactical teams would be positioned, and how to avoid getting caught in the crossfire. Room service arrived, and we moved on to the legal portion of our day.

I was granted confidential status to further insulate me from being part of the actual criminal proceedings. It required an agreement to provide a statement of any and all events which might transpire and to relinquish any physical evidence to the Police Nationale. As I signed the dozen forms, Reneaux read my personnel file.

"Madame, you have a stellar reputation."

"Thanks." Hopefully, we were almost done because I wanted to continue prepping for tomorrow evening and take a nap.

"We're lucky to have stumbled upon you at this particular time." He relayed the story of Ryan's undercover assignment, emphasizing how the entire case almost crumbled when Jean-Pierre was killed.

"It's better to be lucky than good," I said seriously.

Reneaux nodded, and he and DuVall excused themselves. If I were to encounter any problems or if the meet at the warehouse was moved or rescheduled, I was to contact Reneaux personally. That was the essence of deep cover. Only a select few ever knew what was going on until the very end. With any luck, by the weekend, this would be over, and I could go home.

Performing a mental check of everything I was told, I mapped the entire scenario out in my head with a few different outcomes. There were obviously quite a few potential negative possibilities. Abelard may not be present. The address I was given could be a complete hoax. Delacroix could arrest me between now and tomorrow night, or the promise of table games might be ping-pong and pool. I sighed. There were always a lot of unknowns.

Before calling Mark, I took a two-hour nap. I phoned him around noon, his time. I wanted to run through the entire thing with him just to make sure there weren't any other obstacles I hadn't considered. Mark was enthused by the game plan. It was, after all, a lot better than my own plan to do everything by myself. The information on the bomb materials and the DNA analysis of the charred remains were almost complete, and Mark promised he'd try to get that information before I went to the warehouse, just in case. After all, surprises were never good.

"I got a call from Interpol today," Mark said. "I heard you pissed off one of the supervisors in Paris."

"It's a good thing I don't work for you anymore. It means I don't have to play nice for the sake of interagency politics. Delacroix's a real ass. He has no idea how to run an investigation."

"Try to behave," Mark reminded me. "Even if you currently don't work for the OIO, Interpol might still take your malevolence out on my department."

"Sure," I begrudgingly replied. "Hopefully, everything will be over by tomorrow night, and I can come home before I make any more enemies."

"When you have a definite exit strategy, let me know. I'll pick you up at the airport. Farrell wants the chance to debrief you."

I made an ugh sound and hung up.

I was in pre-op mode. I hadn't felt this kind of energy surge since leaving the OIO. This feeling was one of the few things I actually missed about my old job. It was a complete high of emotions, anxiety, fear, aggression, and a bit of bravado and arrogance thrown in for good measure. But I needed to relax and wind down in order to sleep tonight, so I would be ready for whatever tomorrow would bring.

Going down to the hotel gym, I burned off as much energy as possible, running five miles on the treadmill before returning to my room, showering, and ordering some dinner. Finally, I began to feel subdued, but my anxious energy was replaced by an unsettling feeling. My subconscious was scratching at the surface of something I had yet to realize, and I was getting skittish.

To take my mind off things, I dialed Martin's number. It was after midnight here, so with the time difference, he'd be off work, probably at home or out to dinner.

"Hello?" He answered on the second ring.

"Hey. What are you doing?" Why did I call him? Something was eating away at me, and I knew I should hang up before saying something I might regret.

"Making dinner. Is anything wrong?"

"Nothing." I took a breath. "If you're busy, I'll let you go."

He paused, and I wondered what he was thinking. The sound of a chair scraping across the floor filled the silence, and I pictured him taking a seat at his kitchen table. "I'm not busy." I had a feeling he was smirking. "How's everything coming along?"

"With any luck, I will be done by this weekend." Unless I just jinxed myself into being condemned to Paris for another few weeks.

"If you want, Luc and Genevieve Guillot are flying in on the company jet Friday morning. He needs to finalize some things here, and she wanted to check out the houses we've found for them. You could hitch a ride, my treat."

Instinctually, I was going to decline his generous offer immediately, but after that horrible layover in Heathrow last time, I thought better of it. "What time are they departing?"

"8:30 a.m., Paris time. I'll have your name put on the manifest."

There was no way to know how long it would take

to wrap things up with Abelard, but if everything ran smoothly, there was a chance I could make the flight. However, I knew better than to assume things would run smoothly. "I don't know if I'll make it."

"Okay. If you do, you do, and if you don't, that's okay too."

"Just for the record, I wasn't calling to bum a ride on the company jet," I teased, but my tone betrayed me.

"I know." Martin paused. "Why did you call? Did you need me to read some more French articles to you?" His tone was much more teasing than mine.

"No. I was feeling homesick." I shut my eyes and sat on the bed. "There's a slight chance I miss you." The impending tactical op made me more nervous than I cared to admit. If I was confident things were going to be fine, I never would have said something quite so sentimental and girly. Comments like this were the equivalent of throwing lit matches at a powder keg.

"Really?" I heard the swagger in his voice.

"Don't be a pompous ass." That was the kind of comment more typical of me.

"Alex," his voice betrayed a smile, "I miss you, too."

"Jerk."

"Oh, the security equipment we ordered is being installed next week. Monday, I think. If you're back by then, would you care to supervise the installation?" Thank goodness he was back to business.

"We'll see. I don't know if I'll make it. Best case scenario, I'll be there. But worst case, I don't know what'll happen." My thoughts went to the indelible images of Jean-Pierre's car blowing up. Something was off about the explosion, but I couldn't put my finger on it. Optimistically, I wouldn't meet a similar fate, but it never hurt to have a realistic perspective in order to stay alert.

"I'm sure the security guys can take care of it if you're not around."

I needed to get some sleep, so I'd be set for tomorrow. "Martin." The uneasiness returned full blast, and it was getting the best of me. I knew I shouldn't say or do anything at the moment. Potentially making life-altering changes was a result of anxiety and fear, not rational, clear-headed thinking. This was constantly preached in psych classes and seminars, but the nagging feeling wouldn't go away. "When I get back, maybe we can discuss what happened in the hotel hallway." I grimaced, awaiting his response.

"I'm not sure I remember what happened. You might need to stage a reenactment, just to refresh my memory," he said good-naturedly. What possessed me to think opening this can of worms was a good idea? After a few moments of silence passed with me failing to come up with a good comeback or quip, Martin decided it best to back off. "Or not," he added quietly. I was confusing the hell out of him. Me, too.

"It's late, and I'm in desperate need of a good night's sleep, especially before tomorrow." I couldn't tell him what was going to happen, but he was intelligent enough to read between the lines. "We'll talk when I get home."

"Good night. Remember, Friday morning, 8:30."

EIGHTEEN

Twisting and turning most of the night with pre-op jitters, I eventually rolled over and checked the time. It was eight, and I didn't need to be up for another four or five hours. Staring at the ceiling, I couldn't shake the overwhelming feeling of impending doom. With my luck, nothing would happen tonight, and Ryan and I would continue to chase ghosts until we were old and gray. I buried myself under the blankets and tried to go back to sleep. Inevitably, I gave up and got out of bed. I did everything deliberately slow, from showering and selecting clothes to wear to carefully slicing into the wedge heel of my boot in order to slip the GPS chip into the now hollowed out space.

I ordered lunch and ate in my room while I went over my notes on the warehouse and the plan of attack. I memorized both Ryan's number and Reneaux's because, in the event I needed to call either of them in a hurry, I didn't want to be screwed. I went online, looking at street maps and global images in order to see what the warehouse and surrounding area looked like.

The tactical teams would be waiting in a staging area for my call before they would move in. There were a couple of contingency plans in place, and I had been assured the police would be there when I called or at the first sign of trouble. What constituted the first sign of trouble? I picked up the phone and dialed Ryan.

"Everything okay?" he asked. His voice mirrored my anxiety.

"Yes, I'm just running through everything in my head. What are we going to do if Abelard's not there?" This was my main concern.

"If everything else is there, we'll move in and hope we can get some corroboration in exchange for reduced sentences." Ryan didn't sound very pleased with this option.

"And what if my cell phone is confiscated, and there's some kind of glitch with the earwig?" I was being a nuisance, but it was my ass on the line.

He didn't respond immediately, probably because he wasn't sure what they would do in that situation. The entire mission was based upon my outgoing message. "If we don't hear from you within a reasonable amount of time, we'll move in on your location." He swallowed the unspoken implications. "More than likely, this won't be the case. I've got your back, Alex."

"Okay." If nothing else, someone would at least recover my boot with the tracking chip.

"Are you psyching yourself out? Because if you want to back out..."

"No," I said firmly, mostly for my own benefit. "All in, right? Just like Texas hold'em."

"All in. I'll be at the raid. If you run into any trouble, I'll verify your involvement, or Reneaux will."

Great, that was something I had forgotten about. Being caught in a raid meant being on the ground and held at gunpoint, just like the bad guys. Fun times.

"Sounds good," I said, even though it didn't. "Be careful out there. You don't know what kind of lunatics you might be dealing with."

"You be careful. You're walking into the lion's den."

Thanks a lot for the vote of confidence.

* * *

It was getting late by the time I got into my rental car and headed toward the address. On the way, I unsuccessfully phoned Mark. He didn't call like he promised, and when I tried to get in touch with him earlier, it went straight to voicemail. I was annoyed but decided to let it go and not worry about it. There was nothing I could do, and it was almost go-time.

Picking up the burner phone, I dialed Reneaux and was instructed to perform an equipment and sound check once I arrived at the agreed upon destination, a few blocks away from the warehouse. Acknowledging this request, I continued on my way, running through the plan over and over in my head. Get inside, locate Abelard and the gaming tables, contact Reneaux, and keep my head down until the police raided the building. Simple enough. I took some slow, deep breaths in order to put my game face on as I pulled into a metered parking space, four blocks from the warehouse.

Performing a final assessment of my clothing and gear, I was as prepared as possible. In a past life, I must have been a boy scout. Dressed in jeans with wedge-heeled boots that went halfway up my shin, I had my knife strapped to my ankle. Hopefully, they would miss this again, if and when I was frisked. The slice cut out of the heel was not noticeable, and the GPS chip was working properly. I wore a white button-up dress shirt and tucked the earwig securely in the center of my bra, hoping the underwire would mask the metallic properties in the event I was wanded.

During equipment check, Reneaux assured me the GPS was transmitting on both the tracker and the cell phone. I was instructed to turn on the earwig. We conducted a sound check, and then I turned it off and slipped it back into its hiding spot. The burner phone was in my purse, which was empty except for my pepper spray and a stack of Euros. Perhaps the Police Nationale would reimburse me the $750 I lost at the pool hall, but there was no reason to worry about that now. Locking the contact information and content on my personal phone, I slipped it into my pocket. If I was questioned about having two phones, I could come up with a feasible lie. More than likely, they would assume I was involved in some type of illegal activity and let it go.

Walking purposefully in the direction of the warehouse, I tried not to seem suspicious, but I couldn't help but look around. I wanted to know if I was being watched or followed. Less than a block away from the warehouse, the phone in my pocket vibrated. It was Mark.

"Hey, you called just in time." I stopped my procession.

"Parker," his voice sounded urgent, "the results just came in from the bomb and the body. It wasn't Gustav in the car."

"What?" I spoke too loudly, and I glanced around before slowly resuming my stroll. "Who was it?"

"The remains belong to Jacques Marset."

"Shit, I have to go. I need to warn Ryan." If Gustav

wasn't in the car, where was he? Was he still alive? And if so, there was a good chance tonight was a trap. Suddenly, the delivery notification for the VHS tape made perfect sense. "Gustav's alive. The video was a fake. It was delivered a day too soon." Even with the time difference and overnight airmail, if Gustav had been killed Monday morning, the earliest I would have gotten the package would have been Wednesday or perhaps Tuesday night, but not first thing Tuesday morning. There wouldn't have been enough time. I didn't realize it, and apparently neither did Mark or any of the Interpol agents. Instead, I had been blinded by Clare's hysterical phone call and Gustav's alleged murder. Clare, how did she fit into this? My mind raced.

Turning around, I headed back to my car. Mark was still speaking, and I needed him to stop so I could disconnect. He was discussing the bomb schematics, but his words weren't processing in my question-addled brain. As I rounded a corner, a man wearing a gas mask stepped out of the shadow and sprayed something in my face. I stepped back, trying to make sense of the world which had begun to spin.

The phone fell from my hands as the ground teetered, and someone grabbed me from behind. A cloth was shoved over my nose and mouth, and I resisted the urge to inhale. But my lungs betrayed my resolve, and I gasped for breath. My lungs burned as a sickly, sweet smell filled my nostrils, and then the world pitched forward. The last thing I saw was a foot smashing down on the fallen phone before everything turned dark.

NINETEEN

The sound of moaning roused me from my sleep. It took a moment before I realized I was emitting the noise. How the hell did I fall asleep in such an uncomfortable position? My eyes were still closed, and my head was pounding. My hands were numb, and every muscle from my wrists to my lower back ached. Opening my eyes and squinting against a single, harsh light, I slowly lifted my head. My chin had been on my chest, and just the slight movement sent sharp pains down my spine. *What the hell?* I thought miserably. As I focused on my surroundings, terror overtook my senses.

Calm down, my internal voice commanded. Leaning my head all the way back, I looked up. My wrists were tied with rope, and I was dangling from a metal hook, similar to ones used to move heavy objects from one conveyer belt to another. There were a good six inches between my feet and the ground. Between my bound wrists and the ground being so far away, I had no leverage. I shut my eyes and tried to think logically, pushing the frenzied thoughts away. I needed to concentrate and not panic. Start with a simple task. Moving my fingers in the hope of getting some sensation back in them would be the first step in getting myself off the hook, literally. Each motion sent the painful pins and needles up my already sore arms and through my numb hands, but any feeling was better than no feeling.

The room was dimly lit and seemingly abandoned. I turned as far to the side as possible, trying to survey the entire area. It was an old, dilapidated warehouse. Was this the same warehouse where I was supposed to meet Abelard, or was I someplace else entirely? I kicked my legs out, which made my body swing, and the thick rope cut painfully into my wrists. From what I could tell, the GPS was still inside my heel.

"Looks like our guest has awakened." Abelard's voice immediately drew my attention, and I froze, holding my breath.

The man, along with three of his goons, entered the room from a set of double doors directly in front of me. They made their way toward me. I recognized two of the men from the back room of the bar, and the third was Jean-Pierre.

"You son of a bitch," I snarled at Jean-Pierre. "How could you?" I didn't remember Mark's conversation until now. Jean-Pierre stared at me silently. "I wish you were dead."

"Now, now." Abelard positioned himself in front of me, commanding my attention. "It turns out you haven't been quite so honest yourself, Ms. Parker. Or is it still Agent Parker?" I glowered at him, hoping looks could kill. "If you'd be so kind as to tell me who you are working for and what they are planning on doing, then things won't have to get ugly. If you cooperate, I promise to make this as painless as possible."

"Bite me." There was only one simple truth; once Abelard got what he wanted, he would kill me. "We'll see if you don't change your tune." He was enjoying this. He was a sadistic piece of shit. "Claude, bring out my tools," Abelard called to the man I met at the pool hall. Claude emerged from behind the doors, wheeling out a small cart with what looked to be a cattle prod on top. I really didn't like where things were heading.

"Are you planning on performing some magic tricks as entertainment while I hang around?" I wouldn't give him the benefit of showing fear. He could do what he liked, but he wasn't going to get off on my begging or pleading. I caught a glimpse of Jean-Pierre, and he shook his head ever so slightly in warning. "What's a matter?" I taunted him. "You pulled a disappearing act of your own, but now you're afraid you won't like what you're about to see?"

He didn't reply, and Abelard flipped a few switches on the cart and picked up the humming contraption.

"Maybe my little magic trick will make you reconsider." Abelard pressed the electrified end against my rib cage.

I gritted my teeth as the shock traveled through my body, igniting every nerve ending in an agonizing wave. He pulled the metal away and regarded me. I took a few deep breaths before managing to look at him defiantly. "That was refreshing, and just how I like to start my day, with a nice jolt of energy." He would get no satisfaction if I could help it.

"Hmm." He put the device down and picked up a dagger instead.

He approached menacingly, and I wondered if I could kick him. My hands were suspended in mid-air below the hook, so I was at a disadvantage. My kick wouldn't have much force. I might be able to get my legs around his neck, but with four other men standing by, it was no use. It was best to conserve my attack strategy until I had a solid plan or no other choice.

Abelard stood in front of me, brandishing the blade in an ominous fashion. He turned the knife, so the flat part pressed against my skin as he slowly ran the blade down my cheek, across my lips, and to my neck, taking his time to trace the major arteries and veins with the sharp point. I swallowed and made the conscious effort not to cringe. When he grew bored of the theatrics, he dropped the blade to my clavicle and pressed the edge of the dagger into my skin, drawing it horizontally across the top of my collarbone as he carved open my flesh. My breathing remained steady, and I failed to react against the biting, razor-sharp steel. He released the pressure and continued downward to my shirt, slicing off the top three buttons, before taking a step back to admire his work. I stared at him, unimpressed.

"Who are you working for and what are they planning?" he asked again, a bit more portentously. I tilted my chin up and spit in his face. "Bitch," he cursed and slapped me hard enough to send me spinning around on the hook. The rope dug deeper into my wrists, and blood ran down my arms. I needed to come up with a better game plan than pissing him off until he got bored and finished the job. Fortunately, that stunt afforded me the opportunity to see the rest of the warehouse. There was a loading dock in the back of the room, and although the windows were blacked out, a hint of light came from a street lamp outside. The black hole of hell had a back door. "Claude," he commanded, and the man grabbed my hips and straightened me on the hook.

"Ali," Jean-Pierre spoke from the corner of the room. He was observing the exchange but not partaking in the festivities. "Just tell him what he wants to know."

I glared at him. "Don't you dare call me that. It's your fault I'm here. Whatever happens is on you," I warned.

Before Jean-Pierre could reply, Abelard repowered his cattle prod device. He pressed it against my newly exposed skin, and I gritted my teeth, waiting for the onslaught to stop. At some point, I began screaming as wave after wave of fire ran through my nerve endings. My muscles contracted, and I had the briefest desire to give up when, finally, the torment stopped. My entire body went slack, and my head slumped against my chest. I wondered if I was actually smelling burnt flesh or if it was just in my head.

"I'll let you think about that for a little while," Abelard said as he and his group of merry mercenaries disappeared behind the double doors.

I needed to get free, especially before Abelard's little toy made my heart stop, but I couldn't move. Every part of my body ached, and my nerves were too raw and damaged to properly transmit signals. Hanging there, lifeless, I tried to come up with a plan. I feared I might be drifting in and out of consciousness. *Wake up, Parker*, my mind screamed.

Was the knife still strapped to my ankle? If I could get to it, I could cut myself down. That was the best idea I had. It was also the only idea I had. Slowly, I lifted my knees upward toward my chest. As I did this, the rope cut deeper into my wrists, and I could see the once white sleeves on my shirt turning red. I lowered my legs, and the pressure eased. If I could swing, I might be able to get my legs high enough to wrap around the chain holding the hook and retrieve the knife from my boot.

Before I could attempt this, Abelard, Claude, and Jean-Pierre returned. The GPS chip should still be active, and I wondered how long I had been here. What was the timeframe for the police to move in on my location? Had the electricity shorted it out? Most likely, the earwig was fried, but there was no way of reaching it either. Things were starting to feel hopeless, but I had to keep trying. *Buy time*, I thought frantically.

"Once again, who are you working for?" Abelard asked, sounding bored.

"No one." Maybe my conversational skills would get him to ease up on the electric shock treatment. Hostage negotiation tactics often indicated attempting to humanize the victim, but with Abelard's sadistic tendencies, I didn't think that was a good idea. "I came here to hunt down Jean-Pierre's killer. Guess what, he's not dead. Case closed. You can let me go now."

Abelard looked skeptical. "Forgive me, but I don't believe you." He sneered and picked up the cattle prod, taking his time to intimidate me with the implied threat of another round in the hopes I'd cave and give him the information.

"Maybe you should try turning that on yourself. It might make me feel sorry for you, and I'll talk out of pity."

His face contorted into a wicked smile. "I never imagined you would be this much fun."

My screams were deafening. Wherever we were, Abelard wasn't worried about noise. I prayed for unconsciousness to overtake me and free me from the lightning storm that was trying to make my nerve endings explode from the inside out.

"Stop before you kill her. If she's dead, we won't know who she's working for or what they have," Jean-Pierre said in French. The electric current stopped, and I went limp against the rope. My body twitched and convulsed. I wouldn't survive another round. "Please, let me speak to her alone," Jean-Pierre said quietly.

Did they think I passed out or was incapable of understanding the language? Either way, whatever I was going to do, I needed to do it as quickly as possible. Abelard and Claude retreated from the room.

"Ali," Jean-Pierre spoke in a hushed tone. His fingers were on my neck, checking for a pulse.

"I hate to disappoint, but I'm not dead yet," I retorted, taking a few slow breaths.

"You were never supposed to pursue me. I told you to go on with your life. I sent you the tape so you would know I was gone and leave it alone," he whispered angrily.

"You sent the fucking tape, and I came back to Paris to avenge you. Clare called, hysterical over your death." I shut my mouth. I needed to stay quiet in case I let anything slip. "You're worse than Abelard. You're a goddamn traitor."

"Clare?" He faltered at her name.

The anger helped kick-start my adrenaline. I just needed a few minutes alone to free myself. Where the hell were Ryan and the rest of the Paris police?

"So you're working for Sparky now? Son of a bitch would take you out in a heartbeat if he thought you were going to turn on him. Then again, you turn on everyone, just like a rabid dog." I didn't think I would be able to win him over to my side, and even if I did, there was no way I could trust him.

"I know. Ali, who are you working for? Why aren't

they coming for you?"

"He's going to kill me." I had no other play to make. "It doesn't matter if he finds out or not. He's going to kill me." The words sunk into my subconscious and became a known reality. A random memory of Martin interrupted my thoughts, but I pushed it aside. "Why should I make his life easier?"

"I am sorry. I'll do as much as I can." He headed toward the double doors.

"Think about Clare," I called after him.

For all I knew, she was on the other side of those doors, working with Abelard too, but she was the only weakness I knew to exploit. Jean-Pierre didn't respond as he continued out of the room.

"Okay, Parker," I spoke quietly to myself, "you took all those damn yoga classes for a reason." Gritting my teeth, I swung my legs back and forth, slowly gaining momentum. My wrists were most unhappy by this, and I tried to lessen the pressure by grasping at the ropes. It didn't help. Pulling down on my restraints, I let out a whimper as I swung my legs up and over, finally gaining enough height to cross my ankles together over the chain.

My bound wrists and locked ankles contorted my body into a circle, and I slid my ankles down the chain until they rested on the hook, just above my hands. Barely, I got my fingertips into the space between my boot and my shin and maneuvered my middle and pointer fingers to find the button securing the knife in place. Pulling downward, I unsnapped the button and grasped the knife. My wrists screamed in protest against the rope, which currently felt as if it were cutting through my bones, but I maintained a firm grip on the knife's handle. *Mission accomplished*, I thought, dropping my legs.

Sawing away at the ties holding me in place, I

pondered my next move. If I could get off the hook and on the ground, then I would worry about getting the rope off my hands. As I sawed, I alternated my gaze toward the double doors. Any second, Abelard would be back. It was a sobering certainty. The rope was severely frayed, so to save time, I stopped sawing and tugged as hard as I could. I bit my bottom lip to keep from screaming as the rope gave way, and I crashed to the ground.

Scrambling up and barely able to move, I did a quick assessment, looking for a hiding spot or weapon. There were a few crates in the back corner, and I crouched behind them while I finished cutting my hands free. My sleeves were red, and my wrists were swollen, burned, and bloody. Keeping the knife poised in my right hand, I reached into my bra for the earwig. It was worth a shot. I turned it on but heard nothing but static. Fuck.

The double doors opened, and Abelard barked orders in French. I needed an escape plan. Going straight to the loading dock provided no cover. I would be spotted immediately. The warehouse had been used for storage of some kind. It was large, and I ducked behind some long-abandoned crates. Glancing around, I had a decent shot of moving from crate to crate until my means of escape seemed more plausible. But I needed something better to fight off my attackers than just a knife. How come people didn't leave loaded machine guns lying around?

Creeping around the edge of the warehouse, I moved from one set of crates to another, remaining out of sight. Abelard's men desperately hunted for me. Searching for other exits, I didn't see any air ducts, windows, or anything that might lead to the outside world. Staying inside was a death sentence. The only plus was each of the men searched for me alone, and as far as I could tell, none of them were armed. In the dim lighting, I stayed in the shadows to prolong the inevitable. Everything from here on out was about buying time.

As I slunk around a corner, I stumbled on a metal object. The resulting clang drew attention from two of Abelard's men. I reached down and located the metal pipe I tripped over. Scurrying around the corner, I pressed myself against the wall and waited. One of the men peeked around the corner. My swing connected with the man's jaw, and he went down instantly. Maybe I should have been a baseball player. It was a much safer job. A second goon saw the attack and grabbed the end of my pipe before I could connect with him. I gave it a hard tug, and when he pulled back, I let go and lunged for him.

We rolled on the ground, and I attempted to land as many well-placed punches and kicks as I could. I was acutely aware that I needed to finish this and find another place to hide when the man got to his feet and threw me against the wall. Reaching into my pocket, I pulled out my knife and stabbed him just below the ribs. His grip loosened, providing the perfect opportunity to regroup. Finding the discarded pipe in the darkness, I took out his kneecap. He was kneeling on the ground, howling in pain, when I swung again for his head. He was either dead or unconscious, and at the moment, as long as he didn't get back up, I didn't care.

Retrieving my knife, I ran toward the back of the warehouse. It was time to go. Although my initial count of Abelard's resources showed only three other guys, there were still another two or three in the warehouse. They were fast approaching, and I lost sight of Abelard and Jean-Pierre.

Reaching the back wall, I found a few blacked out

windows. I was just about to smash through one of them when I heard sirens. *This better be the goddamn cavalry*, I thought bitterly as I used the pipe to shatter the window, running the metal cylinder around the edges to break away the remaining shards of glass. I needed to get out of here, now. The men who had been closing in appeared to have retreated at the sound of sirens.

Grasping the window frame, I boosted myself up toward freedom, but someone grabbed the back of my shirt and pulled me down. Knife at the ready, I spun around and confronted Jean-Pierre. He adopted a fighting stance, and we carefully assessed one another.

"It's over," I told him. "The way I see it, you can make a break for it and be on the run forever, or you can surrender and turn state's evidence. You used to be one of the good guys." I wasn't sure if I could reason with him, but in a fight, he would win. He was stronger, more thoroughly trained, and hadn't just gone three rounds with an electric-chair wannabe.

TWENTY

"Go," Jean-Pierre said firmly. I didn't move. "Allez!" he screamed.

I turned and pulled myself out the broken window, noticing the men who had been in pursuit were now crumpled in unconscious heaps on the ground. Did Jean-Pierre take them out and assist my escape? I couldn't be sure, but right now, I had to get out of here. Climbing out the window, I landed face first on the ground and was immediately surrounded by the police tactical unit.

They shouted at me in French, so I stayed where I was, not moving. "You're late," I yelled at them. At least ten weapons were trained on me while a couple of guys held me roughly against the ground, handcuffed me, and secured my knife. Brilliant, arrest the goddamn hostage. If I hadn't just been through the wringer, I might have said as much. Instead, I remained face down on the ground until I heard Ryan's Irish accent breaking through all the French.

"Get off of her," he was getting closer, "and take

- 170 -

those bloody cuffs off. Now." Someone gently released the cold metal from my battered and bleeding wrists.

"What happened? You stopped for a fucking croissant on the way here?" I asked as Ryan helped me to my feet. "I thought you had my back."

"I'm here now." He ushered me out of the danger zone, throwing a jacket emblazoned with the word *police* over my shoulders, and placed me inside one of the SUVs parked on the outskirts of the strike zone.

"Gustav's not dead. He's inside, or he was inside. Abelard, too," I relayed as much pertinent information as I could.

"I know. Agent Jablonsky phoned us. We'll get them," Ryan promised. He assessed my appearance. "Are you okay?"

"Do I look okay?"

He gently rolled up one of my blood-soaked sleeves and looked at my wrist.

"Donough," a voice called, and he turned. "There's something inside you need to see."

"Go. I'll be fine."

He looked at me uncertainly before heading for the warehouse. I shut my eyes and rested my head against the car seat. I wasn't dead. Maybe run over by a steamroller and set on fire, but not dead.

"Madame Parker." Reneaux stood in front of me. I didn't know how long I had been sitting in the SUV or how long he had been standing there. A substantial amount of time must have passed since most of the police vehicles were gone. "It seems you are evidence." I wasn't sure if Reneaux's English was a little faulty or my ability to process words was impaired. "How do you feel about going to the crime lab, where a medic will meet you, instead of the hospital?"

"Okay." I would have agreed to anything at this point. Reneaux nodded, and Ryan got in on the driver's side. Turning in the seat so I was facing forward, I let Reneaux shut my door.

"What happened back there?" Ryan asked, flipping on the siren and driving at breakneck speed to the police station.

I gave him the play-by-play, knowing I would be repeating this story a few more times. "Did you get him? Both of them?" I asked.

He turned and looked at me sadly. "We have Gustav and quite a few people from Abelard's inner circle."

"Abelard?" I hoped his ass was shot full of holes.

"He wasn't there."

"That son of a bitch got away?"

"I promise we will track him to the bloody ends of the earth if we have to. The motherfucker will not get away again."

The rest of the ride continued in silence. I was exhausted. My head pounded, and every inch of my body ached. It was almost five a.m. I spent nearly six hours trapped in that warehouse. No wonder I felt like shit. Apparently, a reasonable timeframe to move in included figuring in the time difference between home and Paris.

Ryan parked the SUV and came around to open my door. His eyes examined the cut on my chest, my opened and bloodied shirt, and my wrists. "It's been a hell of a night. Maybe I should take you to the emergency room instead."

Before I could respond, a group of police personnel gathered in preparation for evidence collection and to take my statement. "Too late now," I muttered as he helped me out of the vehicle.

Immediately, I was greeted by a woman who worked in evidence collection and an overly friendly female EMT. I was ushered into one of the larger lab areas where my shirt was confiscated. Anything covered in blood was considered evidence, which seemed ridiculous, but whatever made these people happy. It's not like I needed a ripped, bloodstained shirt as a reminder of tonight. I had all my fond memories that would never go away, no matter how hard I tried to repress them. My injuries were photographed, from my wrists to the burns on my chest to the slice along my clavicle.

Someone else came in to question me while the medic hooked up an EKG to see if I sustained any muscle damage to my heart. Thankfully, the test came out negative. She drew blood for a toxicology screening, which would probably come back positive for something. After being subjected to a basic neurological exam to rule out a concussion or other head injury, my blood pressure was taken, and I was allowed to put on a shirt, which they apparently stocked for this exact purpose. My wrists were bandaged, and I was permitted to clean up.

Finally, I was escorted upstairs where I gave Reneaux the rundown for his official debrief. When that was completed, I located a couch down the hall from the locker rooms. Ryan found me sprawled out with my eyes closed.

"I didn't know where you went." He sat on the edge, next to me. "I'm sorry we didn't have a pair of those pink, fuzzy cuffs handy when the tactical team got too overzealous doing their jobs."

I opened one eye and looked at him. "What a shame." I shut my eyes.

"Your medical report came back," he continued, not getting the hint I didn't feel like talking. "You tested positive for chloroform. You're also anemic, dehydrated, and most likely suffering from exhaustion. They wanted to hook you up to an IV to replenish your fluids, but I warned them you would probably tell them exactly what they could do with that IV."

I looked at him and snorted. "How is it you already know me so well?" I offered a brief grin, imagining inflicting my own torture upon nurses who didn't understand I had been through enough tonight. "And you forgot the part about how everything aches, but I can't complain. After all, I'm still breathing," I said sarcastically.

Ryan remained tight-lipped but got up and bought a bottle of water from the vending machine. "Drink this."

"I was hoping for something a lot stronger," I muttered, but I obediently unscrewed the cap and took a sip. I really was thirsty and in need of replacing the fluids I had lost. "What time is it?"

"It's almost ten. The evidence team is still working the scene, but we've finished processing Gustav and four of Abelard's guys. The fifth is in intensive care. They're uncertain if he'll pull through." He cocked his head to the side and studied me. "You're more lethal than you look."

I chuckled despite the seriousness of the situation. My emotions were off-kilter from lack of sleep. Plus, I was stuck at the police station until everything was processed, especially since I had yet to make or sign an official statement of my own. It was going to be a long day.

"Madame Parker," Reneaux appeared at the end of the hallway, "there is an urgent phone call for you from Agent Jablonsky. You may use my office."

I stood up and shrugged at Ryan before following Reneaux down the hallway. He handed me the phone and went out to the squad room to give me some privacy. "Mark?" I asked.

"Parker, goddamn, I've been up all night, trying to track you down. What happened? You're making this old man worry. Why didn't you call me back?"

"Sorry, I lost track of time, hanging around," I replied bitterly. Slumping into Reneaux's chair, I hoped he wouldn't mind. "I'm probably not allowed to discuss things at the moment, but I'll fill you in when I get back. If you need anything, leave a message at the hotel. It's the only phone I have."

"I've been hearing a lot of chatter. Are you okay?"

"Still breathing," I said before disconnecting. Reneaux had a nice little sofa against the wall of his office, and I looked at it sadly as I went to thank him for the use of his phone.

"Please, Madame," Reneaux ushered me back into his office, "make yourself comfortable. I'll have a translator and officer sent up to take your statement and file a report, and then we'll find someone to give you a ride back to your hotel to get cleaned up before we interrogate Abelard's cohorts."

Crawling onto the sofa, I tried to get comfortable. I understood why they needed to dot the 'I's and cross the 'T's, but I was tired and achy. Why couldn't we do this tomorrow? Reneaux took a seat behind his desk and typed his report while we waited for the officer and translator to appear. Ryan escorted them in and brought me another bottle of water and a sandwich. He felt guilty for not getting there sooner. Oh well.

I ate as I relayed the entire story once again to the officers. Everything I said was written in English and transcribed in French. Life would be easier if we had one universal language, but that was probably just my exhaustion being bitchy. I reread the entire thing and signed it. They cross-referenced the photos of my torture, as they were referring to it, with my statement and placed it neatly into a case file. Hopefully, the

French prosecutor would be satisfied. I wasn't familiar with France's judicial system, but as long as I was granted some type of confidential status and not required to appear for the actual proceedings, I didn't care.

When we were finished, Ryan gave me a ride to my hotel. We took the elevator up to my room, and he came inside once I opened the door. I just wanted to crawl into bed and never move again.

"Freshen up, we have to be back in a couple of hours," he sounded almost as tired as I felt.

"And I thought the overtime at home was crappy." I dug through my duffel bag for something to wear that would be comfortable and also professional. "You've been on all night. Can't we just play hooky?"

He assessed my appearance carefully. "If you want a doctor's note, I'd be happy to drop you off at the hospital and make sure you are, in fact, okay. I never trust those EMTs and medics. What the bloody hell do they know?"

"I just want to get this over with as quickly as possible." I thought about Martin's offer to use the private jet. "Any way I can get the hell out of here by Friday?" Walking into the bathroom and turning on the water, I plugged the drain so the tub could fill. Then I asked Ryan to cut the bandages off my wrists. The bleeding had stopped hours ago.

"I'll make it happen," he assured, pulling out his pocket knife, and I looked away as he cut through the medical tape. Blades and bindings were making me squeamish. I glanced at the neatly made bed I hadn't slept in.

"If you want to catch some shut-eye, feel free." I went back into the bathroom and closed the door. The hot water relaxed my aching muscles, but it stung my wrists and made the blistered skin on my chest burn more than usual. I was trying very hard not to fall asleep in the bathtub when Ryan knocked on the door. "Are you almost ready?" he asked gently. I got out of the tub and dried off. "Ten minutes." I dressed and tied my wet hair back, opening the door and holding out my wrists for him to assess. "I'm not sure what to do about this. I look like an overzealous suicide attempt gone wrong."

"Bloody hell." He glanced at my wrists, but his eyes were drawn to the burn marks on my chest, clearly visible over the spaghetti strap tank top I was wearing to keep from irritating my skin further. "We should have moved in sooner. Alex, I am so sorry."

"Yeah, yeah." Putting on a jacket, I rolled up the sleeves so Ryan could re-bandage my wrists before picking up my purse and room key. "Let's get this show on the road."

TWENTY-ONE

Interrogations had been going on all afternoon. Claude and Francois had been at the warehouse and detained by the French police. I had no input on Francois' involvement, except he was a bartender. Claude, on the other hand, provided Abelard with his little electric toy. One of the men from the back room had been arrested, but I had little to no interaction with him, so I watched as the questions rambled on quickly in French. Reneaux provided a translator, and as I sat in the observation room, watching the interrogations, she effortlessly changed the words from French to English. In between interviews, Reneaux or Ryan would come in and ask if I could verify details or if I had any input. For the most part, I remained silent.

It was a little after three o'clock when Jean-Pierre was escorted into the interrogation room. His ankles were shackled, and his wrists were bound. He stared at the two-way mirror as if he knew I was on the other side of the glass. Ryan and another detective questioned him in French, but Jean-Pierre kept his responses in English.

"Son of a bitch," I cursed, stalking back and forth like a lion. My eyes never left his form. When I could no longer stand it, I tapped on the glass. Ryan turned, nodded almost imperceptibly, and excused himself for a minute.

"What?" he asked as he came into the observation room.

"I want in there." My pacing stopped, but I was still moving, bouncing up and down on the balls of my feet. I couldn't calm down, and I couldn't sit still.

"Are you sure that's a good idea? He's trying to get to you. He knows you're in here. Why else would he be conversing in English?"

"So we let him." I was ready to play with fire. "You can haul me out of there anytime you want if things get out of hand."

Ryan glanced through the window at Gustav, who stared right at us as if he could see through the mirrored glass. "I need approval." He attempted to dissuade me, but it wasn't working.

"Go find Reneaux."

"You stay here until I get back. I don't want our best lead on Abelard to end up dead while I'm gone."

A couple of minutes later Ryan and Reneaux entered the room. "Madame, are you sure you want to do this?" Reneaux asked cautiously.

"Why not? He's playing some game. We might as well find out what it is."

"D'accord. I will stay here and watch the exchange." Reneaux looked at Ryan. "If you see things turning in a negative direction, get her out of there." Ryan agreed, and we entered the interrogation room.

"Bonjour, Ali." Jean-Pierre gave me a big smile.

I wanted to physically remove it from his face, but

instead, I ignored it and took a seat diagonally across from him. I stared at him, silently seething. There were no words to speak, so I just sat there as Ryan continued the interrogation in English. Jean-Pierre wouldn't cooperate, and Ryan became more and more agitated. Given the fact he'd been out in the cold for the last eighteen months and up all night, I could understand why his technique left a little to be desired.

"Why did you let me go?" My icy tone and sudden interruption surprised both Ryan and Jean-Pierre. Ryan stepped back and leaned against the wall, staring at Jean-Pierre. I was permitted to run the show, at least for the moment.

"What else should I have done?" Jean-Pierre answered my question with a question. I shrugged. He didn't get to ask the questions, and I damn sure wasn't going to answer them.

"How many other people have you tortured and killed?" I asked. "Did you do it all for Abelard or maybe your own personal vendetta, too?"

"I never meant to hurt you. You weren't supposed to get caught up in this. I told you to move on. I sent you a video of the explosion. You were supposed to get the hint and drop the entire thing." He slammed his palms against the table.

"Why?" My lips curled into an evil grin. "Afraid I would figure out you were behind the smuggling and helping to create a crime syndicate with Abelard?" Ryan teetered against the wall, perhaps considering stopping me. I leaned back in the chair and waited, but Jean-Pierre didn't answer. "Did you kill Jacques Marset?"

He took a deep breath, and I saw his cheek twitch. He looked away, staring at the wall. "Marset double-crossed the wrong man."

"So you killed him? And being the sick, twisted bastard that you are, you videotaped it and sent it to me. How did you end up here? When did you become this guy?"

"Ali," his eyes looked pitiful, and I wanted to slap him, "I did what I had to do."

"Did you also send the men to my apartment to beat the hell out of me? Stay away or else, was that the message you wanted conveyed?"

Jean-Pierre looked genuinely shocked. "He sent men to your apartment? I had nothing to do with that. I didn't know."

For once, I was inclined to believe him.

"So who did?" Ryan asked, sliding the chair out and flipping it backward before sitting down. "Abelard?"

Jean-Pierre looked from me to Ryan but didn't speak.

"It must have been your idea to put Clyde Van Buren's name on the wire transfer," I said. Ryan and I might just be getting into the groove of things. "You wanted to fake your death and pin the art crimes on your Evans-Sterling teammates. Was that so you could ride off into the sunset with Abelard?"

"Sounds like you're his bitch," Ryan commented matter-of-factly.

Jean-Pierre swallowed but remained silent.

"Didn't you think scattering suspicion onto the Evans-Sterling team would make Clare our number one suspect?" I asked, pausing briefly before interjecting, "Oh wait, she's working with you and Abelard. I keep forgetting that."

"Clare has nothing to do with this," Jean-Pierre said.

"Oh, come on." I found his pressure point and planned to squeeze as hard as I could. "At first, I thought someone so incredibly upset and distraught couldn't possibly be involved in the murder of her lover, but then, it turns out you weren't dead. She makes one hell of an actress though, almost had me completely convinced." I glanced at Ryan. "Did she have you convinced, too?"

"It's always the girlfriend," he replied automatically. "If they aren't the killers, they're the accomplices." I nodded in agreement. "We brought her in. Maybe if you're lucky, we can place you in adjacent holding cells, so you can say your goodbyes." Everything Ryan said was total bull, but he said it so convincingly I was tempted to double-check the facts with Reneaux.

"Ali," Jean-Pierre tried to appeal to my morality, "Clare is not involved. She doesn't even know I'm alive." His expression was genuine and his voice sincere. I believed him. The suspicions Ryan and I had concerning Clare were based on Jean-Pierre being dead and someone else on the Evans-Sterling team being responsible for the thefts.

"I told you not to call me that," I hissed, refusing to acknowledge any of what he just said.

Ryan interrupted before I could go on a tirade. "Do you have information regarding the whereabouts of Louis Abelard?" he asked sternly. I could see the play he was about to make. I just hoped Jean-Pierre didn't see the same thing. "We might be willing to drop the charges on Clare if you help us locate Abelard."

"How can there be charges against Clare? She isn't involved." He spoke rapidly in French, and I knew we had him. Once his dithering ebbed, I interjected before Ryan could say a word.

"Think logically, Jean-Pierre. Clare is your lover. She worked with you at Evans-Sterling. She knew the location of one of Abelard's warehouses. Hell, she gave me the address herself, in her own handwriting.

She covered up your involvement." Before I could continue, Ryan put his hand on my forearm.

"That's enough, Parker." There was a slight glint in his eye. "I can't have you discussing unrelated evidence with a suspect. Take a break."

I made a pretense of being pissed off and slammed my chair against the table for effect. "Fine." The officer opened the door, and I exited into the hallway. *Who's emotional now, asshole?* I mentally retorted to Jean-Pierre. His game didn't go the way he hoped.

Another police officer entered the interrogation room as I exited. Reneaux was waiting for me in the hallway.

"I believe you failed to mention anything about your American threats," he said. I told Ryan about it, but I guess he didn't fill in Reneaux, probably because it didn't seem pertinent at the time. We went to Reneaux's office where I gave him my account, starting with the retrieval of the painting to O'Connell tracking down Ramirez and making the gang connection. "How may I contact your detective friend?"

I gave him O'Connell's number and waited as he called Nick. The report was faxed over, and Reneaux would add it to the ever-growing list of charges against Abelard. Maybe he would find a connection that hadn't been discovered yet. I also told him everything Interpol had on the case and gave him Delacroix's number. The two of them could argue over jurisdiction.

"Did Interpol find anything useful?" Reneaux asked once he finished reading the American police report.

"Not that I'm aware of. Agent Farrell, the OIO liaison, was helpful in providing specific details on the video footage of Gustav's supposed car bombing, but Delacroix probably couldn't find his way out of a paper bag even if he had a pair of scissors and a map."

Reneaux nodded sympathetically. "I've dealt with Monsieur Delacroix on a few occasions. We are supposedly working the Abelard case in a joint venture. It hasn't quite gone the way I hoped." It was my turn to be sympathetic. I gave Farrell's information to Reneaux, figuring it couldn't hurt. "Is this everything? I don't like surprises, Madame Parker."

"That should be it. I'm sure Donough has already given you the relevant Evans-Sterling information."

He nodded. "Thank you very much for your assistance. My department is indebted to you. If there is anything I can do for you, just ask."

"Actually, I need a favor." I felt a bit stupid asking. "I left my rental car parked on a meter a few blocks from the warehouse."

"It will be taken care of and returned to your hotel by morning," he promised.

Finding my way to Ryan's desk, I awaited his return, hoping to find out how useful Jean-Pierre had been. As the minutes passed, I slid further down in the chair and propped my legs up, only seconds away from sleep.

"Need a ride?" Ryan asked.

"Are you finished for the day?"

"Yes, and it's about bloody time," he sounded exhausted. "Come on, let's get out of here." I followed him out of the police station and to his car. We were on the way to my hotel when I asked about Jean-Pierre's interrogation. "We'll have to wait and see where it leads. We have a few of the higher-up inspectors running with it. For now, I'm off duty. And you, my dear, look like you're in need of some much needed rest."

I snorted. That sentiment felt like the

understatement of the year. "I'm done?" I asked skeptically.

He looked uncertain. "Seems that way. You got us the raid, even if it didn't turn out quite the way we hoped. Gustav's statements should lead to even more concrete evidence and Abelard's location." He turned with a grin. "Smile, you're going to make that flight on Friday."

After what happened last time, I was a bit too paranoid to celebrate.

TWENTY-TWO

I wasn't asleep nearly as long as I should have been when the hotel phone rang. I reached over and pulled the receiver from the cradle and held it to my ear.

"Hello?" My voice was hoarse. I tried to clear my throat, but it didn't help.

"Madame Parker, there are a few men from Interpol here to see you," the front desk informed me. "A Monsieur Delacroix." I shut my eyes and hoped I was in the midst of a horrible nightmare. "Madame Parker?" the woman repeated.

"Wait ten minutes and send them up," I croaked. I got out of bed, dressed quickly, and just finished brushing my teeth when there was a knock. I checked the peephole and unlocked the door.

"Delacroix," I greeted, unenthused.

"Is that your boudoir voice, or are you just happy to see me?" he asked, nodding to the other Interpol agent to wait outside.

"What do you want?"

"I got a call from Reneaux this morning, seems you

were playing ball with the Police Nationale and left me and my men in the dark."

"You have issues sharing."

"Seems they have issues protecting their assets," he countered, staring at the cut and burn marks visible over the neckline of my shirt. "If you would be so kind as to grace us with your presence," he looked at his watch, "in say, two and a half hours. I'm on my way to meet with Reneaux and form a joint task force for the apprehension of Louis Abelard. Your insight might be valuable," he sounded skeptical, but I ignored the jibe.

"Interpol offices or Police Nationale HQ?"

"HQ, and maybe you should try some tea with honey for that throat of yours." He let himself out of my room, and I picked up the plastic ashtray and threw it at the closed door. Since I wasn't a smoker, I was happy to find some use for the hotel-supplied object.

Delacroix had a way of getting under my skin. I crawled back into bed. If Reneaux wanted me at the meeting, he'd call. Since I was still exhausted, I hoped to go back to sleep, but I was too pissed off. I lay there, fuming.

The phone rang again. I picked it up, expecting the front desk to say Delacroix refused to leave. Instead, it was Ryan.

"I'm sorry to wake you," he sounded half-asleep. "We need you for the joint task force briefing."

"Delacroix already stopped by to personally deliver the good news."

"Are you okay? Your voice sounds off."

"Maybe I'm catching a cold." Or I spent a good portion of Tuesday night screaming in pain, but I didn't feel the need to share that tidbit of information.

"I'll pick you up on the way."

Why could I never catch a break? I was still

unnaturally pale and completely drained. Maybe I should have gone to the hospital just to get some rest and fluids without police and Interpol agents knocking on my door. As if on cue, Ryan knocked.

"It's Ryan," he announced, saving me the effort of looking through the peephole. He assessed my appearance. "How's the cold?" he asked, playing along, even though he knew I wasn't sick.

"I'll live." I grabbed my room key, and we left the hotel. On the way to the front door, I was told my rental car had been returned, along with the keys that had been found in my purse. However, the bankroll of Euros hadn't been recovered. I wasn't surprised.

"Here," Ryan handed me a cup of coffee once we got into his car, "thought you could use the caffeine."

"I would have preferred sleep."

*　　*　　*

The roll-call room had been turned into the meeting place for the joint task force. Here, both Paris police and Interpol were briefed on the information uncovered yesterday. Apparently, Gustav provided enough information that a few warehouses full of illegal gambling equipment had been seized overnight. The only issue left was tracking down Abelard. From what I could determine, there were mounds of physical evidence and numerous corroborating testimonies implicating him. The case was solid. They just needed to find him.

"Louis Abelard has countless numbers of safe houses, vast resources, and enough underlings to make his apprehension a difficult endeavor." Reneaux gave the speech to the room. It was in French, but Ryan whispered the translation in my ear, along with his own commentary.

"Abelard is a dangerous sociopath. While we will try to make every effort to bring him in alive, do not put yourself in any undue harm." Ryan added, "When in doubt, shoot first and ask questions later."

I gave him a sideways glance. "I'm guessing you're not working Abelard's arrest."

He shook his head. Reneaux continued running through the facts on Abelard's last known location. He then informed the room of Ryan's undercover work and officially welcomed him back from the cold. I was dazing off when Ryan nudged me.

All eyes were on me, waiting expectantly. Ryan leaned in and whispered I was supposed to give a description of Abelard's appearance, demeanor, and anything relevant I learned from my experiences with him. I blushed slightly and began a discourse over the bar setup, my initial impressions of him as aloof but in control, and his sadistic tendencies.

"Abelard has the classic sadist personality. He surrounds himself with people he can easily control, whether it's due to his commanding personality or outright blackmail. It's about manipulation. Emotional, physical, or even financial. He convinces those under him to follow orders or face the unfortunate consequences, not unlike dons in the mafia." I paused and took a sip of water. My voice was barely above a whisper as I continued. "He doesn't care to get his hands dirty. In fact, he relishes in it. When I was taken, he had his minions present, likely for his own safety or maybe as a way of conveying a warning to them not to cross him. Either way, he gets off on the torture, making people scream." I stopped and looked at Ryan, hoping he'd chime in. I didn't prepare anything for this meeting. I was just reiterating the few facts I personally experienced.

"Thank you for your assessment, Madame Parker,"

Reneaux said.

I nodded and slid down in my chair. Public speaking was not my thing. Ryan caught my eye and winked. At least someone was amused.

Delacroix delivered a speech, dealing specifically with the art thefts and smuggling which linked back to Abelard's numerous resources. "The man has fine taste in all things. If the trail turns cold, keep this in mind." How many asses did Delacroix kiss in order to get to the position he held? Bureaucratic brown-noser.

Agents and police were assigned to teams, and each was given a different location to raid. The raids would be conducted simultaneously in order to ensure Abelard would not be tipped off and able to flee again. The warrants were signed and ready to go. Ryan and I remained seated as the groups scattered. My head was in my hand, and I fought to remain in an upright position.

Reneaux walked over to us. "I didn't expect such a prolific psychological workup," he said.

"Neither did I. But you put me on the spot, and the words just came out. I'm certain it's accurate, given everything I know of Gustav's involvement and everything I endured at the warehouse. There's something to be said for firsthand experience."

"Where do you want us?" Ryan asked. I was amused how we somehow became a team. Maybe that was just my exhaustion keeping me a few steps behind.

"In a couple of hours when the teams move in, I'll need you to coordinate from tactical," Reneaux said.

"I can go back to my hotel and get out of the way," I volunteered happily. Both men looked at me.

"I think it'd be best if you stick around here until we capture Abelard," Reneaux replied, frowning.

"You think he's looking to finish what he started?"

It didn't occur to me until now.

"Seems like a possibility." Reneaux excused himself, so he could coordinate with Delacroix. I looked at Ryan, waiting for some elaboration.

"You never know," he responded casually. I put my head on the table. This was too much to deal with. "We'll bring him in tonight, and you fly home tomorrow. It'll be okay. You just have to get through today."

"I'm counting the hours."

*   *   *

Most of the day was spent camped out on the couch near the locker rooms. The anxious energy permeating throughout the police station seemed anticlimactic, probably since I was thankfully sitting on the sidelines. Ryan did all he could upstairs in tac ops, and when he was finished, he came to find me. I sat up, allowing him to occupy half the couch in exchange for a sandwich and a bottle of water. It seemed like a fair trade.

"When are the fireworks going off?" I asked, wiping my mouth with a napkin.

He glanced at his watch. "An hour or two. Everyone should be moving into position now." It was obvious he wanted to be in the field.

"Sorry, you're stuck babysitting. I would have been fine at my hotel."

"I wasn't allowed on this anyway. I don't know how things work at the OIO, but here, we're expected to be thoroughly debriefed and work the desk for a couple of weeks before getting back on the street in any capacity." He wasn't happy being stuck inside.

"At least you're back."

He gave me a brief grin. Ryan had an attractive

rough and tumble quality I didn't notice until now. "I can't argue with that." We sat on the couch for a while, eating our sandwiches. "Clare's in protective custody. We picked her up this morning and moved her to a safe location. It was one of the terms Gustav negotiated. A few inspectors are checking into her alibi and reviewing Interpol's surveillance logs, but as far as we can tell, she isn't involved."

"I never believed she was, but everything pointed to her. Hell, it still does to a certain extent." I searched my memory for anything that might definitively establish her guilt or innocence, but I came up blank. "Either way, she could become collateral damage. Clare is Gustav's Achilles heel," I surmised. "There's a possibility Abelard knows this and will try to exploit it."

"We better bloody well find him then," Ryan concluded, standing up and returning upstairs.

I remained for a few minutes, giving him time to get situated before following. I might as well make myself useful in the event they needed another set of eyes to coordinate the tactical assaults.

TWENTY-THREE

Ryan worked throughout the night, coordinating raids and assigning locations for evidence and suspects to be held. Delacroix opened the Interpol offices to help deal with the overwhelming amount of evidence and suspects being brought in. Reneaux was on the radio with the team leaders, making sure the timing and coordination went down flawlessly. Whatever else happened tonight, I was sure of one thing; Paris would have one less crime syndicate to deal with in the morning.

I had been little actual help, other than filing paperwork and organizing each raid into its own evidence folder. I also had the important task of keeping the coffeepot filled. I waited all night for confirmation of Abelard's capture. Unfortunately, no positive identification was made.

"I'm sure we got him," Ryan reassured me as we stood near the coffeepot. "They grabbed so many people tonight. He's probably lost in the throng of it all."

"Yeah." I looked anxiously at my watch. I had a plane to catch in three and a half hours. "Maybe I should stick around just to make sure."

"No. You're leaving today, even if I have to drag you kicking and screaming." Ryan offered a friendly smile. Things had died down as everyone cataloged evidence, booked skels, and filed reports. "Let me tell Reneaux we're leaving. I'll take you back to your hotel to get packed and then to the airport." He wouldn't take no for an answer. "In the meantime," he filled a paper cup from the water cooler, "drink this. You look like you're about to hit the floor."

I drank obediently, waiting for him to return.

*   *   *

Ryan was lying on the bed in my hotel room with his eyes closed when I got out of the shower. I had a moment of complete contempt for him and his ability to rest, but I pushed it aside as I unlocked the safe and unceremoniously tossed everything into my duffel bag. I took the bag into the bathroom and repeated the process.

"I don't think you can fly with a taser in your carry-on," he said. His eyes were still closed, and I was amazed he was aware of anything that was going on.

"Private jet. Rules don't apply." I opened the closet and threw everything else into my bag. I was fighting with the zipper when Ryan gently pushed my hands away, zipping the bag in one fluid motion.

"Would you like to explain how a former OIO agent gets to return home on a private jet?"

"Great timing and working private security for James Martin has its perks."

"James Martin?" He eyed me strangely.

"CEO of Martin Technologies."

"Uh-huh," he mumbled. I was beginning to feel like a suspect. "Was it his painting you were retrieving for Evans-Sterling?"

"No. Mark Jablonsky, my OIO commander, got me hired as Martin's bodyguard a few months back. I've been consulting for his company ever since." I didn't see why any of this was Ryan's business, but he was a cop. Inquisitive was in his nature. "It just so happens Luc Guillot, the head honcho of the Paris branch, is flying to the States, and I figured I might as well save on airfare."

"Guillot's the new VP." Ryan was more up-to-date than I would have guessed.

"Yeah. How did you know?"

"It was in the finance section of the paper." He picked up my duffel bag, and I glanced around the room for any forgotten items before opening the door and heading to the front desk to check out. "Bodyguard work?" Admiration lined his face. "You?"

"Ridiculous notion, I agree."

We climbed into his car, and he drove toward the private airstrip.

"I was about to say that makes you one hell of a badass. Clearly, there's no need to rescind my lethal comment from the other day."

"Worst experience ever," I sighed. "I agreed to consult on Martin's security protocols and ended up being a twenty-four hour protection detail by myself." I was still bitter about the way things had gone down.

"Well, he's still breathing, and you're employed. It couldn't have been that bad."

"Trust me, it was." I hadn't talked to anyone about this since it happened. "An entire assault team was hired to kill Martin. He was shot, and I took three to the vest. I watched him nearly bleed to death."

Ryan looked me in the eye, probably to assess how

damaged I was from that experience. "No wonder you get to take the private jet. Son of a bitch almost got you killed." That wasn't quite the way things happened, but I didn't feel the need to argue.

We pulled up to the airstrip with a half hour to spare. A chauffeured limousine was parked near the plane, indicating Luc and Genevieve Guillot already arrived. I didn't know if Martin gave them the heads up about my tagging along, but I hoped to avoid them as much as possible. I looked like hell and just wanted to be left alone to sleep for the next eight hours.

"Alex," Ryan stopped me before I could open the car door, "I just wanted to say thanks for helping out back there. It's been a rough couple of days, but if I had to stay one more night in that apartment with the Interpol surveillance van outside my door, I would have lost my bloody mind."

"Glad I could be of assistance." Hopefully, Abelard had been captured. "Let me know how everything turns out."

"Of course. I'm sure if we need you for something else, you can coordinate through your Interpol liaison." He watched as I slipped on my jacket to hide the burns and my wounded wrists from the more civilized world. "I'm sorry we didn't move in sooner." His voice was softer than I ever heard.

"It's okay. You showed up before things got really bad."

"I don't want to know what your definition of really bad is."

"Do you have a pen?"

"Why? Are you going to write it down for me?" he quipped but handed me the pen from his shirt pocket.

"Paper?" I was asking for a lot. He pulled out one of his business cards, and I scribbled my home phone number on the back. "When you're sure you have

Abelard, give me a call." I opened the car door as Ryan tucked my number into his pocket. He picked up my bag and carried it to the plane, flashing his badge to get us through the checkpoint without any real scrutiny and just a cursory glance at my passport.

"I will," he promised. He handed over my bag and hugged me. "Take care of yourself."

"You, too. Watch your back. And no more deep cover because I'm not coming back here to get Delacroix's surveillance off your ass again."

Climbing the stairs, I flashed my passport and my Martin Technologies ID card at the flight attendant.

"Mademoiselle Parker, so lovely to see you again," Luc Guillot greeted from one of the plush seats in the back of the cabin. "James called last night and said you might be traveling with us today." I gave him a tentative smile, hoping I could talk the flight attendant into letting me sit in the separated area reserved for the crew instead of with the Guillots. "This is my wife, Genevieve."

"Vivi, please," she said.

I nodded at her and smiled, so as not to appear rude. "Alex," I introduced myself. "Pleased to meet you, but if you'll excuse me, this is kind of heavy." I indicated my bag and followed the flight attendant to the storage area at the back of the plane. After properly stowing my bag, I re-emerged into the main portion of the cabin where the Guillots were seated comfortably on some bench seats.

"Please," Luc indicated the seat across from them, "make yourself comfortable."

"I appreciate it, but I'll stay out of your way," I said politely. "Enjoy your flight." I headed toward the other end of the cabin, but Vivi stopped me.

"Alex, are you feeling well?"

"I'm okay. I didn't sleep last night." It was enough

of the truth to suffice.

She nodded, believing she understood the implications. "We won't disturb you."

The flight attendant pulled a curtain, separating me from the Guillots. They were talking, but I couldn't make out the words. Leaning my seat back, I turned on my side and pulled the small shade over the window before closing my eyes. Once we took off and stabilized at the designated altitude, I relaxed and let the drone of the engines and the mumbled chattering of the Guillots lull me to sleep.

"Mademoiselle," the flight attendant woke me, "we've landed." I sat up and winced, amazed that I slept through the landing. I wasn't a bad flyer, but takeoffs and landings tended to be somewhat dicey.

"Have the Guillots disembarked yet?"

"They are in the process at the moment."

"Would you mind letting me know once they're gone? I don't want to get in their way." I hoped my request sounded reasonable, even though I just wanted to avoid exchanging more pleasantries. Would Martin be outside waiting for them?

"No problem." A few minutes later, the flight attendant returned with my bag. I hefted the duffel over my shoulder, almost falling over in the process. It didn't seem this heavy in Paris. Maybe the U.S. had a higher level of gravity, and that was the reason for our levels of obesity. It had nothing to do with supersized, fast food, processed meals.

Putting on my sunglasses, I exited into the bright morning sunlight. Mark's government-issued SUV was parked near the fence surrounding the runway, and he stood next to a familiar town car, chatting with Bruiser. The Guillots were helping Marcal load their luggage into the trunk. Martin was nowhere to be seen, which left me feeling oddly disappointed. When

Mark spotted me, he pulled out his badge and waited on the other side of the checkpoint.

"Government business." It wasn't often he got to throw around his power just for show. "Miss Parker," he greeted, taking my bag and studying me from behind his aviator sunglasses, "did you escape from a motorcycle gang?" He mocked my wraparound sunglasses and leather jacket.

"Not quite." I followed him to his SUV. "Did I tell you to pick me up?" It had been a long couple of days.

"You were supposed to." He shoved my duffel into the trunk. "Farrell called this morning and told me what time you were getting in. He wants to debrief you immediately, if not sooner." I sighed loudly and fought against the seatbelt while desperately trying to get my jacket off. It was rubbing my skin raw. "Also, the director wants to see you."

"What director?" Wrestling my jacket off and pulling it free of the seatbelt, I was finally ready to go.

"Our director. My boss. Kendall." He watched my expression out of the corner of his eye.

"Oh, that director." The last time I had any interaction with Director Kendall was when I resigned, and he chewed me out.

"I've been reading the reports coming out of the Paris Interpol offices." Mark waited for a response.

"Good, you're up to speed." Without my jacket on, I was freezing and reached to turn on the heat. He stared at my unbandaged wrists as I adjusted the vents. "Eyes on the road, Jablonsky."

"You're going to make me ask?"

"No. I just don't have much to tell. Everything is in the report. I spent some time hanging around until the Police Nationale arrived." I didn't want to talk about it, and Mark dropped it. The silence continued until we reached the freeway.

"Did you get checked out afterward?" He could act very fatherly sometimes.

"Of course. A medic cleared me. No muscle damage."

"Last chance for an ER check-up," he offered as we approached the exit for the hospital.

"I'm good." I still felt like crap, but I didn't want to start my morning, sitting in an ER waiting room for several hours to hear I was fine. I already had to deal with a debriefing and getting yelled at by Director Kendall.

We made it to the OIO offices a little before noon. Mark escorted me to Agent Farrell's office where I was then ushered into a conference room and forced to give an entire account of everything that occurred over the last week. Since it was already on record and properly filed, I had a sneaking suspicion Delacroix pulled some strings just to torment me further. Agent Farrell was kind and thanked me numerous times for the assistance I provided.

By two o'clock, I was waiting in Mark's office for Director Kendall to tear me a new one. Mark was behind his desk, working on some reports.

"Any idea what Kendall wants?" I asked, hoping to be prepared for whatever was about to happen.

"I have no idea. Are you sure you're okay?"

I hated being female when it came to these law enforcement types. A majority of them tended to think I was some weakling who needed looking after. I could hold my own, thank you very much.

"I'm fine. A bit anemic and slightly dehydrated but fine otherwise." I tried very hard to keep the annoyance from my voice.

"I didn't mean it that way." He watched my expression. "Although now that you mention it, you do look rather ghostly. Or ghastly."

I narrowed my eyes at him. Before our conversation could continue, the intercom beeped, and our presence was requested in Kendall's office. Following Mark down the hallway and into the director's office, I took a seat and waited patiently for the impending barrage.

As I predicted, Kendall proceeded to rip into me for running amok in a foreign country, not considering any of the potential ramifications my actions could have on this office, and the lack of concern I exercised toward my own well-being. I sat quietly, trying to look ashamed. He was right on all three accounts, but I couldn't have cared less. When the yelling portion of the meeting was over, I glanced up cautiously at Kendall. Mark was seated next to me, looking stern. Teacher's pet.

"Parker, what the hell are you doing?" Kendall asked, adopting a more relaxed posture and flexing his fingertips against the tabletop.

"Wreaking havoc in Paris?" I was unsure what the right answer might be but wanted to demonstrate I paid attention to his tirade.

"That much is obvious." He wasn't pleased with my answer. I guess it must have been the wrong one. "What the hell do you think you're doing? You walk into my office several months ago and resign. Now you're in France working with Interpol. Before that, you were involved in some kind of shootout at a CEO's house. You're more on my radar now than you were when you worked here."

I glanced at Mark. His eyebrows raised, and he nodded in agreement. "I'm in the private sector now, sir. There's some overlap."

"Come back to work. We'll reinstate you," Kendall said.

I gaped at him. "With all due respect, I left for a

reason." I was shocked he just offered me my old job back.

"You weren't responsible for those two agents getting killed, Parker. Things happen. You can't control everything."

"Too much bureaucracy and red-tape, sir." I ignored his comment since I wasn't ready to think about the last mission I worked at the OIO. Mark watched the exchange, hoping I would relent and accept the offer.

"Offer's on the table. Think about it," Kendall said.

"Thanks, but no thanks," I moved to stand, but Mark put his hand on my forearm.

"Would you be willing to consult for us?" Mark asked.

"You've got to be kidding me."

"We could use more people like you, Agent Parker." Kendall was laying it on thick. "If you don't want to be here full-time, consider a consulting position. Or even a temporary consulting position. Come back and work a few of the more complicated cases. Think about it. Give me your answer in a couple of weeks."

"Thank you, Director." Leaving his office, I stood perfectly still, trying to detect if hell was in the process of freezing over. Before I could positively conclude there was at least some snowfall accumulating in Hades, Mark met me in the hallway and escorted me to his office.

"You knew," I accused.

"Maybe. Come on, Alex. You live and breathe this. All you have to do is sign some paperwork, pass the psych eval, and take the physical, and you're back in. I want you back here."

I squeezed the bridge of my nose and opened my eyes, staring at the rope burns and cut marks on my wrist. "Do you think I'd pass the psych eval right now?" I didn't deal well with talking things out. I didn't deal well with emotions and processing trauma properly either, or so I'd been told.

"Just think about it," he insisted. "I need you here."

I laughed bitterly and went to get a cup of water from the cooler in the hallway.

TWENTY-FOUR

Mark gave me a ride to my apartment where I quickly unpacked and changed into a low-cut tank top. Today had been enough of an annoyance without the constant chafing of cotton against my blistered and burned skin. He was flipping through a two week old newspaper, when his phone rang.

"It's for you," he said as I emerged from my bedroom.

"It's your cell phone."

"Trust me, it's for you." He shoved the phone toward me, and I awkwardly answered.

"You're home." Martin's voice contained a hint of a smile. "Just for the record, I wasn't at the airport because I was working and wearing a suit."

"Well, that's one way to avoid getting arrested for indecent exposure."

"Dinner tonight?" he asked. Mark offered to buy a few rounds, probably hoping some libations would lower my inhibitions about going back to work for him.

"Mark's taking me out for drinks, but feel free to

join us. I could use someone on my side," I said for Mark's benefit.

Martin took down the address and agreed to meet us at five or as soon as he could tear himself away from work, whichever came first.

*   *   *

Mark and I were seated at the bar. I ordered a glass of white wine, and after one sip, I realized how incredibly stupid the idea was. Even though I slept on the plane, I still felt off. The room wobbled a little as I glanced around at the lively environment. Exhaustion and maybe a tad of dehydration wouldn't mix well with alcohol, especially given my pallor. I pushed the glass away and asked for water instead. Mark continued to stare, probably expecting me to collapse.

"Alex," he began in a tone I knew meant a lecture was on the way, "you need to talk it out."

I sighed and looked at him. My head was beginning to throb, and I intended to write it off as Mark's fault. "Why? So I can pass the psych eval and come back to the office?"

"No," his voice shifted to a kinder tone, "you were tortured. You can't just pretend it didn't happen. It will fester and eat you alive."

"The only thing torturous is this conversation."

He ignored the embellishment. "I didn't say this to you when Michael and Sam were killed. Instead, I let you disappear. You resigned and holed up in your apartment for months. If I didn't get you a position working for Marty, you'd probably still be hiding out."

"We are not talking about this right now." My blood pressure spiked, and the room spun. I propped my head in my hands to get the spinning under control.

"It wasn't your fault. You were coordinating the

operation from the office. You had no way of knowing it was a setup. Nothing indicated the building was booby-trapped. There wasn't anything else you could have done."

Before I could respond, Martin appeared as if out of thin air. "Sorry, I'm late. I had some final plans to make with Luc. We're having a business dinner tomorrow night." He slid past me. Pressing his palm gently against the small of my back, he kissed my cheek in greeting. I had yet to turn or acknowledge him since I was still reeling after Mark opened this particular can of worms. "Did I interrupt something?"

"No, I think we're done here." I glared at Mark, my voice venomous.

"Alex," Mark sounded apologetic, "I'm sorry, it's just—"

"I'm not feeling well. Coming out tonight was a bad idea. I'll just grab a cab and head home." I stood up, and the room spun uncontrollably. I reached for the bar, but Martin snaked his arm around my waist, steadying me.

"Easy." His grip loosened as I took a couple deep breaths and the room stopped moving. "I'll take you home." He got up from the bar as I freed myself from his grasp.

"It's okay. I can manage."

"I'll take you home," he repeated more forcefully. He shot a glance at Mark as I made my way to the front door.

"Keep an eye on her," Mark said, and Martin trailed me out of the bar.

"Are you okay?" Martin asked as I teetered on the sidewalk. Not waiting for an answer, he wrapped his arm around my shoulders while we waited for Marcal to bring the car around.

"Long day. Long flight. Drinking wasn't a smart

decision." I looked up at him. He had seen my wrists and chest but had yet to mention either. "Thank you." He opened the door, and I got into the car.

"When was the last time you had anything to eat?" He gently brushed my hair from my face, trying to determine why I was the color of a sheet.

"Um, good question." I frowned, unable to recall. "Yesterday, I think."

"Crash dieting is never a good idea," he joked. "How does Chinese sound? We can split some takeout. You did agree to dinner."

"Okay." I was just relieved to be away from Mark and his annoying insistence on continuing an absolutely pointless conversation. Finding some relief in the cold glass of the window, I studied Martin as he called in our order.

When he was done, he put the phone away and looked at me. "I did miss you. How was Paris?"

"Awful. French toast and French fries may never be eaten again because it was just that horrible."

"I'm sorry."

I was mesmerized by those gorgeous green eyes. The eyes I thought I would never see again. God, what the hell was wrong with me.

"How was the flight?" he asked.

"Dammit. Thanks for that, too. It was so much better than commercial."

"Told you." His eyes focused on the burns on my chest, but he kept his mouth shut. His driver pulled to a stop in front of my building, and Martin came around and opened my door. I climbed the stairs slowly under Martin's watchful gaze.

"Why didn't you have your business dinner tonight?" I poured myself a glass of water and some scotch for Martin. He took the glasses and carried them to the coffee table in front of the couch.

"Luc and Vivi wanted a chance to get settled at the hotel to combat the jetlag." He took a sip. It wasn't the fifty-year-old Macallan he was used to, but he didn't complain.

"I know that feeling." Although, my exhaustion was linked to days of not sleeping or not sleeping enough. I slumped against the arm of the couch, resisting the urge to crumple completely into the sofa cushions. Sitting sideways, I pulled my knees to my chest and faced him. "I ruined your evening."

"You didn't. We're having dinner, which is all I want." He looked unsure of what to say since he was on his best behavior. "What was all that about with Mark?"

"Long story, but the short version is he wants me to go back to work."

Martin pressed his lips together, lost slightly in thought. "Back to the OIO?" I nodded and sighed. "But you don't want to?"

"I can't," I replied quietly. Luckily, I was saved by the doorbell. "Who is it?" I didn't want to get up and look through the peephole, find my handgun, and then answer the door. Asking seemed simpler.

"Chinese delivery," a man called.

Martin put his hand on my knee. "I got it." He paid the man and took the box of Chinese takeout. "Where should I put this?"

"Coffee table." An insane amount of food poked out of the box. "How much did you order? Are we having a party?"

"I wasn't sure what you like," he rationalized, handing me a pair of chopsticks. He opened each of the boxes, announcing the contents as he went. I selected the carton of orange chicken, and we ate in silence.

Despite the fact I hadn't eaten since yesterday, I

wasn't hungry. Maybe I was too tired to eat. Picking individual grains of rice out of the carton with my chopsticks, I flexed my wrist to see which tendons ached the most. Martin was curiously observing this when the phone rang.

Getting up, I grabbed the cordless phone from the charger and glanced at the caller ID. It had a French country code. "Sorry," I muttered, answering.

"Alex?" It was Ryan. "How was your flight? Did you get home safely?"

"It was fine." I sat back down on the couch while Martin cleared the table and placed the leftovers in my refrigerator. He wanted to give me some privacy. "Did we get Abelard?"

"Not yet. We have his photo posted at the airports and train stations. His passport has been added to the watchlist. He's not going anywhere. We will find him."

Bad news, that's just great, I thought. I picked up the pillow, placed it flat on the couch cushion, and laid against it. "Any leads?" Under normal conditions, I would be pacing, but right now, I wasn't much for moving.

"We're working on it."

"Was he tipped off? Is that how we missed him? Please don't tell me there's a leak."

"I don't think so. After Tuesday night, he's being careful."

"Can't imagine why. It's not like he tortured a police informant." Something clattered in the kitchen, and I remembered Martin was still in earshot.

"We should have moved in sooner," Ryan said, angry about the way things had gone.

"It's not your fault. It's his, so just make sure you get the bastard. Keep me updated."

"I will."

"Hey, Ryan, be careful. Abelard is a crazy,

dangerous son of a bitch. It's not a good mix." My voice reflected worry, and Martin came over to the couch and studied me. His brow furrowed. I gave him a small smile for reassurance.

"I'll talk to you later." Ryan disconnected, and I put the phone on the table and sunk into the pillow.

"Goddammit." I slapped my palm against the cushion.

"What's wrong?" Martin asked.

Realizing I was taking up the entirety of the couch, I sat up and moved the pillow out of the way. Immediately, he sat down, grabbed the pillow and placed it on his lap, before gently pulling me back down. One of his hands stroked my hair while he wrapped the other around my torso. Feeling at ease for the first time in days, I shut my eyes and felt my rigid posture relax.

"A sick, sadistic son of a bitch got away, again." I opened my eyes and looked up at him. He was staring at my wrist, resting over his arm. Why didn't I bandage everything before going out tonight?

"Did he kill Jean-Pierre?"

"I guess it's time to catch you up. Jean-Pierre's not dead. I wish he was dead. Probably wouldn't have minded killing him myself." I hoped I was only over-embellishing. "No, instead he betrayed everything and everyone."

"Did he do this to you?" Martin's jaw muscles clenched, and it was time we talked about the elephant in the room. He gently lifted my hand in his and brushed his thumb ever so slightly over my scraped knuckles.

"No. Not directly." I paused, considering what to say. "We don't need to talk about this."

"Okay." He studied my face. "But you know, I am a good listener. World class, in fact. In case you ever want to talk about anything, I'm around."

My lips curled at the corners. "World class, really?"

"Close enough. You should know. Didn't you call a few nights ago, just to talk?" My face fell as I remembered the pre-op jitters and the feeling of impending doom. Why didn't I listen to my instincts more carefully? I should have noticed the inconsistency with the VHS delivery. "Alex?" He realized he said something wrong.

"The night I called you, it was the day before this happened. Something was wrong, but I couldn't pinpoint it. I just needed to hear your voice." I swallowed uncomfortably. "The next day, I was grabbed off the street and held in a warehouse for almost six hours." I felt unsteady. Even though I was prone, the room wobbled. "I didn't know if I was going to get out of there." He tensed beneath me and lifted my hand in his, trying to gain insight from my injuries. "That was a combination of fighting with Ryan, the cop who just called, and some thugs in a warehouse." Martin's touch was gentle as it slowly moved to my wrist, careful not to touch any of my injured flesh. Instead, he rotated my arm, watching the rope burns and cut marks circle my wrist like a macabre bracelet. "I was hung by my wrists." I swallowed. Mark better be happy I was talking to someone.

"Wait, what?" His face contorted as he tried to make sense of my words and the picture I was painting for him.

"Tied up and hung from a hook. In case you ever wondered, rope is an incredibly unpleasant object."

His jaw clenched, but he remained silent as his eyes bore into the depths of inhumanity. After carefully releasing my arm, his hand worked its way up to my shoulder and traced the slice along my clavicle.

"Dagger." Part of me was back in the warehouse, experiencing the terror all over again. "The guy who grabbed me liked his toys but thought going a bit old school with a blade might make more of an impact."

Martin's hand stopped moving, and I looked up to see anger and sorrow in his eyes. The things I said were unfathomable to him. His life was business and cocktail parties, a place where maids and chauffeurs catered to his every whim.

"How? Why?" He didn't understand. He couldn't comprehend, and I never wanted him to.

"It's okay." My voice was barely above a whisper. Nodding, I gave him unspoken permission. He hesitated before drawing an outline around my burnt and blistered flesh with his fingers. I locked on to his eyes, afraid if I shut mine, I'd open them to find myself back in that warehouse, having never left. Maybe I should stop now. I didn't need to revisit the warehouse, and he didn't need any more details. Too much had already been said, but I couldn't stop myself. It would never be over if I didn't finish the story and file it away. "Electric shock by something resembling a cattle prod. He wanted information, and in a few more seconds, I would have told him anything. Done anything." I inhaled sharply and shut my eyes tightly, forcing the panic away.

"Alex," his voice was saving me from that place, "you can stop. I don't...you don't need to..."

"I wanted to die." This was the first time I verbalized it, but it was the truth. "I screamed myself hoarse, hoping my heart would stop. I just wanted it to stop." He stopped circling the burn pattern and wrapped his arm around me again, his grip tight against my side, firmly keeping me in the present. "I just wanted it to be over."

Martin was afraid to move for fear of hurting me.

His face dropped, and his features darkened. I said too much, and I moved my hand to rest on top of his forearm, hoping we could both find some solace.

"But you're okay?" he asked. His voice sounded harsh against the silence.

"Just a little worse for wear." I tried to smile since I was safe at home.

"Really?" The green irises bore into me, searching for something to grasp on to.

"Exhausted and dehydrated, but finé other than the occasional room spins." Self-preservation reigned supreme, and my ingrained gallows humor kicked in. "My muscles are a bit achy from hanging around and all the electric shock therapy, though." I chuckled. My defenses were working again. "Nothing major."

He took a deep breath and stopped playing with my hair long enough to swallow the rest of his scotch. "I'm glad you're home and you're safe." He watched me, as if I were a porcelain doll teetering on the edge of a shelf.

Well, since we're being sappy and dramatic, might as well kill two birds with one stone, I reasoned. "For now. Martin, this is where I live. These things keep happening. In the unlikely event I lose my mind and go back to work with Mark, these types of things could be in my future or worse." I looked at him sadly. "Hell, even if I don't go back to the OIO, trouble follows me around. I'm a jinx."

"You're not a jinx."

"Regardless," I took a breath, steeling my nerves, "this is why you should run for the door and never look back." The protest formed on his lips, but I pushed on. "But I'm tired. Exhausted, actually." I graced him with a brief smile. "I'm tired of fighting you on this. If you insist on becoming involved with me, at least now you have all the facts. You have my recommendation to leave and not look back but whatever. You like your unilateral decision-making skills, so have at it."

"Okay." Not quite the response I expected. I wondered when he'd head for the nearest exit, but his arm remained around me. My eyes closed, and I knew falling asleep right now wouldn't earn me any hostess of the year awards. "We'll take things slow," he said at last. I turned my head and looked up at him. "We can re-evaluate when and if the time comes." He leaned down and kissed me compassionately. It wasn't sexy or impulsive or any of the things our kiss in the hotel hallway had been. He was scared, and I was to blame. "Just so you know," he whispered, "I've been waiting to do that all night."

"You need to work on your material. It's old and tired, just like me." Letting out a sigh of relief, I turned toward the television and grabbed the remote off the table. "Sorry, I'm not very entertaining at the moment." I handed him the remote. "Don't feel obligated to stay and keep me company. I'm perfectly content turning in early."

"Nonsense." He flipped on the TV and channel surfed. "Get some rest. I'll get out of here when I'm ready."

Closing my eyes, I laced my fingers over his while he continued to absently play with my hair.

The pillow moved upward slightly, and then it gently eased back into place. Whatever was causing the room to spin was starting to get on my nerves.

"Alex." Martin's voice was barely above a whisper. I opened my eyes to find him standing above me. "I'm sorry to wake you, but I didn't want to frighten you."

I didn't know how long I had been asleep, but I assumed he was on his way out. Muttering something unintelligible, I shut my eyes. He cradled me against his chest and lifted me off the couch.

"You're going to hurt your shoulder," I mumbled as he carried me into my room and laid me gently on the bed.

He pulled the blanket over me and kissed my forehead. "I'll be on the couch, if you need anything."

I was asleep before he made it to the door.

TWENTY-FIVE

There was little recollection from the night before. Everything blended into a colorful blur as I opened my eyes and turned my head toward the intrusive sound. The phone was ringing. I leaned toward my nightstand and squinted at the caller ID. It was Mark. I ignored it and reached for the glass of water instead.

"Ow." My shoulders and back protested. Not moving for an extended amount of time made my sore muscles stiffen into uncomfortable knots. Giving up on the water, I rolled over on my stomach and buried my head in the pillow as I waited for the ringing to cease.

"Alex?" Martin's voice permeated through my sleep-filled brain. "Are you okay?"

Being too tired to open my eyes or roll over to face the door, I couldn't be sure if he was standing in my bedroom or if I was dreaming. The mattress dipped down as he sat on the edge of the bed, indicating he probably wasn't a figment of my unconscious psyche.

"Sore back," I mumbled, nestling further into the

bedding.

Without another word, he swept my hair to the side. His feather-light touch began at my shoulders and slowly and gently continued down my spine. I was on the cusp of oblivion when his hands reached the juncture underneath my shoulder blade and along my ribcage. I let out a whimper, and my body involuntarily drew itself into a ball as his slight touch hit a particularly tender spot. Instantly, he withdrew his hands, uttering countless apologies. If I wasn't so close to sleep, I would have said something, but instead, I let his words turn into white noise as I drifted off.

What must have been hours later, I surfaced from under the covers. Sleep had done wonders. My body was no longer sore, and the room had stopped spinning. Sitting up in bed, I could see Martin at my kitchen table, surrounded by a sea of paperwork. He stayed the night to take care of me, which was not the way I wanted things to begin between the two of us.

I grabbed some clothing and went into the bathroom. As I showered and dressed my wounds, I regretted everything I said to him last night. He shouldn't be aware of the things I experienced. After all, he had gone through quite enough in the last year as it was. This was exactly why we were always cautioned not to do anything life changing after traumatic situations. Assessing myself in the mirror, I knew things were going to get awkward.

When I opened the bathroom door, I found him cooking breakfast. "Good morning," he greeted. A cup of coffee waited for me on the counter. Martin had turned into a man-servant overnight. I sat down on one of the stools and watched him suspiciously. He looked like hell, and I imagined he hadn't slept at all last night.

"Were you wearing that yesterday?" I was out of it but not that out of it.

"No, I went home this morning and changed, got some paperwork to review, and went to the grocery store. The only thing you had in your fridge was the leftover Chinese and a bottle of mustard."

I was positively baffled by everything he had just said. "Then why are you here?" I probably sounded ungrateful in my confusion, but he was used to my rough edges. "You went home."

"Well, I had to return your keys. I couldn't just leave without locking your deadbolts. Plus, I wanted to make sure you had something to eat, and I felt bad about this morning." He confused me again, and I tried to remember what happened.

"You didn't hurt me, but you didn't have to stay. And you really didn't have to make breakfast."

He ignored me as he always did. "You look a million times better today. How are you feeling?"

"Better. About last night," I began, but the phone interrupted.

He lifted the cordless phone from its cradle. "It's Mark, again. He's called four times."

"Just pick up the receiver and slam it down."

Martin frowned and answered the phone. "Hey, Mark. It's James." He paused. "I don't know. Hang on." He covered the mouthpiece with his hand. "He wants to talk to you."

"Tell him I'm not here."

"She says she's not here," he relayed my message, and I rolled my eyes. "Uh-huh. Okay. I will." Brief pause. "We talked last night. She's okay." He concluded the call and replaced the handset.

"Mark says he's sorry and you should consider hearing him out."

Gracing Martin with my 'yeah, right' look, I picked

up my coffee and sat down at the kitchen table where I was presented with a plate of pancakes. "Thanks, but you've already done so much." I looked at the couch. "Did you sleep there all night? You could have taken my bed or went home. I am perfectly capable of staying by myself."

"I wanted to stay, and you needed a good night's sleep." He glanced at the digital clock. "And a good morning's sleep, too." It was almost two o'clock.

I picked at the pancakes while Martin watched me eat. "Not hungry?"

"I ate at home. So, how long are you planning on avoiding Mark?"

I put my fork down and studied the ceiling, collecting my thoughts. "I need to say something first." Martin's expression changed. "Last night, those things I told you, I shouldn't have. There was no reason why you needed to hear about what happened in the warehouse in so much detail." I licked my lips. My mouth had gone dry. "A couple of weeks ago, when I tried to throw you out of my apartment, I shouldn't have told you quite like that either. I just wanted you to understand."

"You have to talk to someone," he said gently. "I can be that someone. I don't like what's happened, but listening is the least I *can* do."

"Have you been talking to Mark? Because that's more or less what we're arguing about. He thinks I need to talk things out." From the look on Martin's face, I knew he discussed this with Mark earlier this morning.

"I guess I should be forthright with you," Martin said. "Mark's mentioned some things to me. If it makes you feel any better, it was for purely professional reasons." I stared at Martin, not knowing what in the world he was about to divulge. "Before I hired you to work as my security, Mark told me the real reason you quit the OIO."

"Oh." My tone turned cold as I remembered the Bureau shrink's assessment that I failed to discuss the incident properly and satisfactorily move past it.

"It's why you were the fourth person I interviewed for the job. It's also why I gave you a few chances to walk away when things got rough." He had a guilty conscience for not saying anything sooner. He and Mark both needed to learn how to take a hint. "The point is I don't care what Mark thinks. You know how much you can handle and what needs to be done. You might have a few scars, but you're not damaged beyond repair. Don't let him make you feel that way. You," Martin paused and corrected himself, "we, can take things at your pace and handle them when and if you're ready."

"Only time will tell," I replied cynically. I wasn't sure how to take any of what he just said. Was it a compliment, criticism, or just words to clear his guilty conscience? I put my plate in the sink and leaned against the counter, attempting to regroup. He came up behind me.

"Are we okay?"

Turning around to face him, I wasn't sure the two of us should even be a we. Maybe things were moving at a pace faster than what I could handle. I shrugged, and he moved to kiss me. It was soft and brief as he carefully touched his lips to mine. His hands brushed against the sides of my torso, just below my ribcage. Maybe things were moving too quickly for both of us. Placing my palms against his shoulders, I rested my cheek against his chest, but he wouldn't return my embrace. One of us had to prove I wasn't completely breakable, even if this wasn't the most comfortable thing in the world right now.

His right shoulder was colder than his left, and I spotted one of the ice packs from my freezer next to the stove. I pulled away and dropped my hands. "You aggravated your shoulder by carrying me to bed last night," I surmised, walking away. We weren't good together. I didn't see what possessed me to think letting him make this decision was a good idea.

"It would have happened anyway. It just gets sore sometimes." There was something he wasn't saying, but we had enough drama at the moment.

I sat on the corner of the couch, curling my legs under me. "You should go home and prepare for your meeting. What time is your dinner with Luc?" I tried to cover my retreat with a work distraction. Martin was a workaholic, after all.

"I have time. We're meeting at five for drinks and going from there. All my files are here, so if you'll allow me the use of your table," he wasn't falling for my distraction tactics, "Marcal can bring something more business appropriate I can change into when he comes to pick me up, if I'm permitted to change in your apartment." His tone wasn't lost on me, but I chose to ignore it.

"Of course." I didn't want to fight with him, even though I hated how emotionally manipulated I often felt when he was being genuinely thoughtful and I was so difficult to handle. Most likely, that had more to do with my own take on the way things were and less on how they actually were, but that was beside the point.

"What are you doing today?" he asked.

"Absolutely nothing," I said. His expression was akin to if I suggested I wanted to live on Jupiter. "I might get the mail. Watch some TV. If I feel overly ambitious, maybe I'll do some laundry."

"Really?"

"Hell, yes. I've been busting my ass for a month

now. It's over. I'm done," I paused, thinking about things, "at least for today." He chuckled and placed the remote control beside me before heading back into the kitchen. Since my one bedroom apartment was comprised of a single large room containing my living room, kitchen, and dining room, it basically meant he crossed from the couch to the counter. "However, if you touch those dishes, I will be forced to kick your ass," I warned.

He stepped away from the sink, his hands in the air. "Yes, ma'am." He detoured to the stack of papers he placed on the corner of my kitchen table. I hated being called ma'am, and I glared at him. He smirked and sat down.

Over the next two hours, he reviewed and made notes for his working dinner while I spent the same time lying on the couch, alternating between reading a magazine and watching television. Marcal knocked on my door, carrying a garment bag. I let him in and offered the few meager items I had in my house, but he declined and went to wait for Martin outside in the car, insisting he parked in a tow-away zone. Martin changed into a designer suit. He went into my bathroom to check his hair with his shirt buttons undone and tie hanging untied around his neck. *Men*, I thought ironically. I climbed off the couch and leaned against the doorjamb, watching him.

"Here, let me." Despite his lackadaisical attitude, his shoulder hurt, and his right hand wasn't as dexterous as it should be. Standing in front of him, I buttoned his shirt. He absently played with a strand of my hair, using his left hand and staring unnervingly at me. "I think it'd be best if you kept whatever this is quiet." I worked on figuring out how to knot his tie.

"I agree." His eyes were getting a little too alluring as I finished the knot, so I turned and walked out of the bathroom and back to the safety of the couch. He double-checked his appearance in the mirror before emerging. "If my meeting doesn't run too late, I can come back later tonight."

"That's okay. I'm going to work my way through those leftovers and go to bed early. I'll see you Monday at the office. New surveillance equipment, exciting stuff," I feigned enthusiasm.

"I'll see you tomorrow, Alex. By the way, you need to work on your compromising skills."

I made a mental note to remind him to have Bruiser escort him from the car to my door and vice versa because who knew what kind of crazies could be lurking in the hallway. I just started washing the dishes when the phone rang. It was Martin.

"Mark's on his way up. I just wanted to give you the chance to run down the fire escape." He mocked my avoidance. "However, he is carrying a pizza, y'know, from the good pizza place, so perhaps you should knock him out and keep the pizza. I can send Bruiser up to help you hide the body."

"Go to work," I insisted, hanging up the phone. I went to the door and unlocked the deadbolts, opening it before Mark even knocked.

"Hey." Mark was shocked I opened the door.

"Is that supposed to be an apology?" I asked snippily, gazing at the pizza box.

"Can I come in?"

"That depends. Mushrooms?"

"Yes."

Stepping away from the door, I gestured him inside. "What do you want?"

"Alex, I believe you misconstrued my words yesterday." I took the pizza and placed it on the counter, opening it to verify the bribe of mushrooms was legitimate. "I was worried about you. You can't blame me for that."

"I'm pretty sure I can blame you for anything I want. Global warming, rising gas prices, lack of good feature films to go see."

Mark sat at the counter and waited for me to stop being ridiculous.

"Although, I guess in all fairness, none of those things are your fault. None of them. If you wanted me back at the OIO, why didn't you talk to me? If it was Kendall's idea, why didn't you prepare me? I went into that meeting, got my ass handed to me, and then ended up blindsided with a job offer."

"I didn't know how you would react. If I said anything, you might have run for the hills." In all likelihood, that probably would have been what happened. "It was Kendall's idea to have you come back full-time. I thought maybe you might want to ease back in by consulting on a few cases first."

"You told Martin why I quit."

"He had a right to know who he was hiring and why you weren't an agent anymore. You could have told him yourself, but you didn't."

"Telling some guy how I got two good men killed wasn't going to cinch my interview," I retorted. Although, in twenty-twenty hindsight, it wouldn't have made a bit of difference since Martin had known all along.

"Regardless of your reasons, you didn't tell him. You never told him."

"And we come full circle." Finishing my slice of pizza, I went to wash the dishes I abandoned. "What part of *we aren't talking about this* don't you get?"

"Fine, we won't talk about it. So why the hell aren't you coming back to work?"

"I quit."

"Why?" he shouted over the running water.

I turned the water off and spun around to face him. Considering the fact we weren't talking about it, I didn't have a good answer. "Screw you."

"Why?" he asked again, his volume only slightly lower.

"I don't want to come back. I'm doing just fine on my own."

"Really? You worked for Marty, and I had to run backgrounds on everyone. You worked for Evans-Sterling, and you ask me for help on the car bombing and the package. Without my resources, the resources at the office, where would you be? You call that fine?"

"I'm not fighting with you." I was done.

"Parker, if you were okay with it, you'd be back on the job." He stood up. "You do realize that, don't you?" He had me there, and he knew it.

I pulled a beer from the fridge and placed it on the counter in front of where he stood. It was a peace offering, and he opened the cap and sat back down.

"I like my freedom. No warrants, no gathering evidence, no court orders. I don't have to make a case." I listed the positive attributes of my current private investigator/security consultant status. "If you can guarantee the same kind of gig consulting at the Bureau, maybe I would consider it on a temporary, short-term basis." I had to prove to Mark I was fine. Martin thought I was. Maybe I should listen to him more often.

"I'll see what I can do." Mark opened the box and took a slice for himself.

TWENTY-SIX

As requested, I worked on improving my compromising skills by allowing Martin to come over Sunday. He reported his business dinner went well. His hesitance over the new hire had ebbed away over the course of the last few weeks. As long as Guillot wasn't a criminal or a killer, everything would be fine.

"Did you talk to Mark yesterday?" Martin asked curiously.

"I agreed to go back to work on a temporary, consulting only basis. Mark doesn't know if the director will agree to it, but..." My voice trailed off. I wasn't happy about this.

"Alex, you don't have to go back. Don't do it."

"We'll see." I didn't have a clue what I was doing, or why I was doing it. "Don't worry. If it even happens, it'll take time to get the paperwork in order and pass the background checks. Then there are the mental and physical evaluations, blah, blah, blah." Just the thought of it was exhausting.

"So, tomorrow," he changed the subject, "are you

sure you're feeling up to coming to work?"

"I'm perfectly fine. I caught up on some much needed sleep, and I'm ready to get back out there."

"The installation isn't supposed to start until end of business. The crew should arrive at four, so if you could be there to supervise and make sure everything gets installed where it's supposed to go, I'd appreciate it."

"That I can do."

Martin and I spent a couple of hours going over building schematics and reviewing the upgrades he approved. By the time he left my apartment that night, I had detailed notes on everything being installed and exactly where it was going.

The next day, I checked my mail, threw out the pile of flyers and junk mail, and stopped by my office to repeat the process. Mr. Sterling sent a letter, expressing gratitude for the assistance I provided. Enclosed was a check in the amount of the reward for any information pertaining to the missing paintings. It wasn't an exorbitant amount, but it would help cover my travel and hotel costs from the last two weeks.

Glancing at the time, I called Detective O'Connell. I owed him my thanks for sending his report to the Paris police, and I filled him in on everything. Nick offered to keep an eye out for any suspicious pings on French travelers entering the country, just in case. Unfortunately, he never identified Ski Mask.

"At least Ramirez is long gone," he offered as consolation. "If I hear he's causing trouble, I'll let you know."

"Thanks. You're still my favorite detective."

On the way to the Martin Technologies building, I picked up a new cell phone to replace the one that got smashed in Paris. Things were getting back to normal, finally. I wondered when Ryan would call with an update. I hated to admit it, but Martin was right. I had issues separating myself from the job. Thoughts of Clare entered my mind, and I wondered if she had been cleared of any involvement. Did she know Jean-Pierre was still alive? As I entered the MT building, I forced all Paris related thoughts from my mind and greeted the security guard, Jeffrey, before heading to the top floor to put my purse in my office and wait for the equipment installation guys to show up.

The seventeenth floor had changed in appearance since the last time I was here. One of the four conference rooms had been modified and converted into Guillot's office. Martin wanted to keep a closer eye on him than he had his former vice president. I was swiveling back and forth in my desk chair when my office phone rang. The equipment installers were downstairs. I went to the lobby to greet them.

Over the course of the next two hours, I supervised the installation and approved the locations for the new cameras. A few locks were changed, and the security office and Martin's office were both upgraded to biometric technology. I was standing in the lobby, watching the equipment specialist code the lock so it would open for each of the security guards, when Martin emerged from the elevators.

"Everything set up?" he asked.

"Yes. I'm just waiting for the lock to be coded properly and that should be it."

"Stop by my office and sign the paperwork before you leave." It was good to know he could act professional in public.

After the men were done, I signed off on the work order and went upstairs, retrieved my belongings, and knocked on Martin's open door. He looked up and smiled.

"Close the door on your way in," he said playfully.

"Two things. First, here is the work order, signed and dated for your records. Second," I glanced at the glass wall and the cameras in the hallway. "before you decide to fool around with any of the secretaries in your office, I'd suggest you remember to change the setting on your wall of windows. If not, the security guards will have front row seats to one hell of a show."

Martin adopted a wolfish grin. "I don't think that's an issue, at least not with the assistants. It could be a problem with a certain security consultant I know."

"I don't think that issue will come up."

He raised his eyebrows, preparing a cheeky response, when Luc knocked on his door. Martin buzzed him in.

"Pardon," Guillot said, "I didn't mean to interrupt."

"You're not. I was just on my way out." Picking up my purse, I went to the door. "If there was nothing else, sir."

"Actually," Martin smirked ever so slightly, "would you mind escorting Madame Guillot up here before you leave."

"Sure," I went downstairs and found Vivi waiting near the elevators. I brought her to Martin's office, making polite conversation along the way.

"I'm taking the Guillots out to dinner before they fly back to Paris tomorrow. Vivi wanted to see the main office building and where Luc will be working," Martin said as Luc and Vivi went down the hallway toward the modified conference room. I nodded and stepped closer to the elevator. "Want to join us?"

"That's not a good idea. Plus, I have a fridge full of leftovers calling my name."

"Leftovers?" Vivi said from behind. "No, you must join us. The boys will be discussing business, documents and mergers, and who knows what else.

Please."

"Well, when you put it that way, how can I refuse?" Tonight would be awkward. I remembered the difficulty in feigning interest in Martin; now I had to do the exact opposite. Catching a glimpse of him out of the corner of my eye, I noticed the rather self-satisfied and smug look on his face.

I followed the three of them to the restaurant. We were seated quickly, and as Vivi predicted, Martin and Guillot were discussing the European markets before the waitress even brought our drinks.

"Thanks for not making me feel like an empty chair." She smiled as she spoke.

"Glad I could help." We chatted easily about her impending move, the best places to shop, good restaurants nearby, and anything else that came to mind. The conversation was light and comfortable. By the time the main course arrived, I was feeling much more social and relaxed. I slipped off my suit jacket and hung it from the back of my chair.

"Alexis, what happened?"

Dammit, my internal voice muttered. Until now, she was unaware of my bandaged wrists. "Oh, this." I played it off as if it were nothing. "Hazard of the job." Martin watched me out of the corner of his eye. "Not this job. Different job." I was a blundering mess. "As a security consultant, I work for different companies, doing different things. The last one didn't go so well."

"D'accord." Vivi nodded uncertainly. She looked confused, and I noticed three pairs of eyes staring at me.

"Ms. Parker used to be a federal agent." Martin attempted to salvage the conversation with some diplomacy. "Sometimes, things can be dangerous in her line of work. It's how she first landed on my radar. I hired her to deal with the issue I was having at MT with a former board member."

"I see." Guillot was aware of who he was replacing and why. There was a pregnant pause before he asked Martin, "Pardon me, I don't mean to be so blunt, but is your upcoming surgery related to the injury you sustained in the shooting? I'm not sure why we're advancing the timetable on my move if your surgery is simply elective."

It took a conscious effort to remain impassive toward this new information. When Martin and I were together in Paris, he mentioned surgery might be a possibility, but it never seemed like a definite thing. God, the ice pack the other day and everything else going on, I understood why he didn't tell me, but he should have.

"It's not a big deal. Just a simple procedure to remove some scar tissue, but I want to make sure you are well-versed in the goings on at the office before I leave for a week or two." Martin made it sound like he was taking a trip and wanted everyone to know the proper way to water the plants before he left.

Vivi prattled on about something, and I tried to pay attention to her. I smiled and nodded, remaining outwardly calm for the rest of the evening. But once the check was paid, I stood up, wished the Guillots a safe trip home, and thanked them once again for allowing me to accompany them back to the States. Excusing myself graciously, I left the restaurant before my meltdown caused a scene.

I paced my apartment because, after all, that is what I do. Some people smoke, drink, or engage in other reckless behavior; I pace. It was infuriating that two days ago, Martin sat at my kitchen table and said I wasn't responsible for all the bad things that happened to people around me while, all the while, he had a surgery scheduled because I failed to do my job.

Unfortunately, self-loathing and pity wouldn't get me anywhere.

In an attempt to be more productive, I dialed Ryan. It only occurred to me after the first ring that, given the time difference, he was probably asleep.

"Alex?" Ryan sounded awake. "What's wrong?"

"Nothing. I just wanted to know how things were going. I forgot about the time difference."

"It's okay. I'm at work." He paused, and I heard footsteps in the background. "Gustav's given us locations for half a dozen of Abelard's private safe houses. We've relocated Clare and still have her in protective custody in exchange for Gustav's continued cooperation."

"Have you moved on the safe houses yet?" Even though I was thousands of miles away, the anxious energy radiated through the phone.

"Soon. His tips better not be total rubbish."

"Wish I was there," I retorted before my mind even had time to process the words.

Ryan laughed cynically. "You're daft, but when we get Abelard, I'll tell him you said hello."

"Please do." My own voice had an edge as we disconnected. At least Clare was innocent and someplace safe. Not everyone had been sucked into Abelard's world or Jean-Pierre's deception.

With not much else to do, I cleaned and re-assembled my two handguns and decided to call it a night. I just got into bed when the phone rang. I ignored it. Martin would leave a message if he felt the need to talk things out.

TWENTY-SEVEN

The rest of the week moved by at a snail's pace. I was once again unemployed with the exception of my retainer status at Martin Tech, so the majority of my free time was spent resting and recuperating. A few nights of rejuvenating sleep helped my wrists and chest heal. There were still a few tender areas, but for the most part, I was fine. It would probably be another month or two before the dark pink scars disappeared or at least faded to a more tolerable level. In the meantime, they served as constant reminders Abelard was still on the loose, possibly tormenting someone else. A small part of me wanted to track the rat bastard to the sewer he was using as his refuge, but I couldn't go back there. Not yet, anyway.

Mark dropped off my radar. I agreed to his insane request to go back to work at the OIO and then nothing. *Thanks so much for the added stress.* Maybe Kendall wasn't too keen on hiring a consultant with all my stipulations. Honestly, it was a relief since I didn't want to endure the interrogative tactics of the

Bureau's shrink asking about every trauma I experienced in my life or at least my work life. The nightmares were barely being kept at bay as it was.

Martin and I had a brief discussion about his surgery a couple of nights ago. His scar tissue was inflamed and pressing against the nerves, limiting his mobility and causing him discomfort. He tried to instill upon me his misguided belief I was not responsible, but I failed to agree. This, unfortunately, led to an argument which resulted in an apology dinner at his place. I made it as far as the driveway before calling and asking if we could meet somewhere else instead. The last time I was inside Martin's house was when I was giving Detective O'Connell a very detailed recreation of the firefight surrounding Martin getting shot. I remembered vividly dry heaving in the toilet and didn't want to relive any of those memories.

It was Saturday afternoon, and I was sprawled out on the couch, reading a book, when there was a knock on my door. I ran through my routine of checking to see who it was and unlocking the various locks. Luckily, Martin learned to listen, and I nodded to Bruiser, who smiled briefly before retreating down the hallway toward the stairwell.

"Did we have plans?" I asked confused as I put my handgun on the end table. I was aware of how paranoid I still was. Moving would be a good idea, but there were no other affordable apartments I liked.

"No," Martin smiled, "I decided to be spontaneous. What do you think?"

His smile was infectious, so I resisted the urge to give him a speech about how crazy and dangerous my life could be. Right now, the threats were at a minimum. "At the moment, I like it but only because I have nothing going on."

"I'll try to keep that in mind." He cocked an

eyebrow up suggestively. "I was thinking we should spend the rest of the weekend together in bed since you appear to be feeling better, but you shouldn't take any chances with your recovery."

"I thought we were taking things slow."

"It's been a week. We aren't dead."

I exhaled. His words, while meant to be playful, still made me take a step back.

"You know what I mean." He sensed my trepidation.

"Maybe we should see how today goes and take it from there." Giving him a tentative kiss, I retreated into the kitchen. He was eyeing me enticingly, but I ignored him.

"Okay, if you're sure you can contain yourself because I do remember someone attempting to molest me in the middle of a hotel hallway," he mused, and I threw a dish towel at him but didn't take the bait. "So, what would you like to do today, sweetheart?"

We spent the rest of the day in the confines of my apartment. I was astounded by Martin's patience on the matter, probably because he never struck me as a particularly patient person, especially when it came to his history of sexual exploits. He prepared dinner, which I would have felt guilty about had I not been aware of his love of cooking. After dinner, I took his hand and led him into my bedroom.

"I take it today went well," he whispered smugly in my ear.

"I'm not sure yet. I'll let you know."

Lying on my back with my shirt unbuttoned and splayed open, I watched Martin trail kisses down my ribcage. "Shit." I jerked slightly, wincing. He sat up immediately, confused and concerned. Tilting my head, I spotted the slight discoloration from Abelard's first electric jolt. It had almost been forgotten since it didn't bother me until now. I pressed my fingers against it. "Son of a bitch." Not only did Abelard ruin that night, but now he was interfering with this one too.

"Again, I hurt you. Are you okay?"

"I'm fine. Just a sore spot." Sitting up, I tried to salvage the moment. I ran my hands down his chest, tracing my fingers along his toned abdomen until I reached the hem of his shirt, quickly divesting him of the garment and gently pushing him down on his back. "Maybe we just need to change things up." I leaned down and kissed him, straddling his lap, as he gently brushed my hair back and over my shoulder. Unfortunately, this just made the entire situation worse.

My lips traveled down to his neck and then to his shoulder, accidentally locating the scar and site of his upcoming surgery. Running my fingertips over it, I looked up to find his eyes. His gaze was on my chest. Instead of focusing on my cleavage or attempting to unfasten my bra, he stared at the tender, pink remnants of my electrical burns. Kissing him softly, I extricated myself from his lap.

"Whatever happened to scars being a sexy turn-on?" he asked, defeated.

"That's a gender biased thing, but the damn battle wounds are a complete turn-off." Nothing was going to happen tonight, and we both knew it. Considering Martin always talked a good game, I was surprised he let my still healing flesh bother him this much. Maybe he wasn't as much of a playboy as his reputation would have me believe. "I'll get you some ice for your shoulder." I went into the kitchen. "Want a beer?"

"Sure, why not?"

I opened two bottles, grabbed an ice pack, and went back into the bedroom. He sat on the edge of the bed.

His elbows rested on his knees as he rubbed his face.

"Just so you know, this isn't the way things normally go," he tried to joke as I handed him the beer and sat beside him.

"I was just about to tell you the same thing." Resting my head against his good shoulder, I gently held the ice pack against the other. "When's your surgery?

"In three weeks. Then another six for rehab."

"Okay. Maybe we'll slow things down until then."

We spent the rest of the night talking about everything from sports scores to economics. Time got away, and it was after midnight when I looked at the clock. Martin planned to head home, but it was late.

"I can still offer you a weekend in bed," I teased. "Except sleep won't be a euphemism, it will be the sole activity."

He hedged, but I insisted.

*   *   *

"Please tell me that's your phone," I muttered, refusing to open my eyes.

Martin rolled away from me as he reached over to retrieve the offending object. "It's yours," he mumbled, handing over the phone and wrapping his arm around me. He nuzzled my neck as I answered the call.

"Parker," I said softly, shutting my eyes.

"I'm sorry to call you in the middle of the night," Ryan said urgently. I opened my eyes, immediately pulling away from Martin and sitting up. "One of Abelard's aliases made it through airport security earlier this evening."

"What? When?" I was much more awake now.

"He was booked on the midnight flight to JFK.

Alex, I think he's coming for you." Ryan had never been this on edge before, and his tone sent chills down my spine.

"Are you sure?" I pulled on a pair of jeans as we spoke.

"I just got word. Delacroix called to inform us we were doing a fantastic job keeping a bloody eye on things. He's notified Farrell, but I wanted to make sure you received a personal heads up."

"Thanks, Ryan. I gotta go. I'll call you later." Disconnecting, I was considering calling Nick when my phone rang again. As I answered, I buttoned my blouse. "Parker." I picked up Martin's clothes and tossed them to him. He was awake and confused. *Get dressed*, I mouthed.

"I heard you might have a friend flying in. Farrell has a team on the way to the airport. I'm not sure if they'll make it in time." Mark relayed the news quickly. "We contacted the airport. Officers are standing by. We've spoken to the pilot and crew. According to them, Abelard's seat is empty. He never checked in. We think he might have switched seats or tickets with someone else after he went through security, but there's no way to tell until the plane lands. He might have taken a different flight. He could be anywhere."

"Okay."

"I'm heading to the airport with a team of our own. If he's there, I'll make sure we stop him before he gets through customs. I'll call as soon as I know anything." Mark hung up.

Martin watched me pace in front of my closet. I picked up his phone and tossed it to him. "Call Bruiser, tell him to meet you at your place. I need him to be on twenty-four seven until further notice." My tone was serious, and Martin didn't question me.

Going into the kitchen, I called O'Connell. *Please be working the night shift*, I silently prayed.

"Detective O'Connell speaking."

"Thank god. I need another favor."

"I am here to protect and serve. It's a slow night. What can I do?"

I filled him in on the current situation. "Martin's here. Can you send a cruiser with a couple of uniforms to my place, pick him up, go back to the precinct, switch to an unmarked car, and take him home?" I was asking a lot, but I didn't want to risk Abelard or someone he hired following Martin home.

"Okay, I'll send a couple of unis over, and Thompson will meet him here and drive him home." From Nick's tone, I knew he was suspicious about why Martin was at my apartment at four a.m. But he didn't ask, and I didn't offer an explanation.

Martin emerged from my bathroom, dressed and coifed as if he didn't just roll out of bed ten minutes ago. "What's going on?" he asked as I fastened my shoulder holster and made sure my nine millimeter was loaded before clipping it into place.

"Did you call Bruiser?" I found my thigh holster and hooked it around my leg with my backup side arm.

"Yes. Are you planning on raiding some tombs?" Martin asked, annoyed that I didn't answer his question yet.

"You never know." I turned on the coffeemaker before sitting rigidly on the couch. "Ryan called. Abelard might be on his way here." Martin wasn't sure who I was referring to. "The man who tortured me." I didn't like using that word, but at the moment, my explanations needed to be succinct. His posture stiffened. "O'Connell's sending a couple of uniformed officers to take you to the precinct where Detective

Thompson will be waiting to drive you home. I need you to be safe and stay that way."

"Alex." He was ready to protest.

"Listen, James, I can't be focused and alert if I'm worried about you."

"I hate it when you use my first name. Every time you do, it's always bad news."

"True." Since I had limited information, I needed to call Ryan back once things settled. "You know the drill. Don't call. Don't show up. Absolutely no contact."

"Alexis, you're being ridiculous. You can't just stay here alone, waiting for some sick motherfucker to come knocking. Do you have anyone watching your back?" He was on the couch next to me, rubbing his thumb absently against my cheek.

"Hopefully, it won't come to that. All of this is just precautionary. Mark called, and the OIO and Interpol are going to head Abelard off at the airport. This is just in case he manages to circumvent them. Plus, I don't even know why he's here or if he's here. His resources are in France." But we all knew why Abelard was on his way here. He was here for me.

There was a knock at my door, followed by police officers announcing themselves. Martin kissed me roughly on the mouth. "I need you to be okay," he said. His eyes were intense. I nodded and briefly wrapped my arms around him before answering the door.

"Gentlemen," I said, and Martin joined us at the door.

"You're not even letting them inside?" Nick teased from halfway down the hall.

"What are you doing here?" I asked.

"I didn't want to be late to the party. It sounded like things might get exciting."

"Detective O'Connell." Martin nodded at him.

"Mr. Martin," Nick replied, "nice to see you again." Nick turned to the uniformed officers. "Take good care of him. We didn't do a good job the first time around."

"If anything happens, call Mark and have him relay a message," I told Martin as he threw me one last look and followed the cops down the hallway.

"O'Connell," he called before they made it to the stairwell, "keep her safe."

I ushered Nick into my apartment and shut the door. When the coffee finished brewing, I filled two mugs. "I didn't expect to see you." I handed him a mug.

"Like I said, it was a slow night," he deadpanned, opening my fridge and pouring some milk into his cup.

TWENTY-EIGHT

I was on the phone, trying to make sense of everything that was happening. There had been quite a few details Ryan failed to mention when it came to the raids on Abelard's safe houses.

"Why didn't you tell me sooner?" I was trying very hard not to scream at him. "I could have been more prepared. There were precautions I could have taken. Hell, I should have stayed in Paris until I knew we had him."

"What would you have done?" he asked, his own tone growing heated. "The dossier he had on you didn't mean he was planning an attack."

"So then what the hell did it mean?"

"He had one on me too. And Olivier, Van Buren, and Langmire. Abelard has all our information thanks to his little lap dog accessing Evans-Sterling's files. Alex, none of it meant a damn thing until he snuck through airport security and switched tickets with someone else."

"Why didn't you have his known aliases on the

watchlist?"

"We did, but he still slipped through. I don't know how, but he did. He must have known we'd catch him, so he traded tickets with someone else at a nearby gate. I'm guessing since no one claimed Abelard's seat, Abelard must have paid the guy not to board the plane or he did something to him. We don't know. We haven't been able to identify or locate the original ticket holder yet."

I sighed audibly. Abelard could be anywhere. Maybe he wasn't here. "If he kept his original ticket, when would he have arrived at the airport?"

"Two hours ago."

I hadn't heard anything from Farrell or Mark, and I knew we missed him. I could feel it. "It's not your fault." I forced the words out of my mouth. I didn't blame Ryan. I blamed Jean-Pierre, the lazy ass airport personnel, and Abelard for being a vengeful, sadistic excuse for a human being. "I need an unbiased opinion. Do you think he's here?" The question was met with silence, and my mouth went dry. "Yeah, that's what I thought."

"Alex," Ryan began.

"Save it." I didn't want to hear it. "See what you can get out of Gustav. If he knows anything at all, I want to hear it."

"I'm on it. Keep me updated."

"Will do." I hung up and turned to O'Connell.

"I'm guessing someone's gunning for you this time?" O'Connell inquired, sipping his coffee. "It's a nice change of pace from you protecting someone else, I guess. Although, either way, you still end up with the shit end of the stick."

"Story of my life." Luckily, Reneaux forwarded the pertinent information about my involvement with Abelard, so I didn't have to go through a detailed explanation of what was happening. "Do you think Ramirez might be helpful?" I asked, yawning. The sun wasn't up yet, and I should have been asleep with Martin. My life sucked.

"Doubtful." O'Connell was doing his best to derail the train to worst case scenario and changed topics. "So, you and Martin?"

"Late night meeting. We were discussing the new security equipment that was installed on Monday and his upcoming surgery. We lost track of time."

"All right." He didn't believe a word I said.

"Thanks for the police escort. I don't need him to get roped into this."

"Like I said, I'm here to protect and serve."

There was a noise outside, and O'Connell and I both drew our weapons, aiming at the door. It felt good to know I didn't have the market on paranoia.

"What the hell?" Mark exclaimed as O'Connell threw him against the wall.

"Mark?" I holstered my gun and went to the door, shutting it as O'Connell released Mark. "What are you doing here?"

"I thought you could use some support. I didn't realize I was the B-team." Mark straightened his shirt and sauntered into the kitchen to pour a cup of coffee. "I assume you already heard, no love."

I sighed and went back to the table. We were too late to catch Abelard, but it still hurt to hear it. The three of us sat at my kitchen table, discussing Abelard and drinking coffee until the sun came up. O'Connell looked at his watch.

"Get out of here. You're on the clock." I jerked my head toward the door. "Go protect and serve the rest of the city."

He put his cup in the sink. "I'll be back later to check on you."

I smiled and thanked him before shutting the door and locking the deadbolts.

"Are you okay?" Mark asked.

"Yeah, just tired."

"Go back to bed. I'll keep an eye on things."

I shut the bedroom door, climbed into bed, and took off my two holsters and put them on either nightstand. I was aware of two things. First, there was no way I was actually going to sleep. Second, if Abelard was here, one of us wouldn't survive the encounter.

* * *

A few hours later, I emerged from my bedroom, having done nothing except stare at the ceiling and force my mind to go blank. Mark was on the couch. The Abelard file was opened and dissected on my coffee table. I went to the coffeepot and poured a fresh cup.

"Any idea where he is or if he's here?" I asked.

Mark shook his head. "Any chance he just wanted to visit Disneyland?"

"I highly doubt it."

"So what? You're camping out on my couch until someone tracks him down? Maybe he's in the wind. He might be in another country. Perhaps he fled to Mexico." I was running out of ideas. It was nice Mark was here to watch my back, but right now, having some solid facts or a decent lead would have been preferable.

"Actually, I want to put a tactical unit in the building across the street. It'd be good to have eyes on your apartment, just in case. Once they're set up, it'd just be a matter of waiting."

"You're using me as bait to flush him out? Because

I'm not sure I'm the damsel in distress type."

"You're not. You're more the knight in shining armor. I swear, whoever read you fairy tales really screwed you up."

"Slaying dragons and riding horses sounds like more fun than sitting in a tower brushing my hair or whatever," I retorted. "So you're certain he's here and he's coming for me?"

"No. Not in the least. We have nothing, but while we wait for the Police Nationale to sort through this mess, we need to be proactive."

"Wonderful," I replied cynically.

Mark and I spent the rest of the morning familiarizing ourselves with all the minute details of Louis Abelard. Abelard's criminal career began in his adolescence, running Bonneteau, or three card monte, on street corners. At some point, he became involved with a couple of gangs. After learning the ropes, he broke away from his associates and started his own enterprise. There were some peripheral ties to drugs, weapons, and prostitution from his old gang days, but much less involvement than I would have imagined. Abelard's two main passions were gambling and the finer things in life. He dealt only with top of the line antiquities and art. There were no small-scale robberies in his history. He was meticulous and stayed below the radar for almost all of his adult life. Until three years ago, he barely existed as far as the authorities were concerned.

"For someone so careful and methodical, why the sudden change? He either killed or orchestrated the hit on Marset. He was going to kill me. What happened? It's like he cracked."

"Donough and the rest of the Paris police were moving in," Mark reminded me. "Desperate times and all."

"Why not start over someplace else?" I was trying to apply reason to an illogical situation.

"If someone took everything from you, would you just turn the other cheek and start over?" Abelard was intent on revenge, but I wanted to convince myself it wasn't the case.

"I get it." I rubbed my wrists absently. "Not to mention, given his sadistic personality, I stopped being fun before he got his rocks off."

The phone rang, interrupting my thoughts, and I answered.

"Parker," O'Connell said my name carefully, "would you mind coming to a crime scene? We have a body."

"Who?" Fear gripped my insides as I waited for an answer.

"I don't know, but the corpse has a message for you."

I let out a slight sigh of relief, which was completely inappropriate under the circumstances. O'Connell gave me the address, and Mark and I were on our way.

*   *   *

We were in an abandoned warehouse in the old meatpacking district. The area had been cordoned off, and O'Connell waved us through the crime scene tape before Mark had to flash his credentials. I wasn't prepared for the sight in front of me, but in all honesty, I wasn't surprised.

"We got an anonymous tip two hours ago about a body starting to stink up the place. 911 dispatch relayed the message, and a couple of officers came down to investigate. Heathcliff got the call and bumped it to me once he saw your name," O'Connell explained as Mark and I circled the body. "Recognize him?"

"I don't know."

Hanging chained from a meat hook was a man, late-thirties, average height, maybe two hundred pounds. It might have been Ski Mask, but I wasn't sure. Electrical burns covered his bare torso, and his wrists had been cut cleanly with a knife. Stapled to his bare chest was my name written on a plain white piece of paper.

Mark blanched. "Is this what he did to you?"

Not wanting to respond to the question, I posed my own. "Cause of death?" I didn't know if the electricity killed him or if he bled out. Although, if he had been killed here, the lack of a significant pool of blood indicated he was dead long before his wrists were slashed.

"Coroner's not sure yet. We haven't established a TOD either," O'Connell answered as he continued assessing the scene. "It's recent, less than twelve hours."

"Gloves?"

O'Connell handed me a glove which I slipped on before lifting the paper off of the man's chest to see if it said anything besides my name. There were no other markings on either side.

"You don't know him?" O'Connell watched my expression.

"Might be the goon with the ski mask, but I honestly can't tell. It was dark, and I was tired and preoccupied with fighting off Ramirez." I shut my eyes, thinking if there were any distinguishing features. "I don't know."

The three of us surveyed the rest of the scene. The place had been abandoned for years, and the corners held a collection of refuse from vagrants who used the space as refuge from the elements. Some forensic technicians were sifting through what appeared to be plastic wrap and half a dozen destroyed cell phones. Below the body, scene markers were placed, indicating wire cutters and a pair of needle-nose pliers. Were they used in this man's torture? A spatula and bowl sat on top of a crate, possibly left by one of the squatters in the warehouse. This wasn't a good place to die. Then again, what place was?

"Okay." O'Connell turned to me. "What do you want to do?"

"I'm not sure." My mind was a million miles away. The recreation and murder were threats, but in case I was too dense to get the message, Abelard was kind enough to staple a name tag to the deceased. If the corpse was Ski Mask, then he was cleaning up his mess.

"Look," O'Connell said, "I can bring you into protective custody or set up a protection detail."

"No." I wasn't risking anyone else getting hurt.

"Alex," Mark tried to argue O'Connell's point, "I'll keep a tac team on standby. It'll ensure your safety."

"No," I repeated again. Mark's earlier conversation surfaced to the forefront of my thoughts. "Now that we know he's here, let's give the son of a bitch exactly what he wants. Me."

TWENTY-NINE

The plan was simple. I was dangling myself like a worm in front of a fish, waiting for Abelard to take the bait. I refused protective custody. As far as any onlooker could tell, no police officers were stationed in my building or outside my door. On the surface, I was alone and unprotected.

O'Connell volunteered to work undercover and watch my back. It might have been professional courtesy because we were friends, or he was afraid to deal with Martin in the event of my demise. Regardless of his reasoning, it was comforting to know he was there. O'Connell and Thompson took shifts, running surveillance from the apartment down the hall.

Mark and the OIO were working with Interpol to track Abelard and any of his known associates who might pose a threat. I called Ryan and updated him on the situation. He was working his ass off to get answers from Gustav, but he had met little success. The Police Nationale questioned Abelard's men, but no one had anything useful to say regarding his intentions for coming to the U.S. or what he might do now that his gambling syndicate was disbanded.

It had been two days since we found the body in the warehouse. The coroner placed TOD around six a.m. Sunday morning. My working theory was Ski Mask met Abelard at the warehouse, possibly to collect payment or take another job, but was double-crossed for failing to keep me out of the investigation or for not killing me when he had the chance. Either way, Ski Mask was dead for pissing off the wrong person.

'Accidentally' bumping into Nick in the hallway of my apartment building, I invited him over for a cup of coffee, just to be neighborly. We exchanged the relevant information we had.

"I'm sorry to do this to you. Your wife is going to kill me."

"It's okay. I volunteered. Plus, if I make this bust, I might get a pay increase. First grade detective here I come. She'll be happy about that," he said good-naturedly.

"Glad to help," I teased, "but I hate the waiting. I'm thinking of going to my office. Maybe see if anything or anyone is waiting for me there."

"I'll call Thompson and get a few plainclothes to shop around while you check in. I don't want you going anywhere alone."

"I never knew you cared."

"If you kill him, I won't get my promotion. It's more for his safety than yours."

After waiting a couple of hours for everything to be arranged, I left the building, armed with my nine millimeter in a shoulder holster and my backup strapped to my ankle. I got in my car, afraid of turning the key and exploding, but luckily, that didn't happen. I drove to my office at the strip mall, keeping a watchful eye on my rearview mirror for a tail. When I got there, I unlocked the door and performed a full check of every nook and cranny inside. As I watched the shoppers outside, I tried to determine who the undercover cops were, and with the exception of Thompson, whom I recognized, I couldn't make the rest. Hopefully, since I couldn't tell, neither could Abelard.

Having nothing better to do, I dialed Patrick Farrell. He graciously divulged every fact on the car bombing that killed Marset. The incendiary device had been constructed out of plastic explosive. It wasn't anything special, just your garden variety C-4. Given its chemical composition and limited range, Interpol speculated the bomb was handcrafted.

Gustav might have the knowledge and know-how to make the device since he spent years in the military, but despite everything he put me through, he didn't seem like a cold-blooded killer. Then again, bomb creation was a skill that could be learned. With enough time and an internet search engine, I could be a bomb expert or have Homeland Security knocking on my door. Hoping not to be put on a terrorist watchlist, I skimmed through the basic ingredients necessary, such as plasticizer, other commonly found chemicals, and the rudimentary method of combining the ingredients. It was frightening how readily available these items were and how easily someone with a large enough mixing bowl, a spatula, and reading comprehension skills could wreak havoc if they had access to a couple of detonators.

It was dusk when I left my office and returned to my car. The unsettling feeling of being watched made my stomach twist in knots, but I didn't see Abelard. Maybe it was just the police presence making me jumpy. I didn't risk glancing toward Thompson as I pulled out of the parking space and headed for home.

Constantly checking my rearview mirror, I spotted a silver sedan, four cars back, that made the last two turns I did. To mix things up, I turned left down the next street. The car followed. Forcing my speed to remain steady, I turned right, but the silver sedan continued straight.

"I'm probably losing it," I said to myself and continued home. No other cars were in pursuit. I parked and cautiously got out, glancing around as I walked at a decent clip to the building, resisting the urge to sprint inside. Once up the six flights of stairs, I stood outside my apartment door, cursing loudly about my key being stuck, so O'Connell would know I returned, even though the video feed he was monitoring should have indicated this. I checked my apartment for signs of intruders, but nothing appeared disturbed.

I just sat down when my phone rang, causing my heart to skip a beat. "Abelard's credit card was just used to procure a room at a motel. We have a team heading there now," Mark informed me.

"Mark," I exhaled a breath in relief, "don't let the bastard get away again."

Waiting impatiently in my apartment, I stalked back and forth. It had been almost an hour since the call, and I had yet to hear if they located Abelard. I was going crazy. Did O'Connell have any news? Mid-dial, there was a knock at my door. O'Connell stood outside, holding a bottle of laundry detergent.

"It's my cover," he explained after I shut and locked the door. "I was going to ask if you had any laundry detergent, or how to use the washing machine, or something."

"Uh-huh," I replied, amused. "Have you heard anything?"

"The last I heard, the guy's barricaded himself

inside the room. Emergency services are on the way."

"It's definitely him?"

"It looks that way. We're operating off the description the motel clerk provided. We haven't gotten eyes on him. No cameras. No surveillance. It's a run-down motel, the kind you pay for by the hour."

My leg bounced up and down with nervous energy. Something wasn't right. The familiar twinge nagged at the recesses of my mind. "Why would he use a credit card? He used a fake passport to enter the country. He changed tickets with another passenger on a different flight. He knows we're gunning for him. He left us a freaking gift wrapped body for god's sake. Why would he suddenly get so sloppy?"

"Maybe he figured with a fleabag motel like that it wouldn't matter," O'Connell reasoned. "These guys always screw up. It's just a matter of when."

"No, not this guy. Not like this." There had to be an explanation. I quickly ran through the limited amount of information I had on Abelard. "Shit." The random items found in the warehouse weren't left by squatters. They were bomb building materials, and Abelard was clearly a fan of fireworks. I picked up the phone and dialed Mark, hoping it wasn't too late.

"Parker?" he asked, confused by my call.

"Don't breach. It's a trap."

Mark yelled something to the team assembled. "I'll call you back."

O'Connell raised a questioning eyebrow, and I shrugged. Now we had to wait.

Ten minutes later, Mark phoned. "I've never seen anyone with instincts like yours."

"What happened?" I put Mark on speakerphone as I paced.

"The door was booby-trapped with a tripwire hooked to some homemade C-4. There was a remote detonator attached and wires on the windows. No one was inside. The shared connecting door was jimmied open. It looks like Abelard set everything up and escaped before we arrived. We're canvassing the area, but my guess is he's long gone."

Abelard couldn't have had more than a few minutes to set the bomb and get away. Who was this guy and how did he keep eluding us?

"He wants to draw me out," I said. "But I'm right here. Why doesn't he just come and get me?"

"Maybe he wants to make sure you're unprotected," O'Connell offered. "If he thinks you have Interpol or the Bureau watching your back, he might want to distract them, so you'll be left unguarded."

It was a good theory. I had to give O'Connell credit for coming up with it. The problem was it was just a theory.

*   *   *

The next morning, Mark came by my apartment to check on things. There wasn't much to report. We still had no leads. Maybe I should stand in the middle of the street with a giant neon sign above my head, saying *come and get me*, but the electrical bill for that little stunt would be astronomical. Maybe it was part of Abelard's sadistic nature to make me wait. It was torture knowing he was out there, and there was nothing I could do to stop him.

Traffic cam footage from near the hotel had been compiled from the night before. Even though the motel didn't have surveillance cameras, there was still a chance one of the nearby DOT cameras caught Abelard going or coming. Mark brought a copy, and I inserted the disk into my computer and watched a plethora of cars drive past. Only a few made the appropriate turn which would lead to the motel.

"Dammit," I swore. "The son of a bitch was following me." The silver sedan from last night turned and disappeared out of sight. Suppressing the chill that traveled up my spine, I rewound and pointed to the vehicle.

"Parker, it's a silver sedan. It's the most popular type and color of vehicle. How can you be positive it's the same one you thought was following you?" As the footage continued to play, another five or six silver sedans passed the camera. "I understand you're scared, but jumping to conclusions will only make finding him that much more difficult."

I rubbed my eyes. Was I paranoid and hiding from shadows? Probably.

"Plus, if he found you, he would have known you were alone and made his move instead of trying to lure you into a trap," Mark said.

"True." My paranoia wasn't helping the situation. "Did you get the motel's check-in records? Maybe he was there earlier to plant the bomb. That way, he would have time to swipe his credit card and get away before any of us were the wiser."

"You really think a place like that keeps records? They don't even have security cameras. The clerk stays behind a barred, bullet-resistant window."

"Classy joint," I sighed. "Something's got to give. We can't stay three steps behind."

"Are you sure you don't want to move to a secure location?" Mark asked.

"One way or another, this will end. I need to be more proactive since playing defense isn't cutting it."

"We don't know where he is."

"That doesn't mean I can't look for him. I accidentally stumbled upon him in a foreign country. Here, I have the home court advantage."

"You got lucky in Paris. That's the only reason you found him."

"I'm calling O'Connell and taking another look around the warehouse. Do you want to join us?" I asked, ignoring Mark's pessimistic attitude.

"Might as well, since you're going regardless of what I say."

I gave Nick a call. He was presently at the precinct, and Thompson was in the apartment. Since I was leaving, Thompson could go home. It seemed like an all-around win. O'Connell agreed to meet us where the body had been discovered in twenty minutes.

*   *   *

Walking the interior perimeter of the building, I noted its dissimilarities to the warehouse in France, but for Abelard's purposes, I'm sure it sufficed. There were a lot of broken windows and plenty of light filtering in from outside. Aside from the one large door for trucks to enter and exit and a smaller door, there were no other openings. I crouched on the ground and stared at the hook where Ski Mask had been left dangling until the coroner retrieved the body.

"The techs have gone through this place with a fine-tooth comb, but they didn't find anything else," O'Connell said.

There were no separate rooms for Abelard to use as a staging or prep area. Did he take his toys with him when he finished? Or could he have a setup in one of the other empty buildings nearby?

"Did you check the surrounding buildings?" I asked, doing a quick three-sixty before heading for the door.

"Some officers canvassed the area, but they didn't come up with anything."

There had to be more than this. Determined to find something concrete, I went outside with Mark at my heels. Mark pointed to some dilapidated cargo containers.

"Did you have your guys check those out?" Mark asked O'Connell once he joined us after re-securing the crime scene and replacing the police tape.

"Yeah, nothing turned up. They were empty."

Our outing was a bust. I circled the area. This was my last ditch effort before admitting defeat and giving up. "Sorry, I dragged you here," I muttered, annoyed with myself. "We can leave. It doesn't look like this will lead to anything."

"I have a few calls in to a couple of guys I know in the gangs unit," O'Connell offered. "I thought if Abelard follows his previous pattern, they might hear some chatter."

"Thanks." I rubbed my eyes. I was tired of this. "Would either of you care to stop by my office for a couple of minutes, I just want to double-check some things."

O'Connell glanced at his watch. "If you buy me a cup of coffee, you've got a deal."

"Well, if we're talking free coffee, I'm in." Mark grinned.

"Coffee's on me."

THIRTY

I gave Mark a ten dollar bill and sent him to get the coffees while I read my mail.

O'Connell surveyed my small office space. "Glad to see the private sector is booming," he joked. "What do you call this? Pressed wood chic?"

"I call it all I can afford. I swear, you and Martin both have issues with my office décor." The stack of mail went into the recycle bin, and I pressed the message button on the answering machine to make sure there were no missed calls.

"If you want to get business, you have to look like a legitimate company," he chided.

I was preparing a proper comeback when his radio went off. Dispatch received word of a 911 call regarding a gunman. I ignored the radio chatter until I heard the address.

"That's here." I unholstered my weapon and flipped off the safety. O'Connell's piece was already out, and we approached the front door. Abelard stood in the middle of the parking lot, a cell phone in one hand and a gun at his side. "It's him," I hissed.

O'Connell radioed for backup and relayed the pertinent information. Abelard smiled menacingly and tossed the phone away before giving a slight wave.

"You son of a bitch." I was confident I could put a bullet through his skull from this distance. I reached for the door, but O'Connell stopped me.

"We need a plan," he insisted.

"Fine," my eyes didn't leave Abelard, "go out the back and around the building to head him off. I'll keep him occupied until then." Or I'd shoot him. Whichever came first.

O'Connell went out the back without another word, and I carefully exited my office. *A bulletproof vest would have been a nice accessory to have on today*, I thought wistfully. I kept my nine millimeter down by my side so as not to panic civilians as I made my way toward Abelard.

"Madame," he bellowed from his spot in the middle of the parking lot, "it seems we never got to finish our little tête-à-tête."

I turned sideways and leveled my gun at him. "Drop your weapon."

"Tut tut." He shook his head. "You wouldn't want to risk hurting one of these innocent people."

O'Connell approached from the left, and Abelard raised his gun in the air and fired. The resulting gunshot sent everyone in the vicinity running and screaming.

"Dammit," I cursed as a herd of people blocked my view.

"Parker," O'Connell yelled, and we ran through the crowd in pursuit of Abelard.

Abelard didn't have much of a head start. I ran across the street, narrowly avoiding being hit by a taxi. O'Connell was ahead of me, weaving around the pedestrians on the sidewalk, as we chased Abelard another block. Turning the corner a couple of steps behind O'Connell, I caught a glimpse of Abelard descending the stairs to the subway.

Running down steps was my least favorite thing. Pushing past commuters, I was almost to the turnstiles when I caught sight of Abelard's back, heading up the other set of steps.

"Nick," I screamed, reversing direction and running up the escalator. At least going up the stairs was less of an ordeal than going down. At street level, he disappeared down an alleyway, and I followed, hoping for a dead end. Nick was three steps behind me as the narrow alley opened onto another street. Crossing once more *Frogger*-style and narrowly missing getting hit by a bike messenger, Abelard made it into the park. Nick was at my heels, and as we went past a street vendor, we were confronted with a hostage situation.

Abelard grabbed a teenage boy and used him as a shield, the muzzle of his gun pressed against the boy's temple. "I said I wasn't done with you yet," Abelard taunted.

O'Connell and I trained our weapons on the target, but I didn't have a clear shot.

"Police," O'Connell identified himself, holding his badge in his free hand. "Let the boy go." He sidestepped closer to me. "If you have a shot, take it," he whispered.

"Non, non, non," Abelard responded, his French accent thickening his words. "This is because of her, and I'm not through having my fun." Abelard was less stable than I realized. He might have suffered a recent psychotic break since the man I met in the Parisian bar was less of a lunatic than the man before me now. "Our playtime is only beginning, Madame. Now Monsieur Policeman, I would suggest you put down your pistol." Abelard gave O'Connell a wicked smile.

Mark had followed us and appeared behind

Abelard. He edged closer, hoping to keep his presence hidden. I had no idea how he managed to get around, but I was thankful he did.

"Okay, let's just calm down." O'Connell attempted to de-escalate the situation. He made a show of removing his finger from the trigger and holding his gun in the air before carefully sliding it onto his hip. "No one needs to get hurt."

My weapon remained trained on Abelard. If the kid would just move another inch to the right, I would have a clean shot.

"Is that right, Alex?" Abelard asked. "You don't want to hurt me after everything I've done to you and everything I promise I'll do to you?"

"Seems your issue is with me and only me," I said. "Why don't we work out our differences by ourselves?"

"Oh, we will Madame. I'm just not ready for the grand finale yet. Until then, I hope you're enjoying the foreplay," his voice dripped maniacal pleasure.

Before I could say or do anything, Mark grabbed Abelard's gun arm and attempted to wrestle the weapon from him. O'Connell yelled at the kid to move, and I was about to take the shot when Abelard's gun discharged. Mark hit the ground. Abelard turned and gave a two-fingered salute before fleeing into the crowd. O'Connell checked on the kid, and I rushed to Mark.

I swore loudly, frustrated as I knelt on the ground. Mark was properly accessorized with a vest under his shirt, and given the small caliber weapon Abelard had been holding, it only knocked the wind out of him.

"I don't like your friend," Mark said once he caught his breath.

O'Connell's backup arrived, and we had to provide statements and go through the rigmarole of dealing with the hostage situation and letting the suspect get away. O'Connell would have to deal with the fallout. Mark and I returned to my office and locked up before going to the precinct and filling out the paperwork. When we were done, Mark drove me home.

"Are you sure you don't want to go to the emergency room?" I asked Mark, who was, by all accounts, absolutely fine. He barely even bruised, the lucky bastard.

"Shut up, Parker."

"I should have shot him. Why didn't I take the shot or continue pursuit? Hell, I should have done both."

"You didn't want to hit the kid. And you were worried about the old man who nearly took a bullet. I swear I'm getting too damn old for this."

"Then you should be behind a desk, not in the field."

He pulled to a stop in front of my apartment building. "I'll come up."

"No, you go home. Take some ibuprofen before bed. It'll hurt in the morning," I warned. Mark was reluctant to leave when there was a crazy man on the loose. "I'm sure O'Connell will be here momentarily. Plus, Abelard likes to make 911 calls informing us of his location ahead of time." How long was Abelard waiting outside my office before he made the call identifying his location? He must have been staking it out, waiting for my appearance. Maybe he was in the silver sedan and had been keeping tabs on me all along.

"Fine, but be extremely careful."

"You too. Circuitous routes and everything else."

He nodded, and I got out of the car, walking swiftly inside with my hand resting against the butt of my gun. I didn't know where Abelard escaped to today, but he planned to make good on his threat to finish having his fun with me. I forced my mind not to imagine what that might entail. Hopefully, Abelard wasn't the creative type.

After I made my way to my apartment, I verified all my locks were secure before unlocking the door and flipping on the lights and checking the entirety of my apartment before settling down and removing my backup from my ankle. As I heated a frozen pizza, O'Connell knocked on my door.

"The lieutenant doesn't want any more mishaps," O'Connell said as I offered him some pizza. "He has a team set up in the building across the street." There was no room for argument. Today could have been disastrous.

"I'm really sorry." I felt responsible for the flack he had to endure. "How hard did this come down on you?"

"Not too bad. The kid's fine. Shaken up, but fine. Agent Jablonsky barely even flinched. Everyone's still breathing, so it's all good."

I wished Abelard wasn't, but I kept that thought to myself.

"How are you?" Nick asked.

"Still breathing."

"That's one crazy mother."

"Strangely enough, he didn't seem this crazy the first time around," I took a breath, "and he was insane then, too. Now he's completely overboard." I cringed. It was no wonder Jean-Pierre had been afraid to cross him.

*   *   *

The next morning, I stared out my window, wondering if the police were watching from across the street. Mark called and said he and Farrell might be making progress on locating the supplier Abelard used to purchase the detonators for his C-4. I wished them luck. O'Connell dropped by my apartment that morning, after he relieved Thompson from the night shift, and I offered him a cup of coffee.

"Any news?" I asked. O'Connell shook his head. Abelard had vanished again. I hadn't slept. The paranoia and anxiety were getting to me. People I cared about could have been killed yesterday. Mark had been shot, after all.

"You look like shit," O'Connell said, and I snickered at his assessment.

"Thanks. That's exactly what I like to hear."

He gave me a look and refilled his cup of coffee.

"I hate that Abelard is calling the shots and running the show."

"He's escalating. I bet he'll make another run at you in the next few days."

O'Connell's words rang true a few hours later when his radio chirped, notifying him Abelard had been sighted in my neighborhood. I was positive Abelard made the call himself. The tactical team, which was set up across the street, was on high alert, and uniformed officers were moving in to secure the area.

"Showtime," I muttered, unenthused.

Nick checked his side arm. My gun remained holstered but at the ready. However, I was unsure of what to do. This was when having no official job title made life difficult. The waiting was incredibly anticlimactic as I paced my apartment, avoiding the windows. I checked and rechecked my weapon a dozen times. About forty-five minutes later, Nick's radio went off again. Uniformed officers apprehended a suspect matching Abelard's description.

"I'll make sure we have him," O'Connell said. "Stay here this time."

If I saw Abelard again, he would be bloody and lifeless. O'Connell radioed he was on the way and left my apartment. I stood in the doorway, watching him open the door to the stairwell and disappear down the steps. Taking a deep breath, I hoped this was finally over. I just locked the deadbolts when I heard a high-pitched, mechanical squeal coming from outside.

"Shit." I unlocked the door and pulled my gun before exiting into the hallway. Leaving the door open, I put my back against the doorframe and peered around the corner. The hallway was empty, and I strained to hear if the sound had come from a different floor. Lowering my gun, I cocked my head to the side. Maybe I was imagining things. As I turned to go back into my apartment, the stairwell door opened, and a deliveryman exited onto my floor. There was something odd about the man. The warning bells in my brain blared, but lack of sleep slowed my mind and reflexes.

He has nothing to deliver, I realized, raising my gun to take aim. It was Abelard, but I was too slow. He rushed forward, wrapping one of his large hands completely around my throat and shoving me into the wall. I was suspended by my neck in mid-air, choking. His other hand grabbed for my gun, but I refused to let it go. However, my wrist couldn't withstand the torment in its previously injured state, and after being slammed into the wall a few times, the gun slipped from my grip and clattered to the floor.

Had I been able to get any air in or out, I would have screamed bloody murder. Instead, my vision rapidly clouded with the encroaching black bubbles. I wasn't getting any oxygen or blood to my brain, and there was nothing I could do. I made a feeble attempt to knee Abelard or fight back with my one free hand, but it was too little, too late.

THIRTY-ONE

Abelard released his grip just before the entire world went dark, and I crumpled to my knees, fighting for breath. My head pounded as blood rushed to my brain. He slipped something around my neck, grabbed a fistful of my hair, and shoved me into my apartment and slammed the door.

"You didn't think I would let you escape into the darkness, did you?" he asked teasingly in my ear. He pinned my arms and stood behind me, pressing a knife into my side. "That would be too easy, non?" His French accent was thick, making him hard to understand. The blade punctured my skin, but it was meant as a warning. "We should have some fun first."

I was still coughing and dizzy, fighting to rein my thoughts into an attack strategy. He released my arms and tugged on whatever he placed around my neck. Metal dug into my throat, cutting off oxygen and blood. Using both hands, I tried to get my fingers under the metal chain before Abelard could properly garrote me. He pulled tighter, and I tried to fend off the choke-chain more emphatically. The wrist he slammed into the wall bled profusely, making my hand wet and sticky, and it slipped from the metal. The darkness encroached again.

Abelard dropped the knife, realizing he didn't need it since I couldn't fight against him and the garrote. He took the opportunity to run his free hand along the curves of my body as I fought against the metal chain.

"Don't worry. I'll make sure you're coherent enough for everything that's still to come. It wouldn't be as enjoyable for me if you were dead."

I bucked backward, hoping to slam him into a wall, but we were in the center of the room. He was significantly larger and had come prepared. He released the pressure on my neck just enough to ensure I wouldn't pass out. *Waterboarding must be a similarly horrible experience*, I surmised. I choked and sputtered briefly before he yanked again, cutting off my air supply.

There was only one obvious conclusion; I had to stop struggling against the chain and focus my energy entirely on him if I had any chance of escaping. Pulling forward on the metal with all my strength, I gasped down a lungful of air before dropping my hands and slamming my foot into his shin. My elbow came up and struck him in the solar plexus, and I pulled partially away. The chain acted like a tether, forcing me to remain close to him unless I wanted to choke myself out. Turning at a ninety degree angle, I kicked into his kneecap with everything I had. He hit the ground, howling in pain and temporarily losing his grip on my leash. Collapsing onto the floor, I gasped for breath and frantically tried to free myself from my metal captor.

"Salope," he sneered, cursing in French and clutching his knee. He reached for the cold metal, desperate to regain his only remaining method of controlling me. Giving up on shaking the metal collar from my neck, I launched myself away from him and reached for my gun. He lunged and took hold of the metal chain just as I pulled my backup free from my ankle holster. I was nanoseconds away from pulling the trigger when O'Connell burst through the door.

"Let her go," O'Connell barked. His gun was at the ready, and his finger tensed over the trigger. Abelard dropped the chain and put his hands in the air. O'Connell kicked the discarded knife further from Abelard's reach. "Just give me a reason, you sick son of a bitch." O'Connell positioned himself in front of Abelard, separating him from me. Scrambling to my feet, I threw off the choke-collar, coughing spastically as tears ran down my face, but I had yet to lower my weapon. "Facedown, on the ground." O'Connell kicked Abelard over until he was prone on the floor, and then he frisked and cuffed him. "You okay?" he asked me.

I didn't answer. I couldn't. I had temporarily managed to stop choking, but I was having a difficult time lowering my weapon. All I needed was to apply less than ten pounds of pressure to the trigger, and it would be over.

"Alexis." O'Connell took a step toward me. He holstered his gun, and his hand reached for mine. "He's not worth it."

I snapped my glance to O'Connell for a brief second before focusing back on Abelard. "He's a monster, Nick," I whispered. My throat was sore, and I wasn't sure I could speak any louder without setting off another coughing fit. Abelard pulled himself to his knees and grinned maniacally. "I can end this. Right here. Right now." My finger twitched slightly, and Nick faced me completely. If I killed a handcuffed man, he didn't want to be able to testify against me.

"If you're going to do it, at least let me take the cuffs off first." O'Connell was reasoning with me, and I shut my eyes and dropped my trigger finger. Nick turned back to Abelard. "Stay down." He reached for my gun, and I surrendered it to him reluctantly. "It's over," he said quietly, putting the safety on and laying my firearm on the table.

Abelard muttered to himself in French and climbed to his knees, rocking back and forth. O'Connell shoved him to the ground, but in the blink of an eye, Abelard slipped free from the cuffs and pulled O'Connell's backup revolver from his ankle holster. I watched as Nick, without missing a beat, pulled the gun from his hip and double-tapped Abelard in the chest. In one fluid motion, O'Connell kicked his backup out of Abelard's reach and checked for a pulse. Somehow, my gun was in my hand, safety off, and pointed at the now dead Abelard.

Without even flinching, O'Connell unclipped his radio. "The suspect's been subdued. We're in Parker's apartment." He gave them my address. "Send a wagon to pick him up and a bus. She's been injured." He put the radio down. "Now, it's over."

"Finally," I eked out. For some reason, the room spun. I stumbled, and Nick wrapped an arm around my waist and helped me into the kitchen. I sat at the table while Abelard made a bloody mess on my floor. I needed to find a new apartment. "Are you okay?" I asked tentatively.

"Yeah." He nodded and shifted his gaze, thinking. Checking my side and wrist, he went to the counter and handed me a dish towel. Wrapping the towel tightly around my bleeding wrist, I thought about my gun lying on the floor in the hallway. One of the cops could pick it up on their way in. "You're going to the hospital, no argument." He offered a small smile. "I

just dealt with him, so you can do that much for me."
He was worried about the IA investigation that was
mandatory following an officer involved shooting.

We sat silently, waiting for backup to arrive, along
with the ME and some paramedics. O'Connell was
forced to surrender his weapon and was ushered away
for a proper debriefing. He threw a small smile and
nod over his shoulder before being escorted out of my
apartment. The paramedics evaluated my vitals as I
tried to explain what happened. Eventually, I gave up
due to the coughing fits and pointed to the metal
choke-collar on the floor. Thompson and a few
officers watched the exchange. I had yet to be asked
about the shooting, but that would soon change.
Eventually, I was moved downstairs and away from
the scene.

In the ER, my wrist was X-rayed, my side was
bandaged, and my neck was examined. My blood
pressure was elevated, but everything else appeared
normal. I attempted to give my detailed statement to
the police, but my speech was impaired from my
larynx almost being crushed. The authorities would
just have to come back after the doctors finished their
poking and prodding if they wanted more
information.

By some miracle, my wrist wasn't broken, and I had
not sustained any permanent damage to my neck or
throat. However, I was to avoid speaking or straining
my neck in any way until it had time to heal, and I was
to remain a while longer under observation because of
my elevated BP and failure of my wrist to properly
clot. My previous injuries, courtesy of Abelard, were
also reassessed.

At least it provided me the opportunity to evaluate
the pertinent information surrounding the shooting.
O'Connell's review would be expedited after

everything that happened, especially after the police considered my statement, my injuries, and the wireless surveillance camera which recorded the altercation in the hallway. The shooting was justified. O'Connell was acting in self-defense and in the defense of another, namely me. But how did Abelard slip the cuffs? O'Connell secured them tightly, but his comment about taking them off would appear suspicious if these details were divulged. There was a practical explanation, and I wanted to figure it out just in case it became an issue.

O'Connell's commanding officer, Lieutenant Moretti, stopped by my hospital room to ask some questions. Luckily, I wasn't up to talking. Providing him with a brief recount of the events, I agreed to have the Abelard files forwarded to him.

"The Police Nationale can fax over my original report and involvement." I reached for my cell phone and dialed Ryan, requesting the information and promising to call later. I didn't want to give him any details other than the good news that Abelard was no longer a threat to anyone.

About an hour later, I was still in the damn hospital when Agent Farrell appeared at my door. He was given the contact information for O'Connell's precinct, and I felt like a switchboard operator, having to relay one message from one person to another and put people into contact with each other. Finally, after briefly speaking, or squeaking since my voice wasn't cooperating, to a dozen different people, I was left alone. Lying in bed, I shut my eyes. Since the doctors wanted to hold me hostage, I should use this time productively to catch up on some rest. The doctors had given me some kind of painkiller or sedative that made me drowsy.

I was just about to doze off when the doctor

returned. My blood pressure had returned to normal, and my wrist clotted temporarily. But it needed stitches. My neck was a different story. While there was no permanent internal damage, the flesh was bruised and sore. The doctor wrote out a prescription for an ointment to aid in healing, and he recommended ice and time. For my sore throat, some lozenges and sore throat spray should suffice. Why didn't I have a medical degree? He promised to send someone from plastics to do the stitches to minimize scarring.

I lay back against the pillow, my hopes for a nap vanishing. Instead, I watched people walk back and forth until a nurse came in with some forms to sign.

"How are you feeling, sweetie?" she asked as I held the pen awkwardly in my bandaged hand.

"Ready to go home," I whispered. "Or somewhere else." I handed her the papers and noticed a man in a three-piece suit and tailored overcoat throwing a fit at the nurse's station. "Do me a favor and tell the obnoxious guy in the expensive suit to stop making a scene and get in here."

Confused, the nurse went into the hallway and brought Martin to my room.

"Alex." He hurried to my side, unsure of how to proceed, looking both relieved and worried at the same time. "Are you okay? I got here as soon as I could. Obviously, you aren't okay. You're in the emergency room. That was a stupid question." His speech pattern was rushed, bordering on frantic.

I leaned my head against his chest and hugged him awkwardly with one arm. "Calm down. I'm okay." I had no idea why he was here, but I was happy to see him. He wrapped an arm around my shoulders. "What are you doing here?" I tried to speak normally, not quite succeeding.

"O'Connell called. He said you needed someone to pick you up. What happened?"

I shook my head. It was too long of a story to launch into right now. Martin pulled away and scrutinized my injuries. He tentatively brushed my hair away from my neck. His jaw muscles clenched.

"He shouldn't have called," I whispered, but Martin shushed me.

"More importantly, are you sure you're okay?" Before I could respond, a doctor came in. "Is she okay?"

The doctor looked for permission, and I nodded. He gave Martin a synopsis of everything I had already been told. Relieved, Martin took a step closer, and I buried my face in his shirt as the doctor stitched my wrist. When the doctor finished, he promised to send someone in with discharge papers.

"I didn't realize you were squeamish." Martin attempted levity. He was calmer now than he had been when he first entered the room. I was glad because I would have hated to ask the nurse for a tranquilizer.

"After the month I've had, I can't do it anymore."

"You're not supposed to talk," he insisted.

The nurse came back, and I signed my walking papers, got off the bed, and headed for the exit. I hated hospitals. Martin followed closely behind. He had car keys which meant Marcal wasn't here and neither was Bruiser.

"Where's Bruiser?"

"Dammit, Alex, for once, just shut up." He put his hands on my hips and kissed me. I pulled back, seeing the concern evident on his face. "I got a call from O'Connell and thought you were dead."

"Then why would I need a ride?" I teased, my tone not convincing in its whispered state. "Is there a hearse in your garage that I've never noticed?" I really needed to work on my decorum.

"Smartass," he sighed, defeated. "It doesn't matter."

"Wait," I was reaching the limit on my volume, "I'm sorry. I don't know how to turn it off sometimes." We were in the middle of the parking lot, being stared at by too many nosy onlookers.

"Funny, you know how to shut me out all the time. I'm not a complete moron." He spun around to face me. "I've been reading the papers. You cut me off. No contact. All I had was the news. I read about that body hanging in the warehouse, the bomb at the motel, and the hostage situation yesterday." He was seething. "I get a call from the police, and I made the only logical assumption."

Fighting the urge to point out this was exactly why we shouldn't be involved, I shut my mouth. It wasn't fair. I never considered how this would affect him. Martin opened the car door, and I got in.

"It's over," I whispered. He looked hurt and confused. Bad choice of words, Parker. "Abelard's dead." My voice was scratchy, and I fought the urge to cough, only compounding the problem.

"What happened?" He was no longer angry. His short burst of anger was replaced with distress as I proceeded to gasp for breath around my coughs. He swept my hair behind my shoulder and studied the ligature marks around my neck as he gently stroked my back.

"You know the French and their garrotes," I joked, but he wasn't amused. "Nick took care of him." Shutting my eyes, I remembered how badly I wanted to pull the trigger. Thank god, Abelard was dead.

"Good. I hope he gets a commendation." His tone was eerily sincere. I nodded in agreement as he started the car and pulled away from the hospital parking lot. "Where to?" he asked, caressing my back as I got the coughing under control.

"Shouldn't you be at work? You can just drop me off at my place, and I'll take it from there." I put him through enough today, and I didn't want to deprive him of his main joy in life, his job.

"I'm the boss. I can play hooky anytime I want, and right now, that's exactly what I want."

Gracing him with an appreciative smile, I considered my prescriptions. "Drugstore then my place." I rested against the seat and avoided looking at the speedometer. Martin had a habit of driving like he was trying to place at the Indy 500.

"Condoms and sex, got it." He raised an eyebrow and winked.

Laughing slightly, I was glad he dropped the serious edge. "That sounds like more fun than cough drops, painkillers, and something cold to drink. Not to mention, the pool of blood on my floor that I don't want to deal with anytime soon."

"Well, those aren't mutually exclusive events, except for the blood on the floor thing." He missed our verbal sparring over the past week. "You don't have to go home. You can stay at my place," he offered, but I shook my head.

Martin drove to the drugstore where I picked up a few bags of throat lozenges, some sore throat spray, and a bottle of cold water while I waited for the pharmacist to fill my prescriptions.

"If you won't stay with me, at least get a hotel room," he suggested, "my treat." I was about to protest since he shouldn't throw his money around now that we were whatever we were. I didn't want him to think I was a prostitute. This was not a twisted re-enactment of *Pretty Woman*. "Or half the room." He was being appeasing.

"When will you give up on this stupid compromise kick?"

"That's the problem with both of us being alpha dogs. It's a daunting, uphill battle, but maybe one day you'll actually consider me an equal," he said, and I glared at him. "Plus, I plan on spending just as much time in that room as you are."

"Tease," I sighed. "I'm sure my place is fine. The coroner should have removed the last remnants of scum by now."

THIRTY-TWO

Arriving at home, I stared uneasily at the stairwell. My stomach tightened, and I shut my eyes. Abelard had taken these same steps to my apartment. Running through the scenario, I knew if O'Connell hadn't intervened, I would have killed Abelard or died trying. Shuddering, I pushed it aside. This was my place. I would not cower or run away. It was over.

"Hey, guys," I spoke to the uniformed officers inside the apartment O'Connell and Thompson had used for surveillance. "Are you done in my apartment yet?" The two uniformed cops looked bewildered, so I pulled out my identification and handed it to them.

"Body's been removed. Some detectives and techs are still scoping the place out. Did you want a professional cleaning service?" one of the cops asked, relinquishing my keys.

"No, I got it." How much of a mess could one dead guy make? The cops wished me an uneventful evening and a full recovery.

"Are you sure you want to go in there?" Martin

asked skeptically as we passed the bloodstains left on the wall by my wrist.

"Shit," I muttered, handing him my keys, "I'll be right back. Go inside. Don't freak out." Not waiting for a response, I reversed direction to ask the officers if my gun had been recovered. It had been collected as evidence, and I could pick it up in a few days. When I went back to my apartment, the door was open, and Martin was standing on the threshold. "I told you not to freak out."

"I'm not." He was only staring at my blood-soaked carpeting, completely motionless.

"Right," I sighed and edged past him. Luckily, the carpeting only ran from my front door down the hallway. The rest was hardwood floors. With the exception of where Abelard had been shot, he hadn't caused much damage to my apartment. The rest of the blood was mine. Considering my options, I could replace or pull up the carpet, leaving the hardwood underneath, assuming it didn't soak through. At the moment, there were better things to think about.

A number of police and Interpol agents were finalizing their reports. They turned and stared at the two of us. One of the uniformed officers moved to intercept, but Thompson caught my eye.

"Parker," he called and offered a slight nod. Being here and watching the techs catalog my apartment as a crime scene made me realize how much I wanted to leave. The new plan was to pack a bag and get the hell out of here. Martin was right, as irritating as that was.

"What can I do?" Martin asked, tearing his gaze away from the floor.

"Some tea would be nice." Another coughing fit threatened to come on, and keeping him busy was a good idea. He dutifully went into my kitchen and began boiling water as he rummaged through the cabinets, looking for teabags.

"Are you okay?" Thompson asked, staring at the ligature marks on my neck.

"Uh-huh. Not much for talking. What's going on?"

The police and Interpol were photographing my apartment and cross-referencing the evidence in order to finalize their incident reports. Thompson figured they would be finished within the hour, but there was no reason why I needed to wait around that long.

"Check this out," one of the cops called, kneeling over my bloodied carpet. Thompson and I crouched down to get a better look at the object the man was holding. It was a small, blood-covered, strip of metal that resembled a toothpick. It must have been what Abelard used to slip the cuffs. The pieces were coming together, but I resisted the urge to shout *ah-ha*.

"What is it?" Thompson asked, staring at the item.

The tech shrugged, and before I could interject my two cents, another man joined us and flipped through the digital photos taken of Abelard's remains. His left hand was bloody, and there was a deep puncture just below his knuckles. The sicko stowed the lock-pick inside his own flesh to use in the event of his apprehension. Standing up, I knew I needed to get out of here. The more I learned about Abelard, the faster my mind was imagining worst case, what if scenarios.

"I'm going to pack a bag," I whispered. "My ride," I jerked my head toward Martin and regretted the motion instantly, "is dropping me off at a hotel. Whatever you need, I promise I'll give you tomorrow." Getting a few sympathetic looks, I went into my bedroom and tossed the necessities into a bag and repeated the process in the bathroom.

When I emerged, Thompson and Martin were talking in my kitchen. A travel mug waited on the counter. Glancing once more at the dried pool of blood, I reminded myself the bastard was dead, and I was safe.

"I'll hold off the dogs until tomorrow," Thompson assured me.

"Thanks." Picking up the tea, I took a sip. "Lock up when you leave. Clearly, I live in an unsavory neighborhood."

He squeezed my shoulder. "I'm glad you're okay. In my book, any day's a good day when the only one who ends up in the ground is a psychopath."

I let Thompson's comment go, unsure if he was fishing for information or just offering some sage advice. Martin remained uncharacteristically quiet through the entire exchange and simply followed me out of my apartment and back to the stairwell. On the fourth floor landing, I paused to get a grip. As I leaned against the cinderblock walls, I put my face in my hands and took a few deep breaths.

"What can I do?" he asked quietly.

"Just give me a minute." My stomach twisted in knots as I thought about all the things that could have happened or almost happened. I stood up and blew out an unsteady breath. "Guess I might take you up on that hotel offer, after all."

A simple room for one night was all I needed, but Martin insisted on an upgrade, which led to a suite with a separate bedroom and kitchenette. I had no desire to argue since I was completely worn out. Honestly, any place free of blood and police would suffice; it didn't matter if it was a tiny room with a twin bed or a palace.

In the bedroom, I searched for a comfortable change of clothes. When I came out, Martin was leaning against the kitchen sink, staring at the wall. Today must have been just as unsettling for him. He needed to go back to his life and stay out of mine.

"Mind if I take a shower and change into something else?" I asked.

He looked up as if he had forgotten I was in the room. "Take your time. I'll be right here. Did you need me to do anything? I can do whatever you want."

"It's okay. I can manage." I gave him an encouraging smile, and he went back to staring at the sink.

The soap and shampoo were heavenly escapes from everything I endured. With Abelard being all over me and then the hospital, I just wanted every reminder gone. If I could have crawled out of my own skin, I would have. Instead, I shut the water, dried off, and changed into a pair of pajama shorts and a cropped tank top which I normally reserved for running on the treadmill. The mirror was covered in condensation, so I opened the bathroom door as I towel dried my hair. As the humidity dissipated, I stared at my reflection. The image before me made me shudder.

"Would you mind terribly if we turned the heat up?" I called.

"I believe you already did." Martin smiled flirtatiously, watching from the couch.

"What did I tell you about using old, tired clichés?"

"I'm not sure you understand the meaning of the word cliché. Furthermore, how is it a cliché when I speak the truth?" He went to the thermostat and adjusted the temperature before turning back to me. "Honestly, you're the most beautiful woman I've ever seen."

"Then you need glasses or a neurological exam," I scoffed. He came into the bathroom as I searched for antiseptic and gauze. "Look at me." I dropped my bag and stared at the bruised and battered version of myself. "This is because of one sick, twisted motherfucker." My jaw clenched, and I swallowed the lump in my throat uncomfortably.

Martin was not the person I should be pointing these things out to. He stood quietly, his hand absently running the length of my arm. "You'll heal." His voice was a whisper of hope, not only for my physical injuries but the psychological ones which I was sure I had yet to experience.

After properly dressing my wounds, I switched my train of thought to something more productive as he microwaved some water and made a fresh mug of tea. There was a duffel bag near the door. He must have called Marcal to bring him some necessities while I was in the shower. *It must be nice having those kinds of resources*, I thought as I realized the million things I needed to do. Call Ryan, call Mark, remove the carpet, get new carpet, find a new place to live, retrieve my gun from evidence.

"Have you talked to Mark?" I asked. Surprisingly, he hadn't called about the incident.

"Not recently. Why?"

"He's okay, but he took a bullet to the vest yesterday when we were pursuing Abelard. I just wanted you to know ahead of time. He'll probably call once Farrell submits his report, so... yeah."

"Okay." Martin was still uncharacteristically quiet and keeping in almost constant physical contact with me. At the moment, his arm was around my shoulders while we sat on the couch. The morbidity of my apartment hindered all conversation, even after our escape.

As I predicted, Mark called soon after, and I gave him my unofficial report. There was something bothering me about the entire thing, but I couldn't figure out exactly what it was. I kept the thought to myself and promised, once O'Connell was cleared, the three of us would go out for drinks. Hanging up, I checked the time. When I was released from the hospital, I had a brief burst of renewed energy but being in my apartment drained me. It was early, but I was tired. Martin insisted on ordering dinner, so while we waited, I took my tea and went into the bedroom to lie down. He followed like a lost puppy.

I woke up gasping. Strong arms were around me, and I jerked, desperate to free myself. "Alex," Martin's voice was in my ear, "you're okay. It's just me. Everything is okay." I stopped struggling and opened my eyes, taking a deep breath and coughing. The inside of my throat felt like it was filled with razor blades. "Nightmares?" he asked, knowing my susceptibility to such things.

"Something like that." Being restrained in any sense made my heart race and panic set in. Sitting up, I took a sip of cold tea. Putting the mug down, I tried to think clearly. "Did I miss dinner?"

He chuckled. "No, but I'm glad you have your priorities in order." He turned toward the alarm clock. "Another twenty minutes," he reported.

How long could I have been asleep? Not more than a half hour, unless that was some really slow room service.

"Good. I'm starving." I couldn't resist the draw of snuggling against him. He was turning into a crutch, and I would have to put a stop to it. He wasn't handling this situation well, and it wasn't helping me any. "You know, you don't need to be here. I'm okay. Everything is okay." Maybe I had been a parrot in a past life. Although, I wasn't sure who I was trying to convince of these facts.

"If it's all the same to you," he brushed my hair away from my neck and placed a cool compress along the ligature marks, following doctor's orders, "I'll hang around. The last time I let you out of my sight..."

his voice dropped away. On the one hand, Martin wanting to be here was comforting, but on the other, I was fighting the urge to push him and his smothering habits away. "Look at us, back in a hotel room after a stint in the hospital. Let's not turn this into our thing," he joked. "Next time, we're coming straight to the hotel for some cheap, tawdry rendezvous, instead of stopping at a hospital first."

Once the food arrived, we ate in silence. After dinner, the dirty dishes were tossed onto the tray, and I retreated to the bedroom, allowing him to accompany me. It was still early, but I was done for the day. My wrist and neck throbbed, and I relented and took a painkiller. He didn't mind that I could no longer sleep in the dark and had to have the living room light on or that it wasn't even nine o'clock but we were in bed. He was just relieved I wasn't in a body bag. That made two of us.

It was around two a.m. when I awoke. Going to sleep at such an early hour was a bad idea. Carefully disentangling myself from him, I climbed out of bed.

"Are you okay?" Even half asleep, his voice was etched with concern.

"I'm fine. Go back to sleep." I closed the bedroom door and went into the living room. Pouring a glass of water, I found a towel, filled it with the remaining ice from the bucket, and dipped a washcloth into the melted ice water before finding my phone and dialing Ryan. I took a seat on the couch, icing my wrist and putting the cloth against my sore neck.

"Up all night partying?" Ryan asked.

"No," I chuckled, "couldn't sleep."

"The job will do that to you. What's the unofficial version of what happened?"

I filled him in on the major points. As we were talking, I realized what was bothering me about the

Abelard situation.

"Ryan, he wanted to get arrested. He expected to be cuffed. How? Why? Did he want to make his escape that much more dramatic and hurtful, or was it part of his sadistic game to convince me I was safe just to torture me further when he got free?"

"Maybe he thought he was bloody Harry Houdini. It doesn't make a difference, does it?" It didn't, but it irked me.

"I guess not. So given Abelard's stunt with the C-4 at the motel, have you determined if he was the one who planted the car bomb that killed Marset?"

"I talked to Gustav yesterday after you called." It felt like today to me, but we were dealing with a six hour time difference, which made it yesterday for Ryan. "Marset was Abelard's way of sending a message to whoever the mole in his organization was, and Gustav took advantage for his own personal gains. But now that Abelard's dead, Gustav's not afraid to talk. He's just a chatterbox of information. Reneaux hasn't authorized a move on anything yet. We are waiting for official channels, but if it pans out, we'll have the location of the missing paintings, the buyers, everything. We already made the gambling busts, so the paintings can be the icing on the cake."

"That's great. Your eighteen months of hell weren't a complete waste of time."

"I know, right? If nothing else occurs today, by the end of shift, Clare will be released from protective custody and sent home."

"You said she was innocent, but to squelch my paranoia, did you ever find any connection proving even a slight involvement?" With Jean-Pierre still breathing, I doubted Clare had been involved.

"She's clean, at least as far as I can tell. I'll tell her Gustav's alive and see how that goes." Ryan let out a breath. "It's actually done."

"Thanks to O'Connell." My mind conjured the image of Abelard from the second before Nick burst through the door. "Is it just me or does it not feel done?" My tone changed to something dark and pained, and Ryan heard the shift.

"Alex, he's done. He's gone." The ice on my wrist soaked through the couch cushion, providing a decent distraction. "But a few unanswered questions remain," he added. He was going over the details on the gambling busts when Martin cleared his throat from the doorway.

"Ryan, it's getting late. Call me when your shift's over and let me know how things go." Disconnecting, I looked up at Martin.

"If I weren't completely secure in my manhood, I might be offended that you snuck out of bed in the middle of the night to call some other guy." He crouched down to my level and gently removed the cloth from my neck. After re-dipping it in the ice water, he laid it against my skin. I shivered, and he grabbed the robe from behind the bathroom door and put it over me like a blanket.

"I'm glad you're so secure."

"Even in the middle of the night." He looked tired.

"I didn't mean to keep you up."

He took a seat on the couch and wrapped an arm around me. "It doesn't matter. I haven't been sleeping much lately, anyway. Do you want to talk about it?" Since he had shown up at the hospital, he had barely let me out of his sight.

"No." I shook my head for emphasis. "It's too soon and too close. But if you want to talk about it, that's another story. The week, the worry, your earlier blow-up?"

"I never meant to snap at you. You said this would

be difficult. I just didn't realize everything it would entail."

"The exit is right over there," I jerked my head toward the door and regretted the movement as I winced. Luckily, he didn't notice.

"I just got you back," he murmured in my ear. This wasn't fair to him.

"I'm sorry I put you through this. This whole thing." I never should have hung up with Ryan. At least with him I was calm, rational, and methodical. Now everything was coming back, the fear, the pain, the pure evilness Abelard exuded. If O'Connell hadn't shown up when he did, I would have killed Abelard and been genuinely okay with that, which was frightening, or Abelard would have gotten the upper hand again. Who knows what that might have led to, but given his psychotic, sadistic personality, I could only imagine. "But I'm glad you weren't there, that you stayed away, and that's how I'll always want it to be. It's how it has to be." After being exceptionally forward, I realized I was trying to pull the trigger on our attempt at a relationship before it ever had a chance.

"Alexis, as far as I'm concerned, we're even. You can stop protecting me. You are no longer my bodyguard. Bruiser is. We'll see how things go, one day at a time, so stop making rash judgments and proclamations." He kissed my temple. "Especially not at three a.m."

"I am sorry for everything you went through." My words didn't just apply to this last week, or telling him how I had gotten roughed up, or even our failed attempt at intimacy. Those eight words were meant to convey how I felt about him getting shot. All of it. Maybe I was just overly tired and emotional. Martin was right. No more three a.m. proclamations for me. I needed a clear head and sound reasoning before making snap decisions. I got up from the couch, and we went back to bed.

THIRTY-THREE

Martin woke up the next morning at seven a.m. I felt responsible for his lack of sleep, but he insisted it was fine. Staying in bed long past check-out, I only emerged when my phone rang.

I arrived at the precinct by mid-afternoon to go over everything from yesterday with O'Connell's commanding officer. A tech showed up halfway through my story to photograph the much more apparent bruising around my neck for verification of its match to the choke-chain and Abelard's hand. Lieutenant Moretti nodded as I continued to explain how Abelard had gotten the jump on O'Connell and the most likely scenario that enabled him to slip out of the cuffs. Once I was finished, the lieutenant thanked me for the files and the information.

"When will O'Connell be back on active duty?" I asked, hoping I wasn't overstepping my boundaries.

"Soon. IA didn't find anything suspicious about the shooting, especially with Abelard's record and international notoriety."

I wanted to talk to Nick, but it could wait until he was cleared, just so there wasn't even a hint of impropriety. "Tell O'Connell thanks for saving my ass."

There was no point in prolonging the inevitable, so I went to the OIO offices to see what else Mark or Farrell might need. Amazingly, everything had already been properly documented and noted. I signed off on its accuracy and was on my way out of the building when Director Kendall stopped me in the middle of the hallway.

"Parker, my office," he ordered, and I obediently followed him down the corridor. Sitting down, I waited for him to yell at me, but instead, he took a seat behind his desk and inspected my appearance for a few moments. "You doing okay?"

"Today's a hell of a lot better than yesterday."

"Good," he said before falling silent. I stared at him for what felt like an eternity before edging off the seat, thinking our meeting was over. "Sit down." Apparently, we weren't through yet. I raised my eyebrows and waited. Finally, he leaned forward in his chair and spoke. "I know you've had a hell of a week. Maybe you've reconsidered my offer."

"Look, I told Jablonsky I'd consider a one-shot consulting thing just to see how it goes. I don't want to deal with any of the bureaucratic red-tape. I know it's asking a lot, but quite frankly, sir, I don't want to be here."

Kendall picked up his pen and tapped it on top of his desk as he thought about my terms. "Are you sure one case won't turn into Pandora's Box?" His eyes had a knowing quality to them, but I overlooked it.

"Highly doubtful."

"We'll see." He reached into his desk drawer and pulled out a stack of paperwork. "You might as well get started on this." He turned the papers to face me. "Come back in two weeks. I'm sure medical will clear you by then." Picking up the paperwork unenthusiastically, I went to the door. "Parker," he called, and I turned on my heel, "good job getting Abelard."

"Thank you, sir." My reply was automatic. My damn training was already kicking in just by being in the building. I needed to get out of here as soon as possible before the radio waves could completely brainwash me.

*   *   *

It was time to face the music. I returned to the hotel, retrieved my bag, and checked out of the room. I had just gotten to my apartment when there was a knock at the door. Really? My neighbors must be stalking me now or planning to run me out of the building with pitchforks. I had no firearms, so if someone wanted to kill me, now would be an exceptionally good time to knock on my door and do just that. However, the knock at my door was Martin. Even though I kept him up most of the night, he wasn't planning to kill me.

"No welcome greeting from the nine millimeter today?" he quipped, giving me a quick kiss and proceeding, uninvited, into my apartment.

"What are you doing here?" My packed bag had barely made it into my bedroom before he arrived. He needed a refresher course from Emily Post.

"You checked out of the hotel twenty minutes before I got there."

I rolled my eyes and ignored him as I attempted to tidy up my apartment. Retrieving the bloody kitchen towel from the table, I threw it in the garbage can, hoping he didn't notice. From the linen closet, I collected the pile of old, ratty towels I kept for just this type of occasion and placed them over the bloodstained carpeting.

"It was time to come home and clean up this mess," I said. "Shouldn't you be at work?"

He tapped his watch as he went to my liquor cabinet and poured a decent amount of scotch. "Want something to drink?"

It was already 6:30. Another entire day had been spent dealing with the Abelard situation. "Maybe I'll make some tea," I replied off-handedly.

"Sugar, honey, lemon?"

"Whatever." Tea wasn't my favorite beverage, so I didn't particularly care what went in it.

"Actually, I was trying to figure out which pet name you'd prefer."

"Lemon?" The comment at least got him to laugh.

"Fine, you caught me. I left work early and rushed over here just so I could offer you a hot beverage." As he said this, the kettle whistled. "Ta da." He was being snarky, but I let it go. He sat at my kitchen counter and drank his scotch while I tried to figure out what to do with the carpeting. Finally, I took a tentative sip of the tea, found a box cutter, and put on a pair of gloves.

I cut an outline around the towels. Martin watched, intrigued, as he poured another glass of scotch. It was obvious he was trying to get a handle on the way this week had gone. What better way to do that than by drinking copious amounts of mid-priced scotch?

I cut a six foot by three foot rectangle out of my carpet that had been the last earthly spot Abelard had taken a breath. As I finished cutting out the rectangle and pulled the carpet free, I rolled it up. Going through my kitchen drawers, I found the large black trash bags. I took the rolled up carpet and laid it inside one bag. Then I took another bag, wrestled it around the other end of the carpeting, and taped the two bags together in the middle. The wood floor underneath didn't appear damaged, but I poured some bleach over the wood, wiped it away with a clean towel, and washed my hands.

"I spoke to Luc today." Martin's tone had an odd quality that I had never heard before. Turning off the water and facing him, I waited for him to continue. "Apparently everything that's happened has been in the Paris papers." Martin stared at the remaining scotch in his glass and intentionally avoided my gaze.

"Well, Abelard operated an underground gambling syndicate," I pointed out, confused where this conversation was heading. "That seems newsworthy to me."

"Yeah." He took a sip and put the glass down, focused intently on the remaining scotch. "I might have unintentionally implied your involvement."

"It's fine." It didn't matter if Guillot knew. The situation was resolved anyway.

Martin glanced up. "He has strongly suggested that given your," he frowned, looking for the proper terminology to use, "availability to work dangerous jobs, it might be best if your contract isn't renewed at Martin Technologies."

"Okay." Being personally involved with the boss wasn't kosher in my mind. "Do you want to wait until the contract expires, or do you want to nullify it now?"

"I don't agree with Luc. If he insist on this, he can put it to a vote before the Board. I just wanted to give you a heads up."

"Don't fight him on this, Martin. It's not worth it. You can find just about anyone to supervise your camera installations. You don't need me. I shouldn't be working for you anymore anyway, given our history."

"That's exactly why you deserve the job," he replied angrily. He was angry at Luc, not me, but I was the only one in the room for him to yell at.

"Director Kendall gave me my consulting papers today. I might not be around much if I get scooped into some extensive, long-term situation."

He looked forlorn, burning through my insistence and resolve with his green eyes. "We'll wait until your contract is up for renewal, and then we'll worry about it," he concluded, knowing there were another four months remaining.

"Fine." I sat next to him at the counter and leaned my head against his shoulder. His surgery was in less than two weeks. Closing my eyes, I wished life wasn't this complicated, that murderers didn't exist and try to kill me in my own apartment, and everything would just work itself out.

"Hey, it's going to be okay," Martin said soothingly. He turned sideways and embraced me fully in his arms. "What is it?" He wiped some moisture from my cheek. When did I start crying? Everything had gotten to me. I shook my head, refusing to pull away until I could calm down. I hated crying. It made me feel weak and inferior. He held me tightly, only exacerbating the situation as my silent tears turned into choked sobs. Once I got myself under control, I pulled away from his embrace. "Sweetheart, what is it?" he asked again.

I took a slow, deep breath. "Everything just hit me all at once." Pressing my lips together, I shut my eyes to make sure I wasn't about to relapse.

"I know you don't want to stop working for me," he kidded, and I gave him a lopsided smile.

"You've got me." Before either of us could say anything else, his phone rang. "Go ahead," I urged, taking the opportunity to escape to the bathroom to clean up after my unfortunately timed hysterics, "you should take that." By the time I returned, Martin had his jacket on and was standing near my front door.

"The research department hit a snafu."

"Get out of here. I'm okay, really. I just need some alone time to process things."

"I'll give you a call tomorrow, okay?"

I nodded, and he left. I locked the door and turned around, surveying my apartment. Resisting the urge to open my fire escape and throw the bagged up carpet out the window, I made dinner and went to bed. It had been an incredibly long six weeks.

THIRTY-FOUR

As promised, Martin called the next day to make sure I hadn't checked myself into the loony bin. Even though it was the weekend, he had a million things to do. He had to prepare the office for Luc's impending arrival and find a solution to the current production error. He was keeping busy which was a relief since I had to deal with a million issues of my own. Despite our full schedules, he insisted on staying at my apartment every night, listening for my screams as my nightmares raged on. We were still taking things slow due to his concern over my injured state. Yet, he constantly needed to touch my hand or stroke my hair to ensure I was next to him. The physicality of our relationship was downright baffling. *Hazard of the job*, I reasoned. As his schedule became more hectic, he finally agreed to some much needed time apart.

Over the course of the week, I had spoken with Ryan. As more information was gleaned, the stronger the gnawing became in the recesses of my mind. There was something amiss concerning Jean-Pierre's involvement with Abelard, but I couldn't pinpoint it. I was on the phone with Ryan as he prattled on about the art recoveries that had been made.

"Gustav gave us the location for the three missing paintings, the buyers, and the fences. He even rolled on that bogus third party authenticator Evans-Sterling used when you brought the forged painting to the States," Ryan said. "Interpol made two of the recoveries since they were sold internationally, and Reneaux personally took the collar on the third."

"At least Salazar Sterling will be relieved," I said cynically. I told Ryan how Sal sent me a letter of gratitude and the reward for information on the paintings.

Ryan made a disgruntled noise. "It's amazing how these brokerage firms and insurance companies can be involved in the purchase and retrieval of possible forgeries. No one on the team even knew, or if they did, they didn't tell me."

"It's big business. Think about the countless number of masterpieces that have gone missing during times of war or upheaval and add in all the art that has been in private collections for centuries and other works that were thought to have been destroyed that have surfaced. None of us have any idea what's even out there. So how would we know what's real? Strangely enough, Evans-Sterling isn't doing anything illegal, even though quite a few people on the payroll were."

"It was mainly Jean-Pierre and whatever contracted, third parties recreated the stolen masterpieces and claimed the fakes as genuine articles. That's why tracking the missing art turned into such an ordeal. Every museum and gallery that reported a theft had a different art restorer and different authenticator. If Jacques Marset had been working at all the museums, the dots would have connected faster, and we would have been able to track the smuggling ring to Louis Abelard that much sooner. Instead, the only lead the police had was the Evans-Sterling investigative team."

"Wait a minute." I leaned back in my chair and bit my thumbnail, thinking. "Le Galerie's paintings are real, so Marset had to switch them with the fakes."

"Yeah. The place is practically a museum," Ryan replied, confused by my thought process. "They wouldn't mistake a forgery for a masterpiece."

"But Marset was a forger. He worked for Abelard."

"Right." Ryan waited for brilliance to strike.

"And Jean-Pierre worked for Abelard. Is he still in police custody?"

"We have him in holding. We didn't want to transfer him yet, in case he has anything else to offer."

Flashing back to the shootout in the parking garage, I remembered the men firing at Jean-Pierre. The men in the SUV weren't working with Abelard. If they had been, they never would have fired on one of their own. They must have been working for Marset. The forger probably offered them the real painting and as much money as he could carry in exchange for getting him out of the country and away from the unstable Abelard. But how did Jean-Pierre stumble upon that tip? There were two possibilities. Either Abelard heard whispers of betrayal and sent Jean-Pierre to act as an enforcer to stop the escape, or Jean-Pierre had gotten the intel another way. But who thwarted Marset's exit strategy and killed him?

I had an odd feeling about the whole thing. Jean-Pierre intentionally sent the videotape a day too soon, even though I failed to make the proper connection because of the time difference, and he knocked out the two men in the warehouse and assisted in my escape.

Did Gustav ensure I would have enough time to free myself from the hook before Abelard and his goons returned with another round of shock therapy? Maybe the reason I was left in possession of my knife was because Jean-Pierre let me keep it.

"Alex?" Ryan asked, probably assuming we had been disconnected.

"I'm here. Has Agent Delacroix attempted to take custody of Gustav?"

"Funny you should ask," he snorted. "Reneaux was bitching about it earlier today."

"Son of a bitch."

"What?"

"I think Jean-Pierre's a plant."

Before the police could arrest Gustav, the car exploded. I wasn't sure who killed Marset or how it happened, but the timing was too close for comfort. Following this, Delacroix placed round the clock surveillance on Gustav's apartment, even after his alleged death, and Interpol kept a watchful eye on Ryan in order to keep his movements on a tight leash. Were they afraid Ryan would blow their investigation? And what about me? Delacroix loathed my presence, but he provided me with additional information to ponder. Although he pissed me off, his annoyances ultimately led me in the right direction.

"You're telling me Gustav is in deep cover?" Ryan didn't sound convinced. "What about the three years' worth of stolen paintings? Would Interpol authorize thievery for their UCs? Plus, what about his gambling debts? Were those faked too? And why wouldn't he have told Clare, especially when she's former Interpol too? She could have been his backup." Ryan made several valid points. Given Jean-Pierre's protective attitude toward Clare, I knew she was clueless and uninvolved.

"Then why did he let me go? Why did he protect me?"

"Maybe he has a soft spot for you. Or he was afraid you'd piece it together and ruin him. Possibly both."

I rubbed my face, thinking. There was something off about the entire Delacroix/Gustav situation, and it was going to bother me until I figured it out.

"A call just came in, so we'll wrap this up next time, Alex."

"Do me a favor and see what you can get on Marset's murder and the bombing. I'll do the same from this end. And Ryan, stay safe."

*   *   *

Over the next couple of days, I made little headway in unraveling the questions regarding Interpol and Jean-Pierre. I tried to let it go since the likelihood of ever finding the answers seemed slim. It was Saturday when O'Connell called, thanking me for my thorough retelling of the events leading to the shooting. He had been cleared, so I offered to meet him and Thompson later and open a tab in their honor. It was the least I could do. Phoning Mark, I extended an invitation to him, too.

That night, the four of us sat at the corner of the bar, and I hoped my credit card wouldn't be declined. Since we'd been drinking for the last few hours, it was a legitimate concern.

"You do realize by inviting Feds into a cop bar, we're totally losing our street cred right now," Thompson teased.

"I'm not a Fed. Plus, I'm buying, so it wouldn't hurt if you could show some appreciation. A tiny bit of gratitude might be nice." I winked.

He lifted his tequila shot in my direction before

downing it. O'Connell chuckled and sipped his beer. He had been quiet all night, but I wasn't going to ask why.

Thompson eyed the girl across the room, who he had been flirting with most of the evening. "Thanks for the drinks, Parker." He got off the barstool. "I'm outta here." He walked over to the girl, and the two of them left together.

Mark waited a reasonable amount of time for them to leave before getting up and patting my shoulder. "Thanks for buying," he said. "I have an early morning, so I should probably head out too. You're coming back next week, right?"

"Yes. Kendall seems to think two weeks is ample time."

Mark was killing my buzz with shoptalk. He nodded to O'Connell and started for the door.

"What?" O'Connell called after him. "You don't want to find a badge bunny to take home, too?"

I rolled my eyes. Men could be pigs, and I found the whole badge bunny concept particularly degrading. It gave women a bad name, or maybe I was just jealous that scantily clad men didn't clamor about for women in uniform.

"I have three ex-wives collecting alimony. That would be the last thing I need," Mark said, leaving Nick and me alone at the bar.

"So," I finally decided to broach the subject, "how did this come down on you?"

"It wasn't too bad." Nick turned to face me. "The hostage situation the day before the shooting might have been a blip on the radar. Y'know, looks like a cop was out for revenge, but the fucker had it coming."

"That would be an understatement."

"I got my balls busted a bit, but the mayor was impressed. He's throwing some award ceremony."

O'Connell shrugged as if this were nothing new or special.

"Congratulations. Maybe you will get that promotion, after all." We sat in a comfortable silence, drinking our beers. "Shouldn't you be at home with your wife?"

He glanced at his watch. "She's working graveyard at the hospital tonight. I'll pick her up in the morning and take her out to breakfast to celebrate. It's a Saturday night. Shouldn't you be having a late night security consulting meeting with Martin?"

"No, I don't think that would be a prudent idea. After you called and told him to pick me up at the ER," I gave him my annoyed look, "it's just, I don't know."

"Great use of the English language."

"You know how this life is. There are days we go to work and might not come back in one piece or at all. It's not fair to put someone through that. Honestly, I don't think he can handle it." O'Connell tilted his head back and laughed. "What?" I asked, completely bewildered.

"You don't think he can handle it? What the hell kind of Fed were you, Parker? I always thought you were more competent than that." I remained silent, waiting for some elaboration. "Look, I don't know him that well, but the few times we've met, he can be very intimidating, particularly when it comes to you." I snorted and gave him my best 'yeah, right' look. "Let me put it another way, if you let him, he would walk through fire for you."

"Maybe that's the problem. What if I don't want him to get burned?" I understood what O'Connell was saying. "It's not fair for any of us to expect someone to be there waiting or risk getting caught in the crossfire."

"You have to realize you can't control everything. You cannot make these decisions for him or anyone else. The only thing you can decide is if you want him there or not, and if not, then just say so. I know you have a history, but honestly, you don't owe him a damn thing." O'Connell had a point. "I wouldn't be doing this without my wife," he continued, lost in his own story. "Seven years ago, I got grazed, and she was the nurse working the ER. We got to talking, numbers were exchanged, and one thing led to another." He smiled at his memory.

"Do you worry?"

"I have to, but at some point, you realize life's just too damn short. There are too many negative possibilities and not enough time for anything." He got up from the barstool. "And now that you've made me this damn nostalgic, I'm going to see if she can get off work a little early tonight." He headed toward the door.

"Nick," I called after him, "thanks."

"Anytime."

THIRTY-FIVE

The next morning, I planned on staying in bed for the majority of the day and doing the proper hangover thing. Unfortunately, the universe didn't agree with my carefully laid plans. My phone began buzzing around ten o'clock that morning, and whoever was calling refused to stop until I answered.

"Parker," I growled into the receiver.

"The biometric locks have seized up," announced a panicked voice.

"What?" I wasn't awake enough for that grouping of words to make sense.

The phone on the other end was shuffled around before I got any type of response. "Miss Parker, hi, this is Jeffrey Myers. I'm sorry to bother you on a Sunday morning. It appears the new biometric locks you approved are malfunctioning, and we have no way of getting into the security office."

"Did you call Heller?" I didn't provide the equipment, so why exactly was this my problem?

"Yes, but it's the weekend. She's trying to find

someone to fix it, but we thought maybe you'd have a solution in the meantime?"

"Did you call Mr. Martin?" There was mumbling in the background.

"He thought you might be able to bypass it."

"Fine. Give me the model number, and I'll get some equipment and be there as soon as I can." Performing some quick searches, I made a few calls to a couple of security specialists, grabbed my own lock-picking gear, and stopped by the local electronics store.

Arriving at the MT building an hour and a half later, I planned to break into the security office. Worst case, the lock could be shot off. It was a good thing I collected my weapon from evidence lock-up on Friday afternoon. Flashing my MT credentials at the man guarding the front door, I went to the security office.

"Call Mr. Martin and let him know he needs to notify your security firm that any recorded breach is not a break-in. I don't want the cops all over my ass when I screw up," I informed Jeffrey.

"Um," he stammered, "maybe you should tell him yourself." He jerked his head at one of the armchairs across the room. "Just so you know," he whispered, "the lock on his office isn't working either."

"Great." I sighed.

"Morning," Martin greeted, sounding rather annoyed.

"I'm glad you decided to leave the word good out of that salutation," I said. "I don't know if I can bypass the system or not, but I'm willing to try if you're game." He was in agreement. "Did you give your security firm or the police the heads up? I'm not qualified to do this, and there's a good chance I'll trip the alarm."

"I'll make the call." He was in total business crisis mode, which would explain why he was being short with me.

"You might want to tell Heller exactly what you think of her shoddy equipment," I snapped.

It took almost forty-five minutes to disconnect the biometric reader from the door and manually jimmy the lock open. Jeffrey Myers and the other two security guards applauded, and I rolled my eyes.

"I'm not sure what to do in the meantime, but you might want to get an actual locksmith to install a regular lock until Ms. Heller replaces this one." I was less than pleased with how my recommended security improvements had gone awry.

"I'll check with Mr. Martin and see what he wants to do," Jeffrey said. Glancing at the armchair across the lobby, I realized Martin was gone. "Oh, if you can unlock his office, he'd greatly appreciate it." Wondering when Martin disappeared, I went to the elevator and debated if I was intentionally getting the cold shoulder or if I was just imagining things.

Forty minutes later, I was still standing in the hallway outside Martin's office with an electronic reader in my palm, a metal lock-pick hanging from the corner of my mouth, and a pair of wire cutters sticking out of my back pocket.

"Don't ask me why I find you incredibly sexy right now. I just do," Martin came up behind me and whispered in my ear. I ignored the distraction and continued to adjust the scanner to detect which wires to disengage. Pulling the wire cutter from my pocket, I short-circuited the biometric sensor. It had taken almost half an hour to get the front panel off just to expose the wires. Whoever made these faulty locks should have considered making it easier to bypass them.

"Do you say that to all the locksmiths or just the ones you want to sleep with?" I teased, clipping a few more wires. "My office key is in my pocket if you want to wait in there until I finish." Even though the biometric sensor was inactive, the electronic lock was still fully engaged, and there was no way to determine how to manually disengage it.

"How would it look for me to be rummaging through your pockets?" I could hear him smirking, but he had a point. "Can I help?"

I handed him the electronic reader and my wire cutters. "I'm sorry the biometric locks aren't working. If I had known they were glitchy, I never would have recommended them." Best to remain professional while at work.

"It's not your fault. Dani's called five times to apologize and offered a full refund in addition to new upgraded locks which are being installed tomorrow."

Failing to turn the tumbler in the proper direction, I growled at the door before starting over. Martin remained silent and let me focus as I finally managed to pick the lock and pry the door open.

"There," I said resolutely, sliding my lock-picks into their case. "Sorry, it took so long."

"That's okay." He entered his office, waiting for me to join him. I was paranoid the door would close and the lock would reengage, trapping us inside, so I found a doorstop and propped the door open, just to be on the safe side. "It's been a hell of a weekend."

"Now that your office is functioning again, I'm going to go. But just to be on the safe side, don't close the door," I said. He nodded, staring at the paperwork on his desk. "I know you're busy, but do you think you might have some free time tonight? Maybe we could have dinner."

He looked up, smiling. "I'd like that. Giovanni's at seven?"

"I'll be there."

* * *

I went home, took a shower, and tried on almost every single article of clothing I owned. I didn't know why I was so nervous. Martin and I had been to dinner almost every week for the last few months, but tonight felt different. On the one hand, it was kind of like our first date, and on the other, I knew we needed to address the tension between us. Once again, I replayed the intended conversation over in my head. It was time to take a step back, especially when he would be incapacitated with the surgery and busy transitioning Guillot in as vice president. I would be equally busy, tormenting myself with what I hoped would be a brief consulting gig at the OIO. Needless to say, we both had a lot on our plates for the foreseeable future. Slow meant almost total avoidance, at least while I was working for the OIO.

After finding something appropriate to wear, I went to the restaurant to meet Martin. Requesting a table in the back as secluded as possible, I ordered a white wine while I waited. I was nervously spinning my glass on the tabletop when he arrived. He glanced at his watch and then at my empty glass.

"I thought I'd be on time for once," he remarked, sitting across from me and ordering a bottle of wine for the table.

"You are. I was just early. How are the locks?" I wanted to avoid having a real conversation for as long as possible.

"They're being installed first thing in the morning. I've been assured this will never happen again." He folded his menu and leaned back in his chair. "We don't have to talk about work though. You look amazing." He lifted his eyebrows suggestively. His gaze shifted to the stitches on my wrist and then to my neck. The ligature marks from the garrote had finally vanished.

"Thank you." It didn't seem important to mention it had taken over an hour to figure out what to wear. Our conversation was temporarily halted as the waiter arrived and took our orders.

"I'm glad you invited me to dinner." His green eyes sparkled. "I was positive you didn't want to see me anymore." It was meant to be a joke, but he knew something was wrong.

I bit my bottom lip, and the mood shifted. "I have missed you." I hoped he would take what I had to say the way it was intended. "But we need to talk." He waited patiently for me to begin. "These next few weeks will be crazy for both of us. You have surgery and Guillot, and I'm supposed to be back at the OIO on a temporary basis. It might be best if we don't plan on seeing one another until things calm down."

"This isn't working, and for the life of me, I can't figure out why." He pressed his lips together. His eyes turned dark as they met mine. "Then again, I have my suspicions where the problem might be." I remained silent, and he searched my eyes. "Do you want to call things off?"

"No. Not at all." I reached across the table for his hand. "We said we would take things slow, and after Abelard," I looked at him, hoping for some type of understanding, but I was met with frustration, "it's just, we're either all or nothing."

"Funny, unless you're confusing me with someone else, I don't remember us ever actually doing much of anything. If we were going any slower, we'd be in reverse."

"I didn't mean physically." This wasn't going the way I hoped. "I'm sorry I have to ask you to stay away, but I worry about what could happen to you. I can't separate what's already happened," I glanced at his shoulder, "from where we are now."

"I'm only saying this once, and we are not talking about this again, understand? When I said we were even, I was wrong. We aren't even. You saved me twice, once from the explosion and once from bleeding to death in my own home. That means I still owe you. So do not sit here and give me this goddamn song and dance about how you have to protect me. It's fucking bullshit and incredibly emasculating. You were hired to protect me. You did, and now it's done." He stopped to get his tone under control.

"Martin," I tried to interject, but he put his hand up to silence me.

"I want to spend time with you, Alexis, and it's not because I think you'll pull me out of the way of a speeding taxi or jump in front of some sniper's bullet. So do not sit here and tell me you have to protect me, or we will be done." I leaned back in my chair and swallowed uneasily. His eyes smoldered. "Is that what you want?" he asked in a slightly more civil tone.

I replayed the conversation I had with Nick over in my head as I considered my options. I was at a crossroads. I could walk out that door and ensure Martin would be safe from the hazards associated with my life, or I could agree to let him stick around until we could no longer stand one another.

"I was hoping we could start fresh once our lives have settled down."

He stared unnervingly at me as his green eyes burned through my soul. "What happens afterward when life gets complicated again? Will you tell me to stay away and cut all contact?"

"I don't know. I can't promise you I won't."

He looked despondent and poured another glass of

wine. "At least we'll always have Paris," he attempted to joke, but his words lacked any hint of mirth. Our meals arrived, and I picked at mine as we sat through the rest of dinner in complete silence. We were at an impasse. The check arrived, and he put his credit card on the tray, ignoring my attempt to pay for dinner.

"When's your surgery?" I asked quietly, fearing I no longer had any right to this information.

"Thursday morning."

"How long," I swallowed; my throat had gone dry, "are you going to be there?"

"It's a day procedure. Hopefully, I can get back to work by Tuesday or Wednesday. Not a big deal," he said mechanically. "When do you start working for Mark?"

"Friday, I think." I couldn't figure out what was going on, if we were back to just friends or if we had yet to decide. "I have to pass the evaluations, but at least the paperwork is finished."

He produced a small smile that didn't make it to his eyes. The waiter returned with the receipt, and Martin stood up.

"Well." He paused, contemplating what to say. His tone sounded cordial, and I suspected saying thanks for a lovely evening was obviously too phony a comment to utter.

"Martin." I crushed my body against his in a tight embrace. Now that he was leaving, I didn't want him to go. I fought so long against this and never gave it a chance, and now I was perplexed by how much I would miss it. Miss him.

He held me tightly. "You don't have to do this." His voice had a pleading quality to it. "We can..." He stopped, probably realizing there was no simple solution. I pulled back and kissed him. It felt like goodbye. "Alex." He rubbed his thumb across my cheek.

"Goodbye, Martin." I pulled away and turned around, walking out of the building and back to my car alone.

THIRTY-SIX

Over the next three days, I stayed buried under the covers, regretting what happened but unwilling to do anything to change the outcome. The truth of the matter was if I crossed paths with another sociopath like Abelard, I would do the exact same thing, even if it was emasculating and inconsiderate. This fact didn't keep me from running to the caller ID every time the phone rang, hoping it was Martin. I missed him more than I cared to admit and more than I even thought possible. We had barely even started dating, and despite the many nights we spent together, due to my vast number of injuries, we never even had sex. Maybe it was a good thing. I would have been more attached to him, but somehow, I felt gypped. How did we miss the carefree fun part of the dating process? Oh yeah, Abelard, how could I forget?

My phone rang again, and I was disappointed when the caller wasn't Martin.

"Parker," I answered, taking a seat at my kitchen table.

"If you aren't busy today, maybe you'd like to come

for your evaluations," Director Kendall's assistant relayed the message through the phone.

"Fine." I hung up. There was no reason why I had to stay home and mope when I could go to the last place I wanted to be and bring some cheer to Kendall and Mark.

I went through the routine physical and demonstrated my athletic prowess by being forced to do the rudimentary running, push-ups, sit-ups, and firearm proficiency exams. After I showered and dressed, I was sent to see the Bureau's shrink for my psychological evaluation, my least favorite part of the process. Luckily, since my last evaluation, someone new had been hired. He read my personnel file, asked some basic questions, and sat quietly, hoping I would feel the desire to randomly discuss something deep and disturbing nestled in the very core of my psyche. Instead, I stared at my shoelaces, wondering why the plastic tips at the end weren't the same color as the shoestring itself.

"Would you like to talk about your recent run-in with Louis Abelard?" the doctor asked.

"Not particularly."

"It looks like you stopped some agents from entering a booby-trapped motel room. Is that why the director asked you to come back to work?"

"I don't think so, but you'd have to ask him." Succinct answers were always a good idea when dealing with anyone whose job it was to get inside your head.

"It must be nice to know you prevented a tragedy."

I remained quiet, but I knew the doctor hoped to draw a parallel between my last OIO mission and what just happened. It wasn't the same, and it was none of his business. We were in the midst of a mental standoff, which amused him. After a few minutes of listening to nothing but the droning of the white noise machine, he spoke.

"Do you have a lot of friends?"

I looked at him, surprised by the randomness of the question. "Enough. They have my back if I need them."

He nodded almost to himself. "Are you close with your family?" It was his attempt to figure out what made me tick outside of the job.

"Not so much."

He nodded again. "It says you're not married. Anyone serious?"

I almost said yes and realized yes wasn't an accurate answer. No was the accurate answer. I was single. Martin was a dalliance, casual and brief. I wasn't even sure it counted as casual, maybe just brief. But nothing about our relationship seemed casual, probably because we had been close friends for so long.

The doctor looked up from his notes. A smile played across his face. "I'll take that as a yes." I didn't say anything. He filled out the rest of the form and handed it to me. "You're clear."

I looked down at the paper, almost positive I hadn't heard him correctly. "Really?" I realized questioning his diagnosis was a dumb idea, but there were times I felt batshit crazy. Right now seemed like one of them.

"Yes. There was a note in your file indicating you didn't have enough outside the job to remain objective, but from your responses, I don't think that's the case any longer."

I stood and took the paper. This guy must have gotten his degree from an online university, but I wasn't about to correct him.

"But if you ever need someone to talk to." He reached for his card.

"Don't push it, Doc," I said and left his office. I went downstairs and handed the paperwork to Kendall's assistant. She glanced at it and stuck it into my file, which just happened to be sitting on the desk.

"The director will call when he has a case for you. Have a good day."

"Yeah, you too," I replied with an equal amount of contempt. Maybe I should have my number changed before that could happen.

* * *

The next morning, I got up bright and early and went to the hospital. Even if we weren't on the best of terms, Martin was having surgery, and I was going to be there. I went to the outpatient waiting area and sat down. I had no earthly idea what time his procedure was scheduled, how long it would take, or even if it was being done in this particular hospital. After sitting impatiently for almost a half hour, I tried to sweet talk the nurse into giving me some information. Unfortunately, she wouldn't budge.

I gave up and went back to my chair to wait. After almost another hour, I spotted a familiar face coming down the hall.

"Marcal," I called to him.

"Miss Parker," Marcal's features brightened, and he adopted a knowing look, "I had a feeling you'd be here."

"Am I that predictable?" I quipped. "What's going on?"

"They are prepping him now. The whole procedure shouldn't take more than an hour or two, and then they'll move him back to his room, wait for the anesthesia to wear off, and send him home if there are no complications." He lowered his voice to just above a whisper. "I don't intrude in Mr. Martin's private life, but he's had a rough couple of days."

"I know the feeling." At least I wasn't the only one upset by the way we concluded things. "I had to be here, just so I'd know he was okay."

"He's in room 315. I have some errands to run, and I won't be back until late this afternoon. He doesn't have anyone else to check on him."

"Thanks."

Marcal left, and I sat in the waiting room, trying to decide if seeing Martin was the best idea. In the end, I gave in.

While I waited in his room, wondering if he would be angry by my presence, my phone rang. "Parker," I answered. I had reverted to my old habit of identifying myself to the caller instead of answering with the much more common *hello*.

"Gustav's been surrendered to Interpol," Ryan said. "Delacroix personally picked him up early this morning. I think you're right."

"Don't you hate it when that happens?"

"You should be a bloody psychic. Go ahead and quit your day job now. I'll vouch for your claims."

I chuckled.

"I got curious and called Interpol, asking for a follow-up to Gustav's last interview. I was told it's not possible since he has been moved to an undisclosed location."

"What about Clare?" If Gustav was still working with Interpol, could she have been moved too? Or maybe he was in witness protection.

"As far as I know, she's still around. Do you honestly believe he was undercover this entire time?"

"I don't know. The only other time I encountered Jean-Pierre was when he was a very convincing UC. Maybe he didn't give up the game. Did you find anything on the car bomb?"

"Since you asked, I read Interpol's file on Marset. I swear I don't see how those blokes manage to do anything right."

"What'd it say?"

"Not much. Before Gustav was taken away, I asked him about Marset's murder," Ryan said. "According to Jean-Pierre, Marset wanted to escape Abelard's clutches, and Claude killed him on Abelard's order. Jean-Pierre didn't find out until after the body was presented to Abelard. It was Jean-Pierre's idea to put the corpse in the car and light it up. He thought it would help throw everyone off his scent."

"Do you believe him?"

"I don't know. If your theory's right and Gustav's an Interpol agent, then yes. After all, policemen aren't in the business of killing people, at least not in cold-blood. If I hear anything else, I'll let you know, but I'm not digging. After shutting down the gambling and recovering the art, I'm ready to let sleeping dogs lie."

"That would probably be best." I listened to the silence fill the air space. "Ryan, I'm relieved the sick son of a bitch is dead. Is that a sign I shouldn't be doing this anymore?"

"I would say if you didn't feel relieved, then there would be something wrong." His words were just the reassurance I needed. "It's good you're going back to the OIO. You're a cop, or agent, or whatever you bloody well want to call yourself. It's in your blood. It's who you are, Alex."

"Thanks, Ryan. Maybe I'll see you around." Why did I need his encouragement? After all, no one else had to deal with the fallout except me. As I continued to process this line of thought, Martin's bed was wheeled into the room.

"You and me back in a hospital room," I said to the

unconscious Martin. "Honestly, something should have changed by now." I settled into the chair and watched the machines beep away with his vitals. While I debated if I should leave before he woke up, a doctor came in and told me how the surgery went.

"James will need extensive rehab, but we've removed almost all of the scar tissue. He should regain at least ninety if not a hundred percent of his feeling and dexterity back." At last, some good news. "He'll wake up soon, but he'll probably be groggy," the doctor cautioned. "We should be able to discharge him in a few hours." After the doctor left, I reached over and grasped Martin's left hand.

"Well, at least we know your shoulder is fine." It was time to leave, but Martin squeezed my hand.

"Alex?" he asked, confused. He had a goofy grin on his face, and I was sure he was still feeling the effects of the drugs.

"You caught me. I wanted to make sure you were okay."

"I'm okay now. I'm sorry." He did his best impression of a sad puppy dog.

"Don't be." For all intents and purposes, he was inebriated, so I couldn't rely on the things he said. "You made a valid point. I can't ask you to wait around, not knowing what might happen, and expect you to be okay with it." By the time I finished speaking, he had shut his eyes.

"Please don't leave," he beseeched before falling back to unconsciousness.

I leaned back in the chair and took a deep breath. Now was the perfect time to make my escape, unless I was willing to agree to his terms. Maybe there was a compromise somewhere in the middle.

I sat in his hospital room for the next hour while he slept off the remnants of the sedation. I ate the pudding cup they brought on his lunch tray while I tried to determine what exactly I hoped to accomplish. The only thing I was certain of was I didn't want him out of my life.

When he woke up, he looked confused. "Why are you here?" he asked, a bitter tone to his words.

I snorted. "There was pudding. I couldn't let it go to waste." The slightest bit of amusement crossed his features. "And I wanted to make sure you were all right." After I relayed the information the doctor provided, Martin watched me intently.

"I remember waking up before, and you were here." He squinted, hoping to recall what had transpired.

I resisted the urge to tell him he apologized for being an ass since that wouldn't have been fair. "Yeah." I leaned forward in my chair. "I guess I should probably go, right?" Maybe he'd ask me to stay.

"It's up to you. You decide." We weren't talking about if I was staying in his hospital room.

"Honestly, I won't be around much for the next few weeks." This seemed a realistic assessment, given my current status at the OIO. "But when I get back, if you'd be willing to give us another chance, I'd like to try."

"Okay." He tucked a piece of hair behind my ear. I smiled and kissed him. "I thought we were waiting until you got back."

"I'm compromising. Just go with it."

THIRTY-SEVEN

A few days later, my words rang true when Director Kendall called to ask if I could assist on a particularly intricate case. I dressed in black slacks, sensible shoes, white button-up shirt, and a black blazer. My hair was clipped in a bun, and every part of me from my shoulder holster to my ugly shoes screamed out *federal agent*. It felt like going home, and I hated it. I drove to the OIO building and parked in the garage. When I emerged from the elevator, Mark caught sight of me. He exited his office and began clapping.

I turned and glared at him, but before I could force him to stop, he was joined by a majority of the office. *Dammit*, I thought irritated as I felt myself blush.

Kendall came out of his office and joined in. "Welcome home, Agent Parker."

"I'm not an agent anymore, sir," I said as everyone thankfully returned to their business.

"Things could change," he added, unperturbed. "Come to my office, sign the paperwork, and then you can head to ops for the briefing."

I followed orders obediently, hoping everyone was wrong, and I was not getting sucked back into the life I left behind. Some chapters were closed for a reason and didn't need to be revisited.

After the paperwork was filed and I was briefed on the current case, I decided to take advantage of my new status and went in search of Interpol's liaison. Unfortunately, Farrell was out of the office on assignment. Maybe I should follow Ryan's lead and let sleeping dogs lie.

I returned to my apartment that night confused by the day's events. I sat on the couch and stared at the blank television screen. It was just one case to prove my leaving had been a conscious choice and not an attempt to hide or escape. This was the reason I went back, to prove I had chosen to leave. If that wasn't some ridiculously convoluted thinking, I didn't know what was. At least I figured out what I was trying to prove by going back to the OIO. That was progress.

I glanced at the phone, thinking briefly of Martin. I didn't know how things would work. Maybe starting over was like slamming my head into a brick wall, hoping the wall would break away before my skull did. Only time would tell. I was in the process of deciding which takeout menu to order from when the phone rang.

"Hello?" I answered, making a conscious effort to be less agent-like.

"Parker?" Delacroix asked.

"Agent Delacroix, what can I do for you?" Need the name of a good surgeon to remove your head from your ass?

"Just thought I'd let you know you'll be receiving a check in the mail soon," he sounded less than pleased. "I did say we'd give you the reward money."

"You shouldn't have gone to the trouble." I didn't

want to have anything else to do with him.

"Well, you have an admirer at Interpol who insists. He wanted to make it up to you, after everything that happened."

I pressed the phone closer to my ear. Was he talking about Jean-Pierre? "Were you running an undercover operation independently but concurrently with the Police Nationale?"

"Perhaps." His responses were still infuriating. "You're supposedly smart. Can't you piece it together?"

"What will happen now?"

"Oh come on, you know how these things go. New name, new place, same old game."

I wondered if Jean-Pierre really had committed illegal activity that indebted him to Delacroix and Interpol or if that had been hearsay and a planted background. "What if he wants out?" I had no way of knowing if Jean-Pierre wanted out of the game, but that night in my hotel room, before his murder was staged, I thought his words were sincere.

"You and I both know, once you're in, there isn't much hope of walking away." Delacroix disconnected, and I laid the phone on the counter and stared at it. His words resonated throughout my apartment, all the way to my bones. What if he was right and there was no chance of walking away from this life?

DON'T MISS ALEXIS PARKER'S NEXT
ADVENTURE

MIMICRY OF BANSHEES IS NOW
AVAILABLE FOR PURCHASE IN
PAPERBACK AND E-BOOK.

ABOUT THE AUTHOR

G.K. Parks is the author of the Alexis Parker series. The first novel, *Likely Suspects,* tells the story of Alexis' first foray into the private sector.

G.K. Parks received a Bachelor of Arts in Political Science and History. After spending some time in law school, G.K. changed paths and earned a Master of Arts in Criminology/Criminal Justice. Now all that education is being put to use creating a fictional world based upon years of study and research.

You can find additional information on G.K. Parks and the Alexis Parker series by visiting our website at
www.alexisparkerseries.com

Made in the USA
Las Vegas, NV
30 June 2022

50937146R00194